THE DEAD MAN OF STORR

A D.I. DUNCAN MCADAM MYSTERY

THE MISTY ISLE
BOOK 2

J M DALGLIESH

First published by Hamilton Press in 2023

Copyright © J M Dalgliesh, 2023

ISBN (Trade Paperback) 978-1-80080-956-7
ISBN (Hardback) 978-1-80080-340-4
ISBN (Large Print) 978-1-80080-209-4

Look out for the link at the end of this book or visit my website at **www.jmdalgliesh.com** to sign up to my no-spam VIP Club and receive a FREE novella from my Hidden Norfolk series plus news and previews of forthcoming works.

Never miss a new release.

———————

No spam, ever, guaranteed. You can unsubscribe at any time.

SCOTTISH NAMES
PEOPLE AND PLACES

Characters;
    Èibhlin - (Eve-leen)
    Eidlidh - (Ay-lee)
    MacEachran - (Mack-Eck-ran)

Places;
    Portree - (Por-tree)
    Lochalsh - (Lock-al-sh)
    Maligar - (Mal-e-gar)
    Skeabost - (Ski-boost)
    Kensaleyre - (Ken-sal-ayre)
    Neist Point - (Nee-st)
    Dunvegan - (Dun-vay-gan)
    Trotternish - (Trott-er-nish)
    Waternish - (Water-nish)
    Dunvegan - (Dun-veh-gan)
    Raasay - (Raa-see)
    Rubha Hunish - (Roo-ar Hoo-nish)
    An Talla Mòr - (An Talla More)

SCOTTISH PHRASES AND SLANG

Slang;

    Blootered - (Drunk)

    Wee - (Small)

    Stramash - (Uproar / row)

    Cannae - (Cannot / can't)

    Dinnae - (Did not / Didn't)

    Disnae - (Does not)

    Wasnae - (Was not)

    Nae - (No)

    Mind - (Remember / recall)

    Tae - (To)

    Blether - (Chat / conversation)

    Braw - (Good)

    Bùrach - (Mess)

    Weans - (Children)

    Bairns - (Children)

THE DEAD MAN OF STORR

PROLOGUE

Six hours. If she was able to fall asleep now, then she would get six hours of sleep before the alarm would wake her. Watching the hands of the clock pass around the face for what seemed like moments, but in reality had been almost an hour now… another hour since she'd made the same calculation.

How long has it been since I've had six hours of unbroken sleep?

The truth is, she had no idea. It hadn't happened any time recently and it certainly wasn't happening tonight. Her eyes strayed to the window where the warm orange glow of the streetlights filtered through the gently shifting curtains hanging to the side of the bay window, disturbed by a slight breeze that did little to cool her clammy skin on this strange summer night.

Throwing off the sheet, all that covered her bare skin, she made her way into the bathroom without flicking on the light. At this time of the year, even under a night sky shrouded by cloud cover, it seldom ever got properly dark and the resulting light permeated her bedroom stretching as far as the en suite.

Peering at her reflection in the mirror, hanging the full width of the bathroom wall behind the double basins, she stared at the dark circles beneath her eyes. Everything she'd been through in these past eighteen months registered in this expression, every facial line, every strained contour of her skin... and it would all culminate in that short walk she'd need to take tomorrow morning in the full glare of the waiting press, peers... and of course, the police. The thought of the coming day set butterflies away in her stomach and she shuddered. Until this time her anonymity had been secured... at least from the public. Others knew... and had done so for some time, although many never quite believing it was plausible, if at all even possible.

Aren't they in for a wake-up call.

Cupping her hands beneath the cold-water tap, she bent forward and gently splashed her face, running her cool hands down her cheeks and around to the nape of her neck where she pressed firmly. Her head was throbbing and she momentarily thought about the prescription she'd been afforded earlier; painkillers and a mild sedative to aid her sleep before the big day.

That's what the barrister had referred to it as: *her big day.* There were very few people she'd ever come across more arrogant than silk looking forward to their moment... all she is, is a prop in his performance, one no doubt practised in front of a mirror much like this one. Her imagination pictured him standing in his bathroom, butt naked, rehearsing his lines as would an experienced thespian preparing for their performance on stage at *The Royal Lyceum.* Is he likely to be nervous? She doubted it. He didn't seem the type. It had often been said that if they couldn't make it as musicians or stand-up comedians, they became the next best thing; barristers, the centre of attention, commanding all present to focus solely on them as they hammered away at the court.

Oh, how she hoped that would be true but tomorrow... She

doubted that too. A car alarm sounded in a nearby street, the shrill pitch of the sound breaking the silence over the city. Usually, such a sound wouldn't trouble her but tonight was different. Knowing she was on edge, she should just dismiss it as one of those things you find living in a city and normally she would, but tonight she made her way to the window, clinging to the relative sanctuary of the curtain as she peered down into the street below.

The setts were gleaming, a sheen of moisture left by the passing showers earlier in the night; a brief rain storm that everyone no doubt hoped would break the humidity but in the event was too ineffectual to make much of a difference. Nothing moved as she watched, and seldom did in this part of the city in the early hours this far from *Prince's Street*. A yelp behind startled her and she turned to see her dog sleeping on the chaise at the foot of the bed. She hadn't heard him come into the room, so she must have slept after all, at least for a time.

Moving away from the window, she gently sat beside her dog, reaching out and stroking his head. He was dreaming, his front paws and his nose twitching. The movement ceased as she touched him, his eyelids parting ever so slightly as he eyed her warily. She smiled.

"You go back to sleep, darling," she said, scratching behind his ear before standing up. The curtain wafted inwards as the breeze increased, accompanied by a creak from somewhere in the house. Her head snapped towards the open door and beyond that onto the landing. Perhaps that wasn't the breeze but a draught. Had she imagined it? The doors and windows of the ground floor were all closed. She'd checked, and then checked again several times. The dog slipped off the chaise coming to stand beside her, ears erect. It couldn't be her over-active imagination, not if he'd heard it too.

She listened intently, craning her neck to capture even the slightest sound from below, but all she could hear were the night time sounds of the city beyond the window.

"What is it, boy? Did you hear it too?" she whispered.

The dog glanced up at her and then trotted out onto the landing, pausing at the top of the stairs and staring down into the hall below. Realising she was holding her breath, she released it and drew a sharp intake, holding that too as she watched the dog. It growled. A low murmuring sound suggesting he wasn't sure either. Then he barked, startling her, before he took off down the stairs at speed before disappearing from sight.

She waited… hearing nothing but her own breathing, the speed of which was steadily increasing alongside her fear. The dog would be barking if someone was there, surely? He didn't care for strangers and would always go for people in the street if they got too close or startled him. He'd certainly attack if he felt she was ever under threat.

Nothing. No sounds came to her from downstairs.

Pulling on her dressing gown, she edged out onto the landing, her skin tingling either from the heat or her fear, she didn't know which. Should she summon the dog? If no one was there then he'd come, but if she wasn't alone then they'd know where she was. Her mobile was by her bed… and they said to call if there was a problem, but… she was imagining it. She had to be. It was the lack of sleep, nothing more. To be so skittish was unlike her. It had been eighteen months. That was a long time and no one had said or done a thing. Why leave it until now? It's stupid.

Dismissing her fears, she took the first step down, gripping the banister as she slowly descended. Halfway down, a shadow moved beneath her and she shrieked before realising it was just the dog returning to the foot of the stairs.

"Oh… you bloody… thing!"

He clambered up to where she stood and she sat down allowing him to nuzzle his nose into her stomach, his tail wagging furiously.

"You scared the life out of me, do you know that?" she said, petting him.

The dog looked up at her, almost apologetically. She stood, relieved, and made her way down to the ground floor, intent on making herself a drink seeing as she was up anyway. A sneaky gin and tonic might help her sleep. Her four-legged shadow followed but as she entered the drawing room, he sloped off towards the kitchen, no doubt in search of a drink of his own or to find somewhere to get his head down.

Pouring herself a generous double, she dispensed with the need for ice or fresh lemon, instead choosing to fill the glass to the rim with tonic water, but the last of this bottle was barely enough to fill it halfway. Hunting through the pantry for a fresh bottle of tonic in the dead of night wasn't appealing, so she figured she'd make do. Who needs tonic anyway, she thought as she sipped at the liquid. It was strong, too strong and she baulked at the taste, putting the back of her hand to her mouth as her eyes watered.

Swallowing hard, her attention was drawn to the photograph, framed and mounted above the Victorian fireplace. Something was wrong… it didn't look right. It was offset to one side now, the slant visible even in the gloom. Clutching the tumbler, she slowly walked towards it. The sepia picture of the two of them standing together, her with her arms wrapped around his waist, both smiling into the camera… only… her eyes… were missing, both crudely cut out before rehanging the picture. She spun on her heel, looking across the room to the far wall where another picture of the two of them stood proudly on a table beside a lamp... the eyes were missing here too.

The dog barked from the kitchen and she dropped her glass, shattering it on the varnished oak floor. Backing out of the room and into the hall, ignoring the stinging pain from the soles of her feet as she trod on shards of broken crystal, she turned to see a figure in the shadows at the threshold of the kitchen. There was no sign of her canine guardian. The man was tall... powerful and he slowly raised a hand, placing his forefinger silently against his lips.

She screamed.

CHAPTER ONE

DUNCAN SET the rafter in place, wedging a spacer at the base where it met the wall plate and adjusted the line accordingly so it butted up against the ridge board. Nailing the rafter to the wall plate with his nail gun, he scurried up the sheeting he'd already fastened in place earlier, adding nails to where it met the purlins and finally at the ridge.

The wind was driving straight at him across the water but he was pleased to find it had lessened as the morning progressed. The overnight snow left a light powder coating across the surrounding landscape and a glance towards the mountains saw a deeper covering. He'd been expecting rain sure enough, but the sudden drop in air temperature had brought snow a month earlier than one would normally anticipate on Skye. This would likely be it now for the next three months right the way through to February and perhaps beyond, so unpredictable the weather had become recently.

Glad of the thick leather, fur-lined gloves he'd been given by one of the linesman who'd come to connect up the old McAdam croft a week previously, Duncan paused, throwing a leg over the ridge board and turning his attention to the scenery. It was breathtaking. He was staring out across the water, on a clear day he could see the outer islands but today they were shrouded in sea mist and thick cloud. A glance south and there were the mighty Cuillins, towering out of the clouds, a permanent feature of the island landscape. People would pay a fortune for these views, and often they did, but for Duncan it was simply home. A home he'd shunned for years but now one that'd drawn him back.

A car descended from the main road a quarter of a mile away and he looked across, recognising it as it picked its way along the undulating track passing each croft house. He knew it was coming to him. Over the years various inhabitants of the sprawling township had made a play of resurfacing the road and it was now a patchwork of tarmac, shingle and in other places, mud, pitted and crumbling in many places but still passable even by the average car.

Adjusting his woollen beanie so he could scratch an itch, the material irritating his scalp, he watched the occupants of the car as they drew nearer. There were two. One was his sister, Roslyn, and the driver would be her husband Ronnie. They'd already been across to bring the sheep down from the high ground ahead of the forecast weather change. Duncan figured it was unnecessary as the animals were quite capable of surviving the rain, but as it turned out Ronnie had been correct.

Somehow Ronnie had foreseen snow and Duncan recalled how little fun it'd been as a child when he'd had to trudge out through knee-deep snowfall alongside his father to locate and often dig out trapped animals who'd found themselves buried against walls or in dips in the land whilst searching for safety from the elements. A brutal storm could see them lose a fair number of their flock and on a small croft such as theirs at the time, that was a result they couldn't countenance.

The car pulled up beside Duncan's old caravan, his temporary home that had been such for three months now since he'd made the decision to resettle back home and patch up the old family croft house. At the present rate of building, he'd be in there for another three months at least. Roslyn got out and shot Duncan a smile in greeting. Ronnie clambered out his side, slower than his wife, but his cumbersome bulk made his movements that bit stiffer. He was a powerhouse of a man, solid and well suited for an outdoor life. Quite the opposite of Duncan, not that he'd admit it if pressed.

"You should have got that roof on weeks back," Ronnie said, wiping his nose with the back of his hand before zipping up his gilet and donning his own woollen hat. "Like I told you, you're leaving it late."

"Aye, you did," Duncan said. It would be churlish to argue. The truth was that Duncan would like nothing more than to have a handful of people up at the croft hammering out the joinery and getting the place wind and watertight, but he didn't have that kind of money to hand and besides, his case load also impacted on the available time he had spare to work on the old place. Arriving in Portree in place of the incumbent who was off on long-term sick leave, he'd been surprised to find as great a backlog as he had. Seemingly, even the most remote and picturesque locations had just as many villains per capita as he'd found in Glasgow. Not that that surprised him, not really. The people of Skye were long used to dealing with their own matters, and seldom let such things as national law get in the way of that. Not if they could help it at any rate.

"When is the roof going on?"

"End of the week," Duncan said. Ronnie scowled, clearly

unimpressed. Duncan cast a glance heavenward. "If the rain holds off, it'll be grand. Snow isn't a problem as I can sweep it off."

Ronnie snorted and turned away, heading for the barn where the sheep huddled in relative sanctuary.

"Aye, if you say so."

Duncan arched his eyebrows, but his brother-in-law didn't see. Ros sent him an apologetic look and he waved away the need before sliding down the boarded section of roof to the scaffold at ceiling level.

"How is the build going?" she asked as Duncan made his way down the attached ladder, dropping lightly into the inch of snow that covered the ground. His breath exhaled into a cloud of vapour as he clapped his hands together. Sitting still for even a moment in these conditions was enough to make you feel the cold regardless of how many layers you were sporting.

"Slowly," he said, grimacing and following her eye as she cast a glance over his progress. The old McAdam family croft was in a poor state of repair. Uninhabited for years and left for Mother Nature to consume, she'd done so with ease. The old roof, battered by the Atlantic storms had sprung leaks, rotted and subsequently collapsed in on itself, taking the ceilings of the ground floor down with it. It'd taken Duncan weeks simply to clear away the vegetation sprouting from the stonework and to re-point the mortar where required, which was pretty much every facing of the building, let alone cut in new stone in order to raise the height of the gable ends to allow space for a second floor.

Duncan had plans, but even he was realising that maybe he'd bitten off a little more than he could chew on this occasion.

"I wish you'd come and stay with us," Ros said, turning her gaze back onto Duncan. "At least until you have somewhere warm and dry to stay."

Looking at his caravan, Duncan inclined his head towards Ronnie. "Have you run that by him?"

"Och… don't you worry about what he has to say. He's full of nothing but pish and whinge."

Duncan laughed but shook his head. "Nah, I'm all right where I am, sis. Don't worry."

Her expression seemed dubious that that was the case, but she knew better than to press it.

"Besides," he said, "it may seem like a good idea now, but once it's been a few weeks you'll be sending me back out here with a canvas tent under my arm. Do you remember how we used to go at it when we were bairns?"

"A tent might be a better option than that thing over there," she said, unfolding her arms and flicking a hand towards his caravan.

"It's dry and warm," Duncan said, then tilted his head, "for the most part."

"At least come over for your supper later?" she asked. Duncan smiled. It was kind of her. They'd never been particularly close as children, and certainly not as adults, but she'd really been making an effort since he came back to the island.

"Sure, that sounds nice."

She reached out and gripped his forearm, squeezing it affectionately. Ronnie glanced over and caught her eye.

"I'd better go and help," she said, "otherwise I'll no' hear the end of it the rest of the day."

Duncan smiled warmly, hearing another vehicle approaching. He couldn't see who it was until the vehicle rounded the bend and crested the rise a hundred yards from his house, but he knew it was a 4x4 by the sound of the diesel engine. The black Nissan Navara came into view, easily navigating the uneven surface and pulled up just over the cattle grid at the entrance to the croft.

Alistair MacEachran popped open his door and stood on the footplate, leaning on the cabin roof with one elbow and holding onto the door with the other hand.

"Good morning, boss. Sleep well?"

"Morning, Alistair!" Duncan said, walking over to him, nodding. "As well as I usually do, aye."

DS MacEachran frowned. "That bad, huh? Shame." He looked around the haphazard building site, spying Roslyn looking over at them. He waved and smiled, and she returned it with one of her own. "In such a beautiful spot like this, I can imagine peace and solitude... a roaring fire in a wood burner... all warm and cosy. The perfect place to relax away from the trials of the day, hunting the great unwashed of Skye."

"Aye, thanks for that image," Duncan said, glancing at the shell that was his work in progress. "Maybe one day, eh?"

Alistair pointed at a pile of old timbers gathered to the east of the croft where Duncan had been dumping anything he couldn't recycle in one way or another. "That'd make a decent bonfire."

"I'm saving it for a special occasion."

"Such as?"

"Maybe when division send me a new DS... who isn't so irritating," Duncan said with a wry smile.

The jibe passed by Alistair without causing him to stutter in the least. He smiled. "Haven't you heard? I'm the model for the new service. The Federation are making me their poster boy for the new recruitment strategy."

"Aye, right. What are you doing all the way out here at this time of the morning anyway?"

"Well, you're not answering your phone."

Duncan glanced towards his caravan. "That's because I'm rostered off today… and I've got to get the roof boarded out before the sheeting is delivered in a couple of days' time."

Alistair looked at the roof and then sceptically at Duncan's target. "You'll be going some to do that. What have you got coming, aluminium or zinc?"

"Neither… steel."

Alistair sucked air through his teeth. "It won't last as long or look as good."

Duncan sighed. "Why is everyone on this island a master builder… and yet no one actually works as one?"

"Just a bit of advice, like, you know?"

"Yeah, well if you can see fit to boost my salary, then I'll happily raise the materials budget."

"That's higher than my pay grade," Alistair said. "Which is significantly lower than yours," he added with a wink.

"And I think your next performance review is going to disappoint you this year too," Duncan said. "Very sad." Alistair offered him an exaggerated frown. "So, what do you need me for?"

"Someone called in a body out in the hills," Alistair said. "Mountain rescue have been out to recover it, but they reckon we need to take a look before they will bring it down."

That piqued Duncan's curiosity. "Where?"

"The Old Man."

Duncan thought on it. It wouldn't be the first person to be caught out by the elements whilst hiking in the hills. Alistair must have read his mind.

"Fraser went up there an hour ago to take a look." Alistair

inclined his head. "He reckons we need to see it ourselves too."

If uniform had already been to the scene and saw fit to refer it to CID, then Duncan knew his inclusion was justified.

"The forecast has the weather deteriorating throughout the day, so we need to get a move on," Alistair said, glancing at his watch.

"Give me a minute to put my tools away."

Alistair nodded and got back into his cab, closing the door and rubbing his hands together to warm them. Duncan wasn't pleased to be losing a day working on the house. The roofing was another material he was compromising on for the sake of his budget, but he'd booked the roofers to fit the sheeting this week and therefore giving him a watertight roof at least, prior to the arrival of the windows he'd ordered which were due next week. This was pretty much the story of this renovation at every turn, one step forward and then several back.

Duncan had locked up his caravan and was walking to Alistair's waiting pick-up as Roslyn fell into step alongside him.

"Problem?" she asked.

"A work thing," he said, always reluctant to discuss the nature of his job with anyone outside of the station, family in particular. "It'll probably no' take long."

"Will you still make it for supper?"

"I'll see what I can do," he said. She looked glum. He stopped and turned to face her. "It looks like someone's died on the mountain, over Staffin way."

She gasped. "Oh, that's terrible."

"Aye. I have to take a look, and then we can go from there."

Her eyes narrowed. "Do you go out to see everyone who gets into trouble climbing a mountain in the winter?"

He smiled, kissed her cheek and resumed his walk.

"You'll let me know though, right?"

He waved a hand over his shoulder and pictured her rolling her eyes at the gesture. Looking back, he read her expression knowing he was right.

"I'll call," he said, reaching the pick-up and getting in. Roslyn nodded pensively.

"What have you done now?" Alistair asked as Duncan reached for his seat belt.

"To Ros? Nothing."

"No, not your sister. Him," Alistair said, flicking his eyes towards Ronnie who was standing with his hands on his hips watching the two of them. Duncan smiled and waved, but Ronnie remained as he was, watching on with an impassive expression.

"Lack of trust," Duncan said through the smile as Alistair put the pick-up into reverse and shot him an inquisitive look. "He's the suspicious sort. Not sure of my motives, I reckon."

"Trust? Hasn't he known you for years?" Alistair asked, finishing his manoeuvre and engaging first gear.

"That's just the problem, Al," Duncan said, smiling ruefully as they moved off. "He knows me too well."

"Your brother-in-law? Sheesh, remind me not to lend you any money then," Alistair said, with a snort of laughter.

"Aye, probably wise."

"If we get short maybe he could join up... suspicious people are always needed in uniform."

Duncan didn't respond. Ronnie said something to Roslyn as she approached and his sister at least, looked in their direction as they drove away. Ronnie had his back to them, annotating his speech with a casual fling of his hand roughly in Duncan's direction. His relationship with his brother-in-law wasn't strong. At school they'd been in different year groups and Duncan always found Ronnie to be somewhat aloof. A teenager, then adult, prone to brooding moods and keeping his thoughts to himself. Beyond cursory greetings and small talk over coffee if he happened to be at the house on the odd occasion Duncan called in, they spent little time together.

Duncan figured they had little in common but since his return to the island a few months back, he'd seen something else entirely. Ronnie didn't think much of him, not that he'd say as much. His silence, however, spoke volumes.

CHAPTER TWO

APPROACHING the parking area where most walkers set off on the hike up to The Storr they found a number of vehicles stationary along with several smaller groups milling around; some individuals were in discussion with uniformed officers and Duncan spotted Fraser MacDonald close to the gate at the entrance to the main tourist path.

The Storr trail began a little way back down the road and took a more circuitous route up to the view point and the rocks beyond. The Storr was a vast stretch of hillside along the peninsula with an imposing rocky outcrop above, grasslands sweeping away from it on the down slope. Fashioned by thick basalt lava flowing over weaker Jurassic rock in the Tertiary Age causing landslips that ultimately formed the unique landscape that is the Trotternish peninsula. People in their thousands flocked to the location every year, primarily to view the Old Man, a slender pinnacle outcrop towering above the boggy moorland and wild grassland overlooking the Isles of Rona and Raasay to the east as well as the Torridon mountain range of the west coast of mainland Scotland.

In spring and summer it is difficult to get near the parking areas, such is the popularity. Efforts had been made in recent years to deter roadside parking, creating a separate car park as well as lay-bys where visitors could park, at a price. Further along the A855 to the north and south, barriers were erected to deter parking on the soft verges on what was the main coastal route and therefore heavily used by traffic and often at speed. Further north, the roads narrowed and became far more difficult to traverse, weaving their way through sprawling townships and crofts. People had been injured in the past; accidents happened and a measure of control was necessary.

This deep into late autumn and early winter, however, saw only the hardiest of walkers heading up the paths. The very same paths that were presently closed to the public, barred with the blue and white police tape that formed the cordon. This appeared to be causing a few fraying tempers. Duncan could understand. In the past visitors would come to the island and stay for a week to ten days in one location, using it as a base to explore the island. These days, in the social media age, the Isle of Skye had become something of a tick-box exercise.

Visitors knew where the key sites were and they made their way around the island ticking them off, often over the course of three to four days, perhaps camping en route or staying a night at a time in various holiday lets. This kept the tourist industry busy, but it also had the knock-on effect of bringing three to four times as many people to the island at any given time, putting pressure on the roads and the infrastructure. For the tourists themselves, they might set aside a morning to conquer the Old Man's view point and plan to be further around the island by nightfall. At this time of the year, sunset came early in the afternoon and no one wanted to be caught out by the elements.

Fraser broke away from his conversation with a red-faced

man in his early forties who was dressed for the weather and probably leading a party of four who were standing behind him waiting patiently. Fraser smiled at the two of them.

"Good morning," he said, in his usual affable manner. It didn't matter what was going on in his life, how bad the weather or his day was, Fraser would always manage the same greeting; one that made you think he was in a calm and relaxed state. How Duncan envied him sometimes.

"Morning, Fraser," Duncan said, zipping up his coat as the force of the breeze chilled his core having stepped from the relative warmth of Alistair's pick-up. "Making friends?"

Fraser chuckled, lifting his peaked cap and wiping his brow before replacing it and sniffing. "Aye, they're not a happy bunch now we've closed off the mountain."

Duncan glanced at the hill walkers who seemed inclined to wait it out. Beyond them he saw two vehicles belonging to the mountain rescue team who would have been first on the scene.

"Who found the body?" Duncan asked.

Fraser pointed past Duncan and back to a VW Campervan parked alongside a liveried patrol car blocking one of the entrances to the parking area.

"That lanky guy over there," Fraser said, indicating a man well over six feet tall and, to be fair to the description, Fraser was correct. He was lean, towering above the three people who were with him. He had a thermal blanket wrapped around him and Duncan wondered if he'd got wet somehow, perhaps fallen into one of The Storr Lochs. Fraser must have read his mind. "He's one of these oddballs... what do they call themselves?" he asked absently, his brow creasing in thought. "Oh yeah... extreme fell-runners or something like that. He sets off while normal people are still in their beds having a long lie, and takes on extreme challenges and the like. The others with him were supposed to pick him up at Brother's Point later this morning."

Duncan looked up towards The Storr, shrouded from view in low-lying cloud. Visibility was barely a hundred yards at this elevation, likely worse the higher they went. "He's a braver man than I am."

"Daft, is the word you're looking for," Alistair said out of the corner of his mouth. "There's wiser on the hill eating grass."

"Aye, daft is another word for it, right enough." Duncan nodded towards the path up. "Who's with the body?"

"The boys from the mountain rescue are up there," Fraser said. He indicated to the gate at the foot of the track. "Willie Mac is waiting to lead you up."

"Ah, Willie's here is he?" Alistair asked. Duncan looked at him inquisitively. "Willie Maciver. Good man. Former NCO of the Black Watch… and a retired linesman with the Hydro. Not a finer man to walk besides on this island."

Duncan inclined his head. "Tell the witness… what's his name?"

"Benjy Macpherson," Fraser said, eliciting a chuckle from Alistair.

"Benjy? That's a bloody dog's name," he said by way of explanation.

"Tell him that we need to see the body before the weather closes in…" Duncan said, eyeing the clouds and the snow on the ground at their feet, "… further. What do you reckon, forty minutes up there and similar back?"

Fraser grimaced. "It's a bit dodgy underfoot. I'd add a bit to that if I were you. You dinnae want Willie and the boys having to carry you off the mountain as well like, you know?"

"All right, just tell him I want to speak to him and we'll be down as soon as possible."

"Aye, will do," Fraser said.

Duncan and Alistair approached Willie and Alistair introduced them. Willie Maciver was a slim but athletic man, apparent despite the amount of kit he was wearing. Mountain Rescue teams took no chances in these parts, never sure exactly how long they would need to be out and how badly the conditions might deteriorate, they came well prepared. He smiled at Alistair, taking his hand and then nodded at Duncan.

"How's it going, Willie?"

"Been out in worse, Keck, I can tell you," Willie said, using DS MacEachran's nickname — only permitted for use by those he was long associated with — his eyes seemingly taking a silent measure of Duncan as he spoke to Alistair. "Your man was long gone by the time we got to him." He turned and set off up the path. Duncan and Alistair followed. Duncan found the path pretty good underfoot, far better than it had been the last time he'd made the trek. Although he had no idea when that would have been. It could have been nigh on fifteen years, perhaps more.

The Old Man was arguably the most visited of the tourist spots on the island, helped by the fact it was only a fifteen-minute drive from Portree along well-maintained roads. It was also absolutely stunning. Not that any of that was visible today. As expected, the further along the trail they went, the thicker the cloud became. Duncan felt the temperature dropping away as they ascended the hillside and dampness in the air was ever present. He hadn't realised how out of shape he'd allowed himself to become in recent times, the climb was something of an eye-opener for him.

Working on fixing up his old family home had given Duncan a false perception of his condition. Manhandling beams into place along with large sheets of plywood, he thought he was in pretty good shape, but this was something different. The climb wasn't anywhere near as arduous as some others that could be visited on the island, notably some of those among the Cuillins, but stamina was required and he could feel his thighs burning within the first hundred metres of their ascent. Alistair seemed better equipped. Although he allowed Willie to take the lead in the conversation, a stance Alistair seldom relinquished without being forced to, he still managed to keep pace with only a steady increase in his breathing.

Duncan lagged behind and the other two eased their pace in order to allow him to catch up.

"Your man here not used to the gradients?" Willie asked, lightly mocking Duncan as they paused for a moment to allow him to catch his breath.

"Too much time chasing the wee bams of Glasgow," Alistair said, smiling. Duncan sought a witty retort but nothing came to mind. He was more inclined to make the most of the break. He did note Alistair's colour had changed in his face, and figured he was also finding the pace a little challenging but was unwilling to lose face in front of his friend.

"Ready to move?" Willie asked. Duncan nodded, although he was far from it.

"How far up is he?"

Willie glanced up along the path in front of them. To Duncan it looked like the path this far had been improved to help manage the volume of footfall but from here on up, the way looked to be more ragged with scree and lose rock to contend with. They couldn't be far off the Old Man now.

"Another ten minutes..." Willie said, then frowned as he read Duncan's expression, "maybe fifteen."

"Best crack on then," Duncan said, grateful for the respite. They moved off, marching further up into the cloud bank. Duncan looked behind them but rather than seeing the view across Bearreaig Bay towards the islands, all he could see was the mass of thick grey cloud, a seemingly impenetrable barrier. To lose your bearings in this could be life threatening. For many over the years, it had been exactly that.

Soon, shrouded figures became visible ahead of them. The cloud didn't thin but the small party of experienced mountaineers, all of whom were volunteers, had made a small encampment, offering some shelter by way of several pop-up tents they'd carried with them.

"Hello the camp!" Willie called once they were within earshot of the figures ahead of them in the gloom. They were greeted with mocking chants decrying how long it had taken them to get back up the mountain, but it was all in jest. "This way," Willie said to both Duncan and Alistair and along with another member of the team, Norman, they were led off the path and down a slippery slope; a mix of scree, frozen grassland and snow. All of which made the descent tricky.

They were descending alongside one of the lesser pinnacles of rock, barely a stone's throw from the Old Man. The body lay face down in the snow which was much deeper here than it was even fifty metres below them. Duncan approached carefully, paying close attention to the lie of the land before taking each forward step. Unable to see what was beneath the surface, and knowing it was treacherous in good conditions, he was keen to avoid a fall of his own. Moreover, until they knew what had befallen the deceased this would be considered a crime scene but the conditions were such that full forensic protocols were impractical at this stage.

Alistair hovered a couple of steps behind Duncan, following directly in his wake so as to minimise impact on the scene. Duncan got as close as he dared, looking down on the left side of the man's face which angled north. His eyes were open, his expression fixed and skin as pale as one would expect after a night exposed to the elements. He'd likely died suddenly. Duncan had seen death many times in his career; men, women and, sadly, children. The last moments of pain, anguish or suffering were often etched into features in a way that was almost impossible to comprehend, as if the last moments of mortal experience could leave a permanent mark at the time of their passing.

"He looks familiar," Alistair said. Duncan arched an eyebrow, but Alistair frowned. "But I can't place him."

Turning his attention to the rest of the body, Duncan found his clothing a curiosity. He was wearing jeans and a pair of trainers, the soles of which had ingrained mud trapped within the treads. That suggested he'd been walking somewhere off the beaten track prior to the ground freezing. Glancing around and considering their current elevation, this hillside would have been frozen beneath the surface for weeks now, but perhaps he'd picked up the earth from lower down, maybe crossing the boggy marsh of the foothills. However, the path up here from the car park was well laid and the packed earth between the treads didn't seem to match. Not that his observation could be considered definitive by any means.

Either way, it struck him as odd that someone would be out dressed this way what with the weather forecast of yesterday. Even his coat, suitable for the cold winter of Skye no doubt, was not one to protect you from the extremes of mountain weather by any stretch.

"How long do you think he's been lying out here?" Duncan asked no one in particular.

"My guess is yesterday, maybe late last night," Willie said. Duncan looked up at him and then at Alistair who nodded. "There's a covering of snow on the body, but only what came down overnight," Willie said. "I was up at the summit the day before yesterday and this whole stretch had visible snow cover. Three inches fell on the higher ground these past two nights but there's barely half an inch over this sorry fella."

Duncan looked again at the body and then at the ground in the immediate vicinity and had to admit Willie's logic was sound.

"Besides," Norman, the other mountaineer said, "there are still people walking this path. If he'd been here during the day yesterday, someone would likely have seen him."

Duncan looked back towards where they detoured from the path and he couldn't see it any more. That was due to the lack of visibility, though and, before this front came in overnight, there had been brighter intervals. Norman's assessment was also sound, but if you weren't looking this way then there was always the chance he could have been missed by a passing glance.

The deceased man's left leg was twisted at an awkward angle just below the knee and Duncan looked up to see where he may have fallen from, however it was possible that he'd slipped higher up on the slope and could easily have broken it in the subsequent tumble rather than being the result of a fall from height.

Blood was visible, matted in the hair at the back of his head and Duncan expected to find a significant injury to the base of the skull. The man's head lay at an odd angle to the rest of his upper body. He found it likely the pathologist would determine a broken neck along with the cranial damage. That wound alone looked severe enough to have rendered him unconscious if not worse.

"Do you think he fell?" Alistair asked, echoing Duncan's own thoughts. Duncan looked up at him from his position on his haunches next to the body. He then looked around the landscape. It was the most likely scenario. He was ill-equipped to be walking the hillside in the conditions of the previous day, or of any given day in these parts during the winter. The footwear he sported would no doubt be comfortable for day-to-day use or for road or fell running in favourable conditions, but they weren't up to hiking steep scree-lined slopes such as these. It was quite possible for him to lose his footing, pick up pace as he went down the hillside and catch one, perhaps two, mortal blows on the way down to his final resting place.

"Aye, possible," Duncan said. "But what's he doing all the way out here... dressed like this?"

Alistair scanned the ground around them, moving out to see if he could find anything else that might shed light on what happened here. The snowfall overnight would make it almost impossible to see anything but the largest of items beneath the covering. The cloud around them cleared momentarily and Duncan looked up at the great cliffs looming overhead. A sheer basalt cliff face, dark and imposing. If he fell from up there, then he hadn't stood a chance.

Despite the popularity of the hike out to the Old Man, very few people ventured on to reach the summit of the cliffs above them. The going got tougher from this point with largely unmarked paths and, from Duncan's memory, the route up required a few attempts at a scramble and the odd steep rocky outcrop to negotiate before you'd reach the summit. When you did though, and if the weather broke, you could see not only across to Raasay and Rona but there were uninterrupted views over to the MacLeod Tables as well as to the Cuillins.

Looking up once more, he contemplated the fall. As bruised and battered as he was, could he have fallen from way up there? If he had then he got off lightly, although he was dead so perhaps it was a moot point. *What was he doing out here?*

"Is there any vehicle in the car park that hasn't been claimed or accounted for?" Duncan asked.

Alistair shook his head. "I'll get Fraser on it. I've no idea."

"Is there another route he could have taken to get here?" Duncan asked as Alistair took a few steps back and began skirting the scene, examining the area in more detail. "I mean, we're assuming he was parked close by but… there are other ways up."

"It's possible to hike in from the south," Willie said. "It's two or three kilometres down the way."

"You think he'd make that hike dressed like this?"

"Aye, maybe. People can be odd, you know? The incline isn't too steep and you start at around two hundred metres. The trig point above us is at around seven hundred. It's a bit precarious though. You have to navigate the rim of a wide, fairly steep scree gully before you come along the escarpment and head downhill to where we are now."

"Is that likely?" Duncan asked.

Willie shrugged. "I've brought people off the mountains in flip flops and T-shirts… so nothing would surprise me."

"Aye, aye," Alistair said. "What's this?"

Duncan traced Alistair's steps, holding a hand up to both mountaineers to ensure they remained where they were. Coming to stand at Alistair's shoulder, he looked down. A camera was lying in the snow. It was damaged, the casing was cracked and some of the internal parts were lying nearby in the snow. Duncan took a couple of shots of the camera in the snow before looking up at the steep slope to their left.

"Suggests he was taking pictures… maybe overbalanced, lost his footing?"

"Aye, that's what it looks like," Alistair said. His head snapped round towards the dead man. "That's who it is. I knew I recognised him. That's Sandy Beaton."

"Aye, you're right," Willie said excitedly. "I can't believe I didn't clock him earlier!"

Duncan looked between them. "I've heard the name, but... who is he? Remind me."

"Local photographer," Alistair said. "He's got a little gallery down in the town. Sells prints... landscapes of the islands... a few paintings as well I think." He looked at Willie. "Wasn't he in the papers a while back for something special?"

"Aye... he won some competition on the mainland didn't he?"

"Aye, that's it," Alistair said. "I thought so."

Duncan turned the corners of his mouth down and nodded. "Is he any good?"

Alistair shrugged. "A photo's a photo if you ask me... but he made a living from it, so he cannae be too bad."

"Right," Duncan said, feeling the snow fall around them. It was light but out here that meant nothing as things could change within minutes. He looked up at the cliff and then over at the still form of Sandy Beaton. "Have a forensic team come up here, quick as you can. We need to keep this immediate area sealed off, no one comes onto the mountain without our say so."

Alistair sucked air through his teeth. "What for?" He looked up at the cliff as well. "The daft sod came up here to catch a wintry sunset and fell. What do we need a SOCO team out here for?"

"You sure about that?"

Alistair looked around once more, meeting Duncan's eye. "I'd say so, aye. What am I missing?"

"His wrist," Duncan said.

"What's that you say?"

"The body. Check his wrist."

Alistair frowned, but carefully made his way back to the stricken form of Sandy Beaton. "What am I looking for?" he asked, clearly unhappy. Duncan followed, dropping to his haunches and unzipping his coat, reaching into an internal pocket and producing a pen. He used it to move aside the sleeve to allow Alistair a better view.

"Are you seeing what I am?"

There was a red mark across the left wrist, the only one visible because the right arm was still trapped beneath the body. It was an abrasion, visible in contrast to the pale skin.

"That looks… odd," Alistair said, "but hardly conclusive."

"Whatever caused that mark also broke the skin," Duncan said. "To my mind… that's a cable tie or something similar. You ever heard of a hiker using cable ties to photograph a mountain before?" Alistair shook his head. "Keep this place closed until we know what happened here last night."

"You'll no' be popular for that decision."

"Tough. We need to keep this place secure until we can examine it properly."

"I can see the headlines already," Alistair said, wincing. *"The Dead Man of Storr…"*

Duncan nodded, looking at Willie and Norman. "We need to keep what's happened here to ourselves for the time being. Right now, we've got a tragic accident on the hillside and nothing more. Can we count on your team?"

Both men nodded solemnly. "No problem."

Duncan shivered, his thoughts momentarily drifting to the roofers due later in the week. He was going to be in that caravan for a little longer yet.

CHAPTER THREE

THE NUMBERS GATHERED in the car park at the base of the walking trail seemed to have multiplied by the time Duncan returned to it. More uniformed officers had arrived to close off the scene, assisting Fraser with the task of managing the people present, both walkers and locals who'd stopped to see what all the fuss was about. Word travelled fast in small communities and a heavy police presence on The Storr had not passed unnoticed.

Alistair was still up on the hillside waiting for the scenes of crime officers to arrive. Duncan was crossing the narrow car park to speak to the man who first reported the deceased when a white minivan turned off the road, passing the black-clad toilet block and pulling up behind it. Duncan caught Fraser's eye, standing stoically at the gated entrance to the path, making sure he'd seen their arrival. Fraser waved to say he had and crossed to meet the team with a member of the mountain rescue team ready to lead them up.

Duncan approached the small group who were standing beside a van. It was one of those multi-use vans depending on how they were kitted out, some commercial, others for camping. This one was the latter and the group were either eating or had their fingers wrapped around steaming cups of tea or coffee. Duncan felt his stomach growl as soon as he caught a sniff of freshly cooked bacon.

"Mr Macpherson?" Duncan asked the group, unsure of who he was addressing. Previous to climbing the mountain, Benjy Macpherson had been identifiable by way of a reflective thermal blanket draped across his shoulders. Everyone present was now fully dressed for the weather. His support team must have brought fresh clothing with them.

"That's me," a tall man said, stooping as he got out of the back of the van, a roll in his left hand as he stepped down. Sauce ran from the bread and he quickly tilted his head and lifted it to his mouth to catch it before it fell with a flick of his tongue.

"DI McAdam," Duncan said, involuntarily allowing his gaze to drift to the food in the man's hand. "I'm sorry to have kept you."

"No problem, I understand," Macpherson said, coming through the group to stand with Duncan. He took his measure. He was comfortably over six-foot tall and had a natural curve of his spine that made him appear to be leaning forward at all times. In his fifties, with very little hair on his head, he wore frameless glasses and had a narrow face with an ascetic expression which fitted well bearing in mind what he did for fun in his spare time.

"I understand you were out running, Mr Macpherson?" Duncan asked. "A cracking day for it."

He smiled. "We're raising money for charity," he said, smiling and turning his back so that Duncan could see the charity name emblazoned on his coat. "It's the great highland challenge; three marathons in ten days taking in the east, west and north coast."

"That's… one hell of a challenge."

"It is… and I've been training hard for months in order to do it."

"You didn't need this to get in the way, I suppose. We'll have you on your way soon enough," Duncan said. Macpherson frowned, nodding. Duncan felt his mouth watering at sight of the bacon sticking out of the roll. Macpherson noticed.

"Can we offer you something to eat, Detective Inspector?"

"Oh… no…" Duncan lied, "but thanks very much for the offer." He glanced at a familiar face loitering nearby, a journalist from the island's best-selling paper. He wouldn't want to be photographed tucking in at a crime scene. "Can you tell me how you came across the body?"

"Not much to tell I'm afraid." Macpherson looked up towards the Old Man as if he could see through the clouds, scrunching up his nose. "I was on the descent… I always planned to come down to a lower level to stay below the snowline if I could. It's safer that way, but there's way more snow than we'd anticipated." He glanced at his team, two of whom were listening in and they nodded. One woman seemed concerned. The way she looked at Macpherson made Duncan think they were possibly married or at least a couple. "Anyway, I was coming down and I was very unsure of my footing. There's a steep gully to the side of the ridge along the summit—"

"Aye, it's pretty treacherous at the best of times, let alone in the dark and the snow," Duncan said. "I'm surprised you took it on."

"See, that's what I said," the woman stated evenly, obviously irritated. Macpherson inclined his head.

"Yes, love… I know. I should have listened," he said to her

apologetically. "This is my partner, Eloise. She told me yesterday that I should alter course."

"And you didn't listen."

He looked glum, not commenting on her obvious frustration. "As it happens, I'd planned to stay along that ridge for a little further. I always prefer to run on wild land rather than made paths... it's an extreme runner thing," he said, smiling at Duncan who nodded politely as if he understood. He didn't. It all seemed like a colossal waste of time and energy but if it was for a good cause, then maybe it was justified. Besides, it would only have taken one misstep and Willie Mac and his team would have been putting their own lives at risk to save this particular daredevil. "Anyway, I was taking my time because I'd almost gone over a couple of times because I couldn't see what was beneath the snow. My torch just happened to pick up something in the darkness that caught my eye. It was him..." His eyes glazed over and he took on a faraway look. "I tried to aid him... but it was clear he'd been gone for some time."

Duncan nodded. "Did you happen to see anyone else around, either up where you discovered the body or after you descended to the car park?"

He shook his head. "No, sorry. There was no one around at all."

"How close were your team?"

Macpherson looked at Eloise, searching her face for an answer. She obliged.

"After dropping him off at the start point, we made for Portree and found somewhere for breakfast." She took a small device from her pocket and held it up to Duncan. "We have Benjy low-jacked with a GPS beacon, so we'll always know where he is, what time he's making and so on. That way we can stay close."

"Handy," Duncan said. "Did you touch the body?"

"I did… but only to check the guy's pulse. Not that I expected to find one. He was cold. I guess he'd been there since yesterday." Duncan didn't wish to confirm or deny anything. "The poor guy. That's not a good way to go out is it?"

"Is there ever a good way?" Duncan asked.

"I suppose not," Macpherson replied with a shrug.

"Has PC Macdonald taken your details?"

He nodded. "Yes, he has. We live over on the Black Isle… and we'd like to get underway again soon, if that's okay?"

Duncan had no issue with that. "Let me have a word with my colleagues first and then we can send you on your way."

"Thank you," Macpherson said and Duncan nodded to them both before walking back across to speak to Fraser.

"SOCO are on their way up. I don't envy them processing a crime scene in this weather," Fraser said. "They know they have to get a move on too. Willie had an update on the weather and the storm front is increasing on the approach to the Western Isles. They're forecasting another two inches of snow to fall in the next six hours."

"It's come early this year," Duncan said with a sigh.

Fraser nodded. "We've got the doc on his way over, too, to make the official certification," Fraser said, referring to the local Forensic Medical Examiner, "seeing as we're calling it potentially suspicious."

"Only between us though, right, Fraser?" The constable nodded. "You got the eyewitness' details, yes?"

"Aye. You happy to let him go?"

"No reason not to," Duncan said, glancing back towards Benjy and Eloise. They were deep in conversation and Duncan figured she wasn't giving him an easy time regarding his decision making. Finding a dead man in the snow would likely exacerbate things, little did she know that Duncan suspected foul play.

Duncan spotted Russell Mclean's arrival in the car park. The detective constable parked his car and then hurried over to them, a small bag cradled in his armpit as he struggled to zip up his coat whilst leaning into the driving wind. He nodded to Fraser and smiled at Duncan.

"The keck called down and asked me to run some number plates for you," Russell said.

"Aye, did you find one belonging to Beaton?"

"Yeah," he said, looking around the parked cars. "Over there, the Mondeo."

Duncan looked, spying a metallic orange Ford parked by itself on the far side of the car park. "I'll go and take a look in a sec. Are you taking over from Alistair and supervising the scenes of crime?"

"Aye, for ma sins," Russell said. He held up the bag that had been tucked under his arm to reveal a zip up cooler bag with a small flask nestling in a pouch at the side. "Got my provisions." He looked up the hillside into the dense cloud as if he could see through it to his destination. "Looks cold up there."

"It's cold doon here," Fraser said quietly.

"I hope you've got a few bags of your crisps in there to keep you going," Duncan said, referencing Russell's penchant for perpetually tucking into bags of crisps. Russell frowned, shaking his head. Fraser laughed. Duncan shot him an inquisitive look.

"He's no' allowed them anymore."

"What?" Duncan asked.

"Aye, Fraser's right," Russell said mournfully. "Wifey says I have to lose a few pounds." He tapped his ample belly with a glum expression. "She says ma' love handles are getting too big like."

"Is that right, aye?" Duncan asked. Russell nodded. "So, what have you got in the bag?"

"Seasonal salad," Russell muttered.

"Seasonal... in a Scottish November?"

"Aye..." Russell said, frowning, "seasonal somewhere... baby leaf and... rocket."

"Rocket?" Fraser asked, smiling. "Ten years ago we were spraying that stuff with weedkiller as it grew through the cracks in the patio... now we're supposed to be eating it in our sarnies."

Duncan sighed, patted Russell on the shoulder and left him to make his way up to where Alistair was waiting for him, and headed over towards Beaton's car. No one standing around was paying him any attention although he had lost sight of the journalist. He'd met Katie outside the sheriff's court following the conclusion of another case he'd attended the previous month. Despite not having been a part of that particular investigation, he attended as a senior officer to help manage the media rather than to actually take part in proceedings. She'd stuck in his mind; efficient, to the point, and one he knew to be careful around when it came to choosing his words. He liked her though.

Walking around the exterior of the car, he looked for anything that stood out, accident damage or similar, but the car seemed well maintained. It was only four years old judging by the registration number. Peering in through the driver's window, he noted the lock of the passenger door was disengaged which surprised him. Not wishing to draw attention to himself, he took out a clean tissue from his pocket and used it to pull the driver's handle, careful not to smudge any fingerprints that might be present.

The interior light came on as he opened the door and he dropped to his haunches to examine the interior. Much of the cabin was pretty clean, far cleaner than any vehicle he'd ever owned. It was obviously a well-used car though, the carpet mats were dirty and there were leaves and small stones present beneath the pedals, likely brought in on footwear. However, there was nothing to suggest anything untoward had gone on. The fabric seats showed no evidence of blood stains nor did the headlining of the roof which was where people inadvertently left trace evidence as they got in or out of cars.

Leaning in as best he could without getting into the car, thereby preserving the interior for the crime scene technicians, Duncan spotted the key fob in the central console storage area. It wasn't necessarily odd to leave the car unlocked. After all, how many people would be passing the previous night and stop to break into cars? Duncan wondered if he'd been up here very late and therefore didn't find security was a concern. To leave the key fob in the car however, that was very strange indeed. He'd never have thought that would be a good idea, no matter how low the risk.

Popping the boot, he made his way to the rear as the lid raised. Inside he found a number of hard case luggage boxes, similar to suitcases but knowing Beaton was a professional photographer, he thought it likely these contained his equipment.

"You're a trusting soul to leave all this there for the taking, Sandy," he said quietly to himself.

"DI McAdam."

Duncan was startled by the voice, believing he was alone. He looked up inquisitively to find Katie Matheson, the local journalist, standing beside the car.

"Miss Matheson," he said, smiling. She returned his with one of her own, broad and warm.

"Katie, please."

"Good morning, Katie. What brings you all the way out here on such a windswept day?"

Her smile widened. "I was going to ask you the same thing, Detective Inspector. Are you usually found wandering the hills in search of missing climbers?"

"Is someone missing?" he asked playfully, looking around. "I wasn't aware of that."

"Oh, come on, Duncan. You can do better than that," she said, looking at the cordon manned by Fraser who had been joined by his partner in uniform, Ronnie MacDonald, the two chatting quietly at the closed gate. "What's with all the drama? I've seen Willie Maciver out and about. Lost a few hikers... or is it something more sinister?"

"You're very observant, Katie."

"Well, it kinda goes with the job, you know? Normally, I'd say a climbing party has got into trouble, but you're all out here... so..."

Duncan shrugged. "I was just passing... thought I'd lend an experienced head to matters. Nothing more."

"Nothing more?" she asked, her tone suggesting she didn't believe him for a second.

"Nothing more," he said flatly. She looked over his shoulder and Duncan followed her gaze. Alistair had appeared from the cloudy backdrop and was now deep in conversation with Fraser and Ronnie.

"And DS MacEachran... the plot thickens."

"There's no plot..." Duncan said but she seemed unconvinced. Her attention turned to the car, casting an eye over the contents of the luggage compartment. Duncan pressed the automatic close button and the motor whined, lowering the boot lid. She still had time to get a look at the interior though, cocking her head and shooting him a broad smile, as if she'd seen something interesting. Unless she had superhuman vision enabling her to see through solid objects, he figured she was baiting him. He wouldn't bite. "Don't stay out here too long," he said, smiling and setting off to where Alistair was standing with the others. "The storm front is going to worsen and I wouldn't want you to catch your death out here."

"But I would have half the island's emergency services here to rescue me," she said, smiling.

He turned to face her, walking backwards and spread his hands wide, smiling but adding nothing. Her smile widened. Rather than being irritated by her persistence, the usual reaction he had to a journalist's intrusion, he actually found himself pleased to have had the exchange and very much looking forward to seeing her again.

"You should be careful around that one," Alistair said as he approached. "She's a canny one. She'll go far."

"She's too young for you," Fraser said bringing a smile to Ronnie's face beside him. "You dirty old man."

Alistair looked at Fraser with a measured expression and that wiped the smile off Ronnie's face. Fraser looked away as if he was surveying the car park, whereas in reality he was probably looking for a hole to drop himself into.

"Aye... and which of you lot is going to be working night shift on Hogmanay this year?" Alistair said. Fraser swallowed hard under Alistair's gaze. "Something tells me it might be your turn, Fraser."

"Aye, I think you're right," Ronnie said bringing a dark look his way from Fraser.

"Oh... like that is it, Ronaldo?" Fraser said indignantly. Ronnie shrugged apologetically. Duncan led Alistair away, leaving the two constables to bicker at one another which was something they were both supremely good at.

"Anything in the car?"

Duncan looked over at it, frowning. "No answers there... but maybe more questions."

"Oh good, for a brief moment I thought we had a simple case on our hands," Alistair said drily.

"It looks like he came out here well equipped to take some pictures or it's been made to look that way."

Alistair inclined his head. "Of course, those marks on his wrist may not be what we think they are."

"There's nothing to say he was brought here under duress. That wrist injury could well have happened earlier in the day."

Alistair arched one eyebrow. "You think this might be an accident after all? A dafty falling from the ridge in search of the perfect photo?"

Duncan smiled. "Let's root around in his life for a bit first before drawing any conclusions. Has anyone informed the next of kin?"

"Aye, I sent Caitlyn and wee Angus over to his sister's place. She lives over in Skeabost; runs a B&B."

"He's not married then?" Duncan asked, sure he'd seen a wedding ring on the victim's left hand but perhaps he was mistaken.

"Not as far I know, no."

"He's got a gallery in town you say?"

"Aye."

Duncan checked his watch. "If Caitlyn and Angus are taking care of the notification, let's call in on the gallery first and see if anyone knows Sandy's whereabouts yesterday."

"Aye, sounds like a plan."

CHAPTER FOUR

THE BEATON GALLERY was on the outer edge of Portree's town centre, one half of a shared retail unit, the other being a small family-owned funeral home. There was room for four vehicles to park at the front but most footfall would likely be from people passing by as they walked around the town. Duncan guessed a lot of business came from the tourists looking to buy something unique to mark their visit to the island.

The gallery was closed, the front door locked and the lights were off. Duncan cupped a hand to the glass and peered in at the selection of images hanging from the walls. The majority of images available were landscapes, which was unsurprising, and most were time lapsed images of sunrises or sunsets over the island's coastlines.

"Hey," Alistair said, drawing Duncan's attention by raising a thumb to next door, "I'll bet he wasn't expecting to use the facilities so close to home, eh?"

Duncan shook his head. The gallows humour of his DS was an acquired taste. A flicker of movement from inside made Duncan peer into the darkness at the rear of the premises. He stepped forward and knocked on the frame of the door.

Moments later a woman appeared from a room at the back, hurrying across the small gallery to unlock the door.

A bell mounted above the door chimed as she opened it, apologetically turning the sign from closed to open.

"So sorry," she said, smiling. "I don't know what's happened this morning but we're all a bit behind."

Duncan looked past her and saw no one, assuming the *we* in that comment meant her. She seemed flustered. "Do you usually get a rush at opening time?" Duncan asked as he entered the gallery, Alistair a step behind, his smile gone, now replaced by his usual expression of stern sobriety.

"Oh… no, not so as you'd notice," she said, wiping her hands on the sides of her dress, a floral print one piece which seemed a bit thin for the weather they were having, and eyeing the two of them. "At least, not at this time of the year."

"Just you here, is it?" Duncan asked. Her gaze narrowed as she looked at him, nodding. Alistair wandered a few steps towards the rear, looking at the artwork on offer.

"I see Sandy doesn't only do photography then?" he asked, checking out the canvases on the wall, his hands clasped together behind his back.

"No… the photography has always been Sandy's primary medium but recently he's been following his other passion for painting. We have been buying and selling artworks over the past few years, established niche artists and their one-off works. It's been steadily taking over the business really. Sandy loves his oils."

"Ah… does he, aye?" Alistair said, leaning in and staring at one painting in particular. "Neist Point… from the south side… unusual."

"Aye, it's one of his favourites… do you like it?"

"Oh aye… I love a painting, I do," Alistair said. "I'm a big fan of Sandy's work."

She looked at Duncan who wasn't sure how genuine Alistair's interest was, but the man was something of an enigma at the best of times. It was a character trait Duncan was certain he fostered if not enjoyed exploiting.

"I'm sure Sandy would love to hear that in person... but I'm afraid he's not in at the moment."

"Is he usually?" Duncan asked.

"Not always... but he was supposed to be opening up this morning. I had... well, I had an appointment and he said he would," she said, lowering her voice although they were the only ones present. "I guess he forgot."

Duncan nodded. He reached into his pocket and took out his ID, opening the wallet to reveal his warrant card. "DI McAdam... and DS MacEachran," Duncan said, indicating Alistair who was still admiring paintings in the background."

"Oh my... whatever is the matter?"

"Can I ask your name?"

"Erin... Erin Henderson," she said, looking between Duncan and Alistair. "I look after the gallery... and do some of Sandy's admin."

"Right," Duncan said, smiling. "You said Sandy was due to open up today. Do you know his plans for the last day or two?"

Erin thought hard, her forehead creased. "He wasn't... planning a photo shoot over the weekend. He likes drama... and the forecast was quite bland for the end of the week."

"Little did he know, eh?" Alistair said.

She smiled awkwardly. "Yes, I suppose so... but none of us should be surprised when it comes to weather in these parts."

"That's true," Duncan said. "So, what did he have planned? Do you know?"

"I can check the diary... see if he wrote anything in but if it was personal... then I'd have no idea," Erin said, moving quickly to the small counter set against one wall of the shop. There was only space for a telephone, a small diary book and a cash register. Duncan cast an eye across the photos available for sale. They were priced in the hundreds of pounds.

"Are these the originals?" he asked, "or are they prints?"

"Oh, prints of course," Erin said, opening the diary. "Sandy would never release his copyright."

"Does he sell many?"

She found the right page in the diary, holding it open with her forefinger and glanced up at Duncan. "Yes and no. The tourist boost is always welcome… and Sandy's photos used to sell better than they do at the moment but…"

"But?" Duncan asked, coming to stand with her.

"Well," she said, checking around them instinctively to ensure she wouldn't be overheard, "he's been trying all manner of new ways to shift the needle, so to speak."

"New ways?"

"Yes… these NFTs… things like that." She rolled her eyes. "I have no idea what he's going on about most of the time, but Sandy's always keen to try new things."

Duncan nodded, looking down at the diary. Erin's eyes went to it as well. The weekend pages were blank. "He had nothing planned work wise then?"

She shrugged. "He could have had something personal on. Why do you ask?"

Duncan ignored the question for now. "How well do you know him?"

She hesitated, only for a fraction of a second, but it was enough to pique Duncan's curiosity. "I… I've worked for him for the last three years." She averted her eyes from Duncan's.

"Would you consider yourself friends?"

"Yes, I would say so."

"And how is Sandy at the moment, within himself I mean?"

Erin fixed him with a stare, perhaps trying to read him. "He is… Sandy."

"Meaning?"

"Well, he's a hard man to read sometimes. He can be a bit up and down," she said, pursing her lips. "Ever since that wife of his left… he's been… erratic."

"Oh, I didn't realise he was married," Duncan said. Alistair came to join them having finished circling the gallery.

"He's not, not anymore," Erin said. There was intonation in her tone that suggested she was pleased about that fact. A response spurred on by loyalty to her friend and employer or something else? Duncan wasn't sure.

"Acrimonious, was it?" Alistair asked with a knowing nod.

Erin snorted. "Somewhat, yes. She really did a number on him. I'm not sure Sandy will ever recover from it."

"Mentally or financially?" Alistair asked.

Erin glanced at him with a steady look. "Both."

Alistair flicked his eyebrows and sighed. "Love can be a brutal pastime," he said quietly.

"Aye, it can," Erin agreed. Alistair looked down, at the diary Duncan thought, but his eyes narrowed.

"Henderson you say?"

"Aye, that's right."

"Are you married to Dougie Henderson… from out Borve way?"

She inclined her head towards him. "Aye, didn't know he was famous."

Alistair smiled. "Ah… no, I just know Dougie well. I go back a long way with him."

"Right… well, Dougie's got a lot of friends. Always has done."

Alistair nodded. Duncan considered the exchange but didn't comment. Erin's gaze lingered on Alistair and he didn't break the eye contact.

"Erin, could Sandy have gone out yesterday for any reason?" Duncan asked.

She turned back to Duncan. "I guess so. We don't get as much snow on the island as many people think, so the weather forecast might have inspired him to do something extra." She looked around at the images on the walls. "Snow scenes tend to sell well. They stand out I guess."

"Business is good?" Duncan asked. She shrugged. "Before, you said that sales have been better."

"Aye, they have been," she said. "Sandy's been doing better with the paintings of late."

"Oh right… the competition win must have helped?" Alistair asked.

"That's right… it's all kind of taken off from that."

"What was that again?" Duncan asked.

"Oh… it was a thing run by the National Arts Council, to encourage new artists in the country. Sandy submitted a piece and it only went and won the whole competition! It was so unexpected."

"To win a national prize must have been quite something," Duncan said.

Erin grinned. "Oh, he was ecstatic. Not just for the kudos from his peers but the prize money really helped things here at the gallery."

"How much did he win?" Duncan asked.

"The prize was a grant of two thousand pounds," she said, "to go towards costs and to help the artist continue to paint, but the real prize was the auctioning off of the winning painting. That's what made the difference."

"And how much did he get for that?" Alistair asked. "At

the auction, I mean?"

"It sold for twenty-two thousand pounds… to a gallery down in Edinburgh," she said gleefully. "They've been in talks with Sandy to host an exhibition of his work."

"Oh… that would be grand," Alistair said, "and so richly deserved."

"Wouldn't it!" Erin said. Alistair caught Duncan looking at him intensely and when Erin wouldn't see, he winked. "The problem for Sandy though is that he hasn't been focussing on the painting until now. If they wanted to run an exhibition of his photography then he could fill a gallery five times over, but the painting is so, so time consuming that he can't keep up with the demand."

"The photography sells at quite a price," Duncan said, glancing at the nearby pictures. Even the smaller prints were three figures. "How much does a canvas go for?"

"Thousands," Alistair said, nodding towards the paintings hanging in the rear half of the gallery.

"That's right," Erin said, "thousands. Although, he doesn't have many to sell."

"And has he always painted?" Duncan asked.

"Oh yes, as far back as I can remember. It's always been a passion of his, but the photography has been what pays the bills. To that end he's been doing more commercial work recently… until the painting started earning at least."

"Commercial work?" Duncan asked.

She shrugged. "Whatever paid really. I mean, he's stopped short of wedding photography, but he's been willing to under-take almost anything. To be honest, it was getting him down at the back end of last year. If the painting side of things hadn't come off, I worry about what might have happened."

"In what way?"

"Well… Sandy is…" she stopped, looking at both of them,

perhaps sensing she was speaking too freely about her employer. "What's this all about?"

"I'm afraid that we've found a body... and although we are awaiting an official identification, we have cause to believe it is Sandy Beaton."

Erin gasped, raising a hand to her mouth. She seemed momentarily unsteady on her feet and Duncan thought she might faint, preparing to reach out and grasp her if needed, but she gathered herself, fixing him with her eye.

"Are you sure?"

"We believe so," Duncan said, glancing at Alistair. Erin followed his gaze to him and Alistair nodded.

"I can't believe it... I was only with him..."

Duncan and Alistair exchanged a look. "With him when?" Duncan asked.

Erin's eyes darted to Duncan and away again as she shook her head, frowning deeply. "The other day... Saturday... the morning. The gallery closes at one on Saturdays and we... we were both here."

"And you haven't seen him since?"

She looked at Duncan, meeting his gaze for a second before looking away again, shaking her head.

"Have you spoken to him?" Alistair asked.

Again, she shook her head.

"I can appreciate this is quite a shock for you," Duncan said.

"Y–Yes, it is," she said, pulling out a little wooden stool from its resting place under the counter, sinking onto it and bracing herself on the counter with her right hand. "Poor Sandy. What... happened?"

"We're not sure yet," Duncan said, "but it looks like he may have lost his footing and fallen."

She looked up at him. "Where was he?"

"Up at the Old Man," Duncan said.

She inclined her head. "That wouldn't surprise me." She laughed. It was a dry sound. "That's one of the most photographed places on the island. I'll bet he was going to paint a landscape... he talked about it often enough." She shook her head. "Damned fool going out there by himself."

"Would he have done so without telling anyone?" Duncan asked. "I know it's a well-walked path, but the weather being what it was yesterday..."

Erin looked bemused. "Hard to say. Sandy... is a whirl-wind of passion... for all that he loves. He never allows anything to get in the way of what he wants." She looked furtively between them. "After that... after his divorce, he said he had a second chance at life. An opportunity that he wasn't going to waste... the painting, the exhibition... nothing was going to stand in the way of seizing what he wanted. It was all there for the taking. That's what he said and I... I love that about him. His refusal to lie down and be beaten... by anything or anyone."

"An admirable attitude," Duncan said. "You say that as if Sandy had problems with someone. Did he?"

She held Duncan's gaze, looking pensive. "Like I said... he is... was... very focussed on what he wanted."

"Has he fallen out with anyone recently?"

"Why do you ask?"

"I'm just trying to get a picture of his life, relationships and so on. Has he?"

Erin thought on it for a moment, then shook her head.

"What about concerns he may have had?" Duncan asked. "You suggested his business was struggling a little until recently. Did Sandy seem down about it... depressed?"

"You're not suggesting he did himself in are you?" Erin said, indignant. "He's not the type."

Duncan smiled. "As I said, I'm just building a picture. It all helps."

Erin nodded. "He's not without his worries, that's true, but that's life, isn't it? We all have our moments, don't we?"

"That's true. What about romantic relationships? Was Sandy close to anyone in particular?"

"No."

Duncan was surprised by the sharpness of her reply. He glanced at Alistair.

"Has there been anyone since his divorce that you're aware of?"

"No... but I wouldn't know about anything like that," Erin said. Her eyes shifted to the door as a woman approached. Before she could enter, Erin slipped off the stool and reached the door placing a hand on it to stop it from opening.

"I'm sorry," she told the customer, "but we have to close early."

The woman looked at her quizzically, then at Duncan and Alistair before retreating and walking away. She glanced over her shoulder at them before disappearing from view.

"I... I don't think I can stay here... not today," Erin said quietly, turning the sign on the door to closed and dropping the latch on the lock.

"Quite understandable," Duncan said. "Would you like us to call someone for you or perhaps give you a lift home?"

"Aye... maybe we could give Dougie a phone?" Alistair asked. Erin shot him a dark look.

"No... thank you. I'll be right."

"It's nae bother at all," Alistair said but Erin declined. Duncan took out one of his contact cards and handed it to her. She glanced at it, holding it with the fingers of both hands. It seemed to Duncan as if she was holding a grenade the way she treated it.

"If you think of anything that you consider we should know about, then please give me a call," Duncan said.

Erin looked at him then back at the card before snapping out of her reverie and nodding. "Has anyone told Morag yet?" Duncan offered her a questioning look. "His sister," she said.

"Of course. Yes, our colleagues are with her at the moment."

Erin nodded gravely. "She'll be distraught."

"They're close?"

Erin inclined her head. "Fairly. As close as Sandy got to anyone, but I know he was good to her. She has chronic arthritis and her condition is deteriorating. The extra money Sandy had coming in... he used some of it to help her, not that he could afford it. Not really."

"Seems like a decent man," Duncan said.

Erin's expression took on a faraway look and she nodded silently.

CHAPTER FIVE

Erin Henderson closed the door behind them, followed by the sound of the latch dropping as she locked it. The gallery had been warm and Duncan shuddered as they walked the short distance to Alistair's pick-up.

"What do you think?" Alistair asked.

Duncan sucked air through his teeth, glancing back at the gallery. Erin was walking towards the rear tapping something into her mobile phone. He found himself wondering who she was calling.

"I think she was diplomatic with the truth."

Alistair laughed. "You need a few more promotions before you can get all political on me."

"All right," Duncan said, turning to him, "I think she's lying through her teeth."

Alistair winked. "That's my boy!"

"Question is, which part of what she said was a lie?"

"Aye, good question."

"So, what was all that about Dougie? He's no' someone I've heard of."

"Dougie Henderson?" Alistair asked. "I nicked him a

couple of years back for a red diesel scam he was running supplying half the people on the peninsula with dodgy fuel."

"Sounds about right."

"Aye, I cannae believe it but he got off with a suspended sentence," Alistair said. "A hefty fine which should have put him out of business but somehow he got by. And as for his missus—"

"Duncan!"

The interruption came from the other side of the street. Duncan looked across to see Becky Mcinnes waving to him. He waved back and she waited for a break in the traffic to cross, bounding over to where he stood.

"Hey, Bex," Duncan said. He caught Alistair narrowing his gaze in the corner of his eye. The DS unlocked his pick-up and got into the cabin, leaving them alone. "You no' working today?" he asked.

She shook her head. "No, it's my day off."

"Ah right. How have you been?"

"Aye, okay," she said, looking down the road briefly. "It's been a while."

He nodded. "Aye, it has. It's been… a bit hectic with the house and all that."

She laughed. "I wasn't looking for an excuse, Dunc."

He felt himself reddening.

He hadn't seen Becky in weeks now, which seemed strange to him. They were childhood sweethearts, on and off, and then they'd been lovers for a few years in their late teens and early twenties. After Becky returned to Skye and Duncan stayed in Glasgow they hadn't been in touch at all, but now he was back, they'd socialised a little. It was tricky on Duncan's part because although their relationship was long over, he still felt a flicker of affection towards her, no, it was far more than that, but Becky was married and had forged her own path and it was one that steered her well away from him.

No matter how much he wondered about the past, it was all there, in the past. He felt a little awkward around her and based on how she seemed to react around him, the feeling was mutual. He'd thought she was avoiding him which, incidentally, was very much his chosen approach.

"Have you seen Archie?"

Duncan hadn't. He'd been meaning to call in on their mutual friend, but he'd been busy and kept putting it back. "No, I haven't. Why?" He read something in her expression. "What's up?"

"I'm worried about him, Duncan. I've called in on him a couple of times in the last week and… can you drop in?"

Duncan felt an unexpected pang of jealousy which irritated him. Why should Becky and Archie seeing one another bother him?

"Archie is a big boy. He can take care of himself."

His tone sounded harsh to his own ears and judging from the surprised look on Becky's, she thought so too.

"Well, good to know how you feel about your friends, Duncan."

"I'm sorry. What's going on with him? I mean, you know Arch… he's not exactly normal, is he?"

"Aye, I know but this is different. He wasn't doing well when I saw him and then Fiona's been around after… and since then, he's really dipped."

"Fiona? What's she want with him? I thought they were done and dusted."

She shrugged. "I don't know… but I think he could use his pals right now, you know?"

Duncan frowned, thinking about their friend. It'd been something of a miracle that Archie could get anyone to stick around long enough to agree to marry him, but once she'd left him then it was a bigger surprise for her to come back.

"I'll see if I can stop by."

"Thanks, Duncan. I know he'll appreciate it." Becky looked down the road towards the town. He followed her gaze, trying to see what she might be looking for but it was just a normal day. "Oh, and take some groceries with you when you do."

"Aye. Is he not eating properly?"

Becky smiled knowingly. "I think he's eating well…"

Duncan wondered what she was smiling about. "I can do that." She looked to her left again and then at Duncan, pensive. "What's up, Bex?"

She shook her head. "Nah… nothing. Who says anything's up?"

"You just seem… I don't know…"

"Listen, Dunc… I kind of want… no, need to talk to you about something—"

A car horn beeped. Becky jumped, looking behind her. A Toyota Hilux pulled up across the street from them. The driver didn't get out or wind down the window. Becky frowned at Duncan, then turned and waved at the vehicle with a smile. It looked contrived. "I have to go," she said, crossing the road. "Another time though eh?"

"Aye, no problem," Duncan said. He watched as she rounded the vehicle and got into the passenger seat, glancing towards Duncan just before ducking her head into the cabin. Duncan recognised the driver. It was Davey, her husband. They pulled away and Davey glanced Duncan's way as they passed but Becky remained focussed on the road ahead.

"I wonder what all that was about," Duncan said to himself as he walked to Alistair's pick-up. The engine fired up as Duncan got in.

"If you're about done with your love life, we can get back to work," Alistair said.

Duncan ducked a little and observed the departing Toyota in the mirror on the passenger door, intrigued by what Becky might have been about to say. Whatever it was, she didn't feel she could say it with her husband looking on. He felt a sensation of optimism and a flutter of excitement before quelling it.

"What was that you said?" Duncan asked as the Mcinnes' vehicle disappeared from view.

"I said, if you're done with Sandy Beaton's love life, then we can get back to work."

Duncan looked across at Alistair, with his ever-present straight face, watching him. He nodded. "Aye, I thought that's what you said." Alistair grinned. "So, you're going to tell me your theory about Sandy Beaton having an affair with his assistant, aren't you?"

Alistair cocked his head. "Aye, that's exactly what I think. You disagree?"

Duncan drew breath, smiling as he exhaled and shaking his head. "I would if you hadn't laced every word around Erin, her husband and Sandy Beaton with sarcasm about her relationship status."

"She wasn't very convincing in the friendship stakes, was she?"

Duncan shook his head. "No, she wasn't."

"About as convincing as you and herself back there," Alistair said, thumbing in the air towards the rear.

"What's that you're talking about?"

"You and the Mcinnes lassie..." Alistair said, grinning. "Let me know if I'm crossing the line, but if you were in the playground, you'd be pulling her pigtails by now."

"Och... away with you man! You're talking..."

"Oh... am I, aye?" Alistair said through a broad smile. "Just look in my eyes and say it. I dare you!"

Duncan shook his head, not wishing to be drawn into a debate. He didn't meet Alistair's eye though, and the detective sergeant laughed gleefully at his obvious discomfort.

"Let's get over to Skeabost and relieve young Angus." Duncan glanced sideways at Alistair who was still smiling but thankfully didn't appear keen to push the conversation any further. "And... you are crossing a line, so how about you just keep your thoughts on the case, aye."

"Aye, will do, Detective Inspector. Have no fear. I'll nae be saying another word about it."

Duncan knew that wasn't likely to be true.

CHAPTER SIX

THE BED and breakfast business owned by Morag Beaton, was located where the River Snizort began narrowing as it came inland. Alistair parked the pick-up and the two of them got out onto the gravel driveway. Duncan braced against the breeze, blowing bitterly cold air from the north down across Loch Snizort towards them. On a clear day, they would have a stunning view up towards the loch with the Trotternish peninsula across the water to the right. The main A850 continued on to the north-west and the Waternish peninsula before reaching the MacLeod clan seat of Dunvegan.

Alistair approached the front door, passing Angus's red Ford Focus, while Duncan looked back the way they had come, eyeing the ruins of St. Columba's Chapel on the far side of the river.

"Are you coming, sir?"

Duncan rolled his tongue across the inside of his cheek, shaking his head, catching up with Alistair as he rang the doorbell.

"You can cut out the formality, DS MacEachran," Duncan said. "It doesn't suit you."

Alistair smiled, wiping it from his face as the door was soon opened. He needn't have worried for it was DC Ross who greeted them at the door.

"Hello, sir," Angus said to Duncan and nodded at Alistair. He stepped back and allowed them room to enter.

The house was a 1960s construction, one and a half storeys with the rear facing north towards Loch Snizort. Angus led them through to the rear and a garden room which was little more than a lean-to bolted onto the back of the house to make space for guests to eat. A wood burner was alight in the centre of the room, its flickering glow casting dancing shadows across a tiled floor. The heat emanating into the room was quite intense and Duncan found himself loosening his coat.

"Sir, this is Ms Beaton," Angus said, introducing him to a woman sitting alone on a cane sofa with floral print cushions. She forced a smile but Duncan could see the news had hit her hard, which was to be expected. Caitlyn Stewart, his DC rose from a nearby seat, nodding to Alistair and addressing Duncan.

"Sir."

"Hello, Caitlyn," Duncan said before addressing Sandy's sister. "Ms Beaton," Duncan said. "My name's Duncan and I am looking into what has happened to your brother."

She smiled gratefully and nodded, gesturing for him to sit down. Alistair hovered a few steps behind them as Duncan picked up a chair from a nearby dining table and set it down in front of her.

"I'm sorry for your loss," he said. "Accidents out on the hills are all too common, especially in treacherous weather conditions like those we've experienced in the last twenty-four hours, but even so, it's never easy to accept when it happens to someone close to us." She nodded, her eyes drifting to a collection of framed pictures on the far wall. Duncan followed her gaze and he could tell that some, if not all, were in the style of Sandy's.

"Thank you," she said.

"I'm sure DCs Ross and Stewart have explained that we are still to carry out a formal identification?" He looked at Caitlyn who nodded. "But we can arrange that for tomorrow morning, once... well... we can arrange that for another time."

"What was he doing up there?" she asked.

Duncan inclined his head. "You're surprised to hear he was out on the ridge?"

"Yes and no," she said. Her gaze turned to the outside. She was curled up on the sofa, her legs tucked beneath her, wrapped in a thick shawl to help keep her warm. She seemed older than Sandy, perhaps by ten years or more. "Sandy was always keen to capture a landscape."

"He liked drama," Duncan said, drawing her attention to him. "That's what his assistant told me a little while ago."

Morag nodded. "Oh, I would say he certainly went looking for drama all right. In every aspect of his life."

"Why then, might you be surprised that he was out on The Storr in that case?"

She frowned, pensive. "Just... that he seemed more involved with his painting this past year. Photography has taken something of a back seat, that's all." She looked at Duncan with a piercing look. "He didn't tell anyone he was going out there. Is that right?"

"As far as we know, that's the case, yes."

She shook her head. "Sandy... never thinks... he's impulsive and just walks headlong towards whatever he's focussed on at that moment without a second thought as to the consequences."

"Would you describe your brother as rash?"

She snorted. "Rash doesn't even begin to cover it!"

"Is it something he would do?" Duncan asked. "Head out there in bad weather without telling anyone?"

She nodded. "It certainly sounds like him, yes. Foolish little boy."

Duncan found that comment interesting. He looked around. "Are you here alone?"

"Yes, I don't have any guests at the moment. That's normal, although I will expect one or two to pass through between now and Christmas."

"You're not married?" She looked at him, her gaze was stern and made him feel uncomfortable. "I'm sorry, it's none of my business."

"That's okay," she said, looking away. "I used to be asked that a lot more frequently… but I suppose it is a question that is asked less and less as one gets older."

"I didn't mean any offence, merely that it is difficult news to receive and to be with people who care for you—"

"You can stop digging that hole," she said warmly. "I understand. I have friends in the village I can call upon if needed. And to answer your question, no, I am not and never have been married. One man asked… once… and it was a long time ago. I declined, obviously," she said with a genuine smile.

"Fair enough," Duncan said. "Can you tell me a little about your brother?"

"What would you like to know?"

"The type of man he was… his friendship circles, business interests."

"Well," she said, sighing deeply, "that will certainly take some time. Maybe young Angus should put the kettle on again?"

Duncan glanced at his DC who nodded and left for the kitchen. Duncan turned back to Morag. "Anything you would like to share would be appreciated."

"Sandy is quite a character… and I am his sister, so there is no perspective of seeing him through rose-tinted glasses, I can assure you."

"Please be as candid as you wish." Duncan sat forward in his chair. "I'll be honest with you, Ms Beaton—"

"Morag, please. You make me sound incredibly old when you address me like that."

"Very well. Were you close with your brother?"

She shook her head. "Not so as you would know. Sandy… he isn't close with anyone, I don't think. He keeps everyone at arm's length… including that woman he was married to. Although… they were a poor match and well rid of each other, if you ask me." She shuddered. "A terrible match."

Duncan smiled. "And your brother, what type of a man was he?"

"There is something of the lovable rogue about my wee Sandy," Morag said, tilting her head to one side. "I love him very much… despite his best efforts to make that difficult, but he is a real chip off the old block when it comes to relationships with the opposite sex."

"In what way, if you don't mind me asking?"

She dismissively waved away his intrusion. "By the way he played the field, both in and out of his marriage, you'd think our father had stayed around to teach him."

"He played the field?"

"Like father like son," Morag said. "The only difference between Sandy and our father is the choice of woman he married. Louise wasn't like our mother… she wouldn't stand for it and ultimately Sandy's infidelity destroyed their marriage. Although, she is so awful that I don't really blame him for straying."

"I see. Louise… is she still around?"

"Oh yes, she is still on the island as far as I know. Not that I see or hear from her. She cut all ties after the divorce. I can't blame her. It's not like they had any children or anything, so a clean break was better for all parties."

"The divorce... was it acrimonious?"

Morag laughed. "Yes, I would say so. She wanted her pound of flesh, that's for certain. Not that Sandy had a great deal... besides his gallery... and his pictures obviously."

"How was he financially?"

She met his eye with an inquisitive look. "Up until recently, he'd been struggling. My brother is many things to many people, but I can tell you he wasn't a businessman. No matter how much he tried to portray himself as... what did he call himself... an entrepreneur." She smiled. "But he wasn't very good with money. Never had been. It passes through his fingers like water."

"Did he have debts?"

She leaned in towards him. "I'd be surprised if he hasn't, but I cannae tell you who he likely owes money to or how much."

"You said up until recently—"

"Oh yes, recently he's been doing quite well. Prior to that he'd been out to see me on quite a regular basis... with his hand out."

"You gave him money?"

"Of course. He's my brother... and," she looked around, "it's not like I have anyone else to spend it on."

"How regularly did you give him financial assistance?"

Her forehead creased. "More often than I'd like, to be honest. I've always been willing to help... but after a while it does start to feel like you're somewhat being taken for granted. Sandy... once he knew you were prepared to help... would... take advantage." She raised a hand to her chest, her expression clouding. "Oh, it sounds awful to speak ill of him..."

"I'd rather you were honest, Morag. It makes our job a lot easier when people are."

She seemed reassured by that and appreciated the comment. Angus returned to the room bearing a tray with mugs of tea, setting it down on the nearest table. He passed a mug to Morag who accepted it with a smile.

"Two sugars," Angus said, "just like before."

"Thank you, Angus. You're very kind," Morag said. Angus flushed as he passed a mug to Alistair who had his tongue firmly planted in his cheek as he accepted the offering. Duncan declined. Duncan watched Morag as she sat back, a flicker of pain visible in her expression as she moved. She seemed fragile to Duncan, more so than one might expect from the emotional impact of hearing of her brother's death. She caught him appraising her, and perhaps read his mind.

"You've noticed then?" she asked.

"Noticed what?" Duncan asked innocently.

"You're a detective," she said, cupping her hands around the mug and seemingly savouring the warmth in her fingers. "You're wondering what's wrong with me, aren't you?"

He felt bad then. She was right, but he didn't wish to draw attention to it. He winced.

"It's quite all right, Duncan," she said. "May I call you Duncan?" He smiled and nodded. "I've been living with cancer for some years now. It is quite literally in my bones... and I fear that my struggle may soon be at an end."

"I'm... sorry to hear that," Duncan said.

"Not half as sorry as I am, I can assure you," she said with a smile. "You wouldn't believe we were only a year apart, would you, Sandy and me?"

Duncan was surprised, thinking the age gap was far greater. Not that he said as much. "You were talking about the money you would give to your brother."

"Oh… yes. For a while I think I was all that was keeping him afloat. You see, he doesn't own the gallery… it is rented… as is his home. The only assets Sandy has are his photographs… and now his painting. As I said… he is terrible with money. Always has been, even when we were weans. Not that we had much back then." She frowned. "We had a wonderful mother who did her best by us… in spite of our father bleeding the family dry with his drinking and gambling."

"You mentioned how Sandy was like his father. Did he share the same tendencies?"

"For the drink and gambling?" she asked and Duncan nodded. "Not to the same extent where alcohol was concerned, although Sandy has his moments. I think our father's habits put us both off the drink a little, but when it came to proclivities like gambling, and especially to women… then yes, very much like his father."

"I see. So, what happened recently to change things… regarding his finances in particular?"

"He got back into painting… and to everyone's surprise, he was able to make money from it."

"He's good at it then?"

She shrugged. "I never thought so… but what do I know?" Her expression took on a faraway look. "I mean, his photographs were doing well for a time… but what with all this digital stuff… computer software… apparently, it's not quite as hard to get these perfect photographs anymore. At least, that's what Sandy said to me when he was here."

"When he was after a loan?"

"A loan? Heavens, if only it had been a loan. I'd never have seen anything but the back of him as he hurried away if I lent him anything."

Duncan smiled. "So, you never expected to see that money again?"

She scoffed. "No, certainly not. Besides... I won't need it where I'm going."

"Can we go back a step? You said your brother was making money from his paintings now?"

"Yes, ever since he won that competition, he entered down in Edinburgh... all of a sudden he was of great interest. People were contacting him for commissions from all over the country... and from abroad, asking to see his work... it was quite a surprise."

"That must have made a nice change for him?"

"Oh, it was, aye. The problem was he hasn't been painting for years and his earlier work... everything he did when he was a teenager really... let's just say it didn't really make the grade, so he was taking commissions in advance for work he was yet to do."

"And, at that point, he didn't need to approach you for financial support anymore."

"That's right. It was the best decision he'd made in years to go back to his painting."

"What made him do it, do you know?"

She shrugged. "I'd say desperation... but no one ever started painting because they thought it'd make them wealthy. I'd say it was that lady friend of his."

Alistair's ears pricked at that. He'd been quietly listening until this point. "Lady friend?" he asked.

Morag looked up at him. "Aye, Lorna... a lass he's been knocking about with recently, from what I can gather. Not that Sandy tells me a great deal, but people talk, don't they?"

"Aye, true enough," Duncan said. "You think he's dating this Lorna?"

"Talks about her enough, so aye, wouldn't be surprised."

"Do you know her surname by any chance?"

"Oooo... Lorna... Laura... Somerton... Sutherland... something like that."

Erin, Sandy's assistant hadn't mentioned her, but if Duncan's instincts were dialled in when it came to Erin and Sandy's relationship, then Lorna could well be a rival for Sandy's affection.

"And you think the two of them have been dating?"

"I'm not sure I'd say that is definitely the case. I mean, Sandy's always been a little... coy whenever she comes up in conversation, which is fairly often I should add. I wouldn't be surprised if she was another one of his interests who is married..." Morag said out of the side of her mouth. "The way Sandy spoke about her... he was keen, I think I know him well enough to say that, even if she was supposedly off limits or declining his advances. He has a way about getting excited when he speaks about certain people... you get to know when he's interested, you know? I don't recall him ever being so talkative about a person since... well... ever, if I'm honest."

Duncan exchanged a glance with Alistair who raised one eyebrow quizzically. They would certainly need to track this woman down.

"Do you happen to know where this Lorna lives?"

She shrugged. "Not exactly, no. From what Sandy said... I think she has a place out the back of Duntulm... somewhere above Loch Cleat, if my memory serves me right."

If Morag's assessment of her brother was accurate then there could be several local men with an axe to grind regarding Sandy's relationships with their respective partners. Perhaps if this Lorna proved to be similarly married or involved with a partner, then it could be yet another angry lover baying for Sandy's blood.

"Forgive me, Morag," Duncan said, "but for someone who

says they aren't very close to their sibling you do seem to know quite a bit about what he gets up to."

She held his eye momentarily before slowly setting her mug down on a small table beside the sofa.

"Forgive me, Duncan..." she said softly, "but since when does a detective inspector trek all the way out here to ask searching questions of a relative of someone who's been the victim of a tragic accident?"

Duncan had to admit it, nothing much made it past her. Beneath the softly spoken veneer, Morag Beaton was as sharp as a surgeon's blade. He decided not to respond to that specific question. Instead, he changed tack.

"We need access to your brother's house, Morag. We haven't found a key... only the fob to his car. Do you by any chance have a key to his home?"

She shook her head apologetically. "Like I said, Detective Inspector, we're not very close."

Duncan smiled. "Never mind. Thank you. We'll find another way in."

CHAPTER SEVEN

SANDY BEATON LIVED in a detached house on the northern edge of the island's capital, Portree. As the town expanded, small estates were springing up on the outskirts of the town. Shepherd's Road was located in one of these modern developments. Sandy's home was opposite an open green space with an enclosed children's play area although no one was using it when Alistair parked his pick-up in the street outside.

The house was in darkness, whereas neighbouring properties already had their lights on. At this time of the year, that was not unusual. There was space for two cars to park in the short driveway to the front of the house and as Duncan approached the front door he cast an appraising eye over the building's exterior. It was lime rendered, commonplace in these large-scale modern property developments. It was discolouring now, far from the crisp cream of the newly finished properties in town and a green algae-like substance was growing along the northern side.

The house as a whole appeared not to be bearing up well in the current climate, although Duncan glanced at neighbouring properties that were faring better. Perhaps their owners took more care with upkeep and maintenance. Underfoot, the block paving of Sandy Beaton's driveway was spawning substantial growth between the pavers, even subsiding at one end where rainwater had pooled. In the corner of his eye he caught the curtains of the neighbouring property twitch as he resumed his walk to the front door.

Duncan rang the bell.

"He lives alone," Alistair said.

"So everyone tells us," Duncan said. No one answered the door and Duncan did his best to peer through the obscured glass floor-to-ceiling pane to the left of the door. It was too dark inside to make anything out. "Let's try around the back."

The side gate was locked but Duncan used the bins to clamber up and climb over the fence, easily dropping to the ground on the other side and sliding the bolt back to allow Alistair to join him. The rear garden was unkempt, the grass growing to shin height except for where the moss had taken over, suppressing all other growth. The window into the kitchen was uncovered and Duncan frowned at the state of the interior.

Alistair found the back door into the kitchen was ajar, pointing it out to Duncan who came to inspect it. The frame was twisted beside the lock plate and there were black marks on both the door and the surrounding frame indicative of someone levering the door open, probably with a wrecking bar or similar. Alistair walked over to the French doors a couple of metres away. He sighed, shaking his head as he peered into the room.

"Aye, aye… that's not what I was expecting," Alistair said. Duncan went to join him, looking into the room beyond. The interior of the living room was a mess. It had been ransacked. Being a modern house, this room spanned the length of the building from front to back, a living and dining room combined. The rear of the room was the dining area and a sideboard set against one wall had been emptied out onto the floor. The drawers were discarded, one of which having come apart as it impacted the floor where it had presumably been thrown. The living room hadn't fared much better with furniture in haphazard places or overturned. Duncan could see the lining at the back of the sofa had been slashed with a blade to reveal the structure beneath.

"Someone's been having fun," Alistair said with a wry grin.

"It's been utterly trashed," Duncan said. Together, they went back to the kitchen door and Duncan eased the door open with his foot. Despite having been forced, it still sat on the hinges well, creaking as it moved. The locking mechanism of the door was intact but the lock plate had been ripped from its housing in the frame, the latter splintering to allow the door to open.

"They don't make them like they used to," Alistair said. There was no indication that anyone was inside, but the two of them entered with caution. The kitchen had a strong odour of rotting food, tobacco and the unmistakable stale smell of beer. "It looks a lot like my place a couple of years back when we left the weans at home for the weekend and came home early."

"I'd pay to have been there to see your reaction," Duncan said quietly as he looked around. "How long were they grounded for?"

"I'll let you know… if I ever let them out of the basement."

"You're a harsh man, Alistair."

"You wouldn't say that if you saw the state of our Persian rug."

"You have a Persian rug?"

"Aye… bought it in Ikea. The Glasgow store. It's quite a

nice place for a day out if you're in the area. Nice café. Avoid Saturdays mind."

Moving from the kitchen into the hall, Duncan signalled for Alistair to go through the other door into the dining room. The hall led to the front door with the stairs to his right. Alistair met him at the front of the house, coming from the living room. The ground floor was clear. Both men stood at the foot of the stairs listening intently. There were no sounds from above and no sign of movement.

Together they went up, reaching the small landing with three bedrooms and a bathroom off it. They quickly found they were indeed alone in the house. Every bedroom had suffered the same fate as the downstairs and even the bathroom cabinet had been emptied before being pulled from the wall, as if there was a possibility of a secret hidey-hole behind it. There wasn't, although the fixings had brought much of the plasterboard off the wall when the cabinet came away, so there was one now.

Duncan exhaled, looking around when they regrouped on the landing.

"Burglary?" Alistair asked. "I mean, it has all the hall-marks. In and out as quickly as possible… leaves a right mess."

Duncan inclined his head. "The homeowner isn't usually found dead, mind you. At least, if they are then it tends to be at the house itself and not a half hour drive away, halfway up a mountain."

"Well… we're going to earn our money on this one, aren't we?"

Someone knocked loudly on the front door. They made their way back down to the hall and Duncan was pleased to find the inside of the door had a manual lock that could be turned without a key. He opened it to be faced with an angry man in his eighties, leaning heavily on a walking stick, hunched over and glaring up at Duncan before looking past him at Alistair. Presumably realising neither of them was Sandy Beaton, his expression softened momentarily before he eyed them suspiciously.

"Where's Sandy?"

Duncan exchanged a look with Alistair, then shrugged. "Who's asking?"

"Who are you?" the man asked, one eyelid twitching involuntarily as his eyes darted between the two men. Duncan took out his identification and showed the man his warrant card.

"DI McAdam… and you are?"

He seemed startled by two policemen standing in the house and he searched Duncan's expression for a moment before nodding. "David… Bannon. I… er… I live next door." He looked past both men, craning his neck to see into the back of the house. "Are you two… er… here because of last night?"

"What happened last night, Mr Bannon?"

His attention returned to Duncan and he eyed him up and down for a moment.

"I did nae think you were going to take it seriously… but I have to admit," he said, cocking his head as a slight smile crept across his lips, "I did nae expect detectives."

"You called us yesterday?"

"Aye," he said, looking past Duncan again, trying to see into the living room this time. He quickly gave up as Duncan casually took a half step to his left to block the view. "A right old stramash was going on in here the night."

"A bit o' noise was there?" Alistair asked.

"Aye, I'd say so," Bannon said, the anger once more clouding his expression, his eyebrows knitting together. "It should nae be allowed… except for special occasions like."

"Loud, was it?" Duncan asked.

"Loud, you say? Damn right it was loud. I thought he was

goin' t' come through ma walls... which would take some doin' bearing in mind it's a detached hoose."

"What was it... a party or something?" Duncan asked.

"Aye... a party for one mind. Wouldn't be the first time. He's at it a lot ever since that wee lassie of his left. He's been a nightmare ever since... drinking... shouting... at all hours of the day and night," he looked around as if indicating the whole house, "letting the place go to rack and ruin. This used to be a nice street, you know?"

"It still is a nice street," Alistair said, looking past the man.

Bannon looked at him, smacking his lips and nodding. "Aye, but it used to be better."

"So... last night," Duncan said, "what was going on?"

"Ah... the man... Sandy... he was on a proper bender."

"Drinking?"

"Aye, blootered he was... absolutely blootered."

"Alone, you say?"

Bannon frowned. "I cannae say either way... he wouldn't let me in."

"So you spoke with him?"

"Oh aye... he was standing right where you are the noo." He leaned in towards Duncan. "Although he had a hand on the door frame so as not to fall over."

"He was the worse for drink then, aye?" Alistair asked.

"Not unusual, as I say," Bannon said glumly. "It's a shame really. He was always quite a good neighbour... willing t' put your bins out on occasion." He sighed. "All changed when his lassie left."

"Does he have many visitors?" Duncan asked.

Bannon thought on it. "He has that wee wifey who works for him... down at the gallery... what's her name now?"

"Erin?"

"Aye... that's her. Erin. Nice lass." He shook his head.

"What she's doing still tied up with that man, I'll never know. Not that her own man is very pleased about it. Mind when he came around here... hollering and shouting."

"Erin's husband?"

"Aye... didn't I just say so?" Bannon scowled at Duncan and then looked at Alistair. "These young people are hard of hearing... and they say I'm deaf!"

Alistair looked sideways at Duncan and smiled. "Aye, they aren't what they were in our day, eh?"

"Not so as you'd notice, no," Bannon said. Duncan was bemused that Alistair could be considered the same generation but hid it well. "You lot had to come and break it up."

"Were they fighting?" Duncan asked. "Erin's husband and Sandy?"

"Well... if you can call it a fight. Back in the day there'd be blood on the floor but... they were both making threats and throwing insults around and as for the wifey herself... I think she kind of enjoyed it."

"When was all this?"

Bannon leaned back, eyes wide, shaking his head as he eyed Duncan. "Well, you should know!"

"My memory is pretty bad... so... humour me, if you don't mind."

"Two, maybe three months back. It was definitely in the summer... the midges were biting of an evening."

"Right," Duncan said, smiling. "And what did you say to Sandy last night then?"

"I asked him to keep the noise down! He had his music on... and was throwing things around in there from what I could tell." He tried once again, unsuccessfully, to see past Duncan who remained steadfastly in the way. "Is everything okay?"

Duncan ignored the question. "But you didn't see anyone else with him? Did he have any visitors last night?"

"No, not that I can say I saw," Bannon said. "A few different cars out front... in the road like, but I'm no one to pry into other people's business. I would nae wanna neb like."

"Oh, you wouldn't, aye," Alistair said, winking at him. Bannon wasn't sure if Alistair meant it as an insult but the accompanying smile put him at ease.

"When was the last time you saw or heard anything from Sandy last night?" Duncan asked.

"Oh... I came round about six-thirty, seven... and it was all quiet a little after that. It's no' like him to listen to me like, but maybe... he fell asleep or something."

"Oh aye, he fell asleep all right," Alistair said knowingly. Duncan shot him a dark look and Alistair shrugged apologetically.

"We'll likely need a statement from you to detail all of this... formally," Duncan said, "but, for now, many thanks for calling by."

Bannon appeared to swell with pride, beaming at them. "Well, anything I can do to help is ma pleasure."

He turned and slowly made his way back to his house next door. Alistair arched his eyebrows at Duncan once they were sure the man was out of earshot. "Things getting all curious."

Duncan inclined his head. "There's no way Sandy Beaton was heading up The Storr in a snowstorm looking to take a picture in the dark, that's for certain. Especially if he was half-cut."

"Well then, that begs a deeper question, doesn't it?"

"Aye, what's that?"

"Who wants us to think he did?" Alistair asked. Duncan nodded solemnly. "Unless the old boy next door has got his days wrong… I mean, to be fair, he could have been asleep for the past week and just woken up."

Duncan laughed. "Aye, we'll have to corroborate it. Speaking of which, have someone dig out the files on uniform coming out here. At least we'll have some idea of how accurate the neighbour's memory is. We might even find out what Sandy and Erin's husband were arguing about."

"I should imagine it might have *something* to do with his personal assistant," Alistair said, pouting.

"Quite possibly. You know Dougie Henderson. How might he take it if he thought—"

"Or found out…"

"*Or found out* that his wife was playing around with someone else?"

Alistair's expression turned grave. "Well, regardless of what your man next door says, suggesting handbags at five paces, the Dougie I know would be locating Mr Beaton in a dark alley with a pitchfork or some other… pointy implement with which to address the situation."

Duncan nodded. "I thought you might say something like that. We'd better check into his whereabouts yesterday as well while we're at it."

"What do you want to do about this place?" Alistair asked. "Have SOCO check it over?"

"Aye, I reckon so. Even if Sandy was on a bender… this place is properly trashed. I'm inclined to think it's more someone looking for something rather than him doing it himself."

"Looking for what though?"

Duncan exhaled. "We'll figure it out."

Alistair looked past him, thoughtful. He stepped outside and walked halfway to the pick-up and turned to look at the neighbours' houses. Duncan followed. Alistair pointed to the house on the other side of Bannon's, and then across the street at the playground and open grassed area.

"That house has one of those camera doorbell things, doesn't it?"

Duncan looked. There was a chunky black and grey box mounted beside the door. "Looks like it."

Alistair looked up and down the street. It's a pity the house isn't opposite, but maybe they recorded someone coming or going last night."

"Worth a look," Duncan said.

"I'll be right back."

CHAPTER EIGHT

DUNCAN AND ALISTAIR arrived back at Portree before Caitlyn and Angus Ross; primarily because Alistair saw speed limits as optional when it came to crossing the island. Duncan went upstairs to brief the DCI on progress and by the time he entered the ops room, the two detective constables had returned and Alistair was already setting them up on their tasks.

Duncan's mobile beeped in his pocket. It was a text from Becky. *Have you spoken to Archie yet?* He silently cursed. It was likely he'd have his hands full for the next few days with this case dropping on them. He checked his watch and beckoned Alistair over to him.

"Listen, I've got a call to make... just a quick one. Can you keep everything going until I get back. Then we can have a briefing, see what we know already."

"Aye, nae bother. Everything all right?" Alistair asked. "You need help with anything?"

"Nah... it's all good, don't worry. Just something personal someone asked me to look into."

"Ah… right," Alistair said, lowering his voice. "Anything to do with seeing that Mcinnes lassie from earlier?"

Duncan met Alistair's eye, trying to read beyond the question but Alistair genuinely seemed to be asking from concern rather than nosiness.

"Worried about a mutual friend. That's all."

"Right you are," Alistair said, inhaling deeply and standing upright. He looked at Angus and Caitlyn. "We'll have things underway in no time. I need to check in with Russell out at Storr and I'll speak to scenes of crime about Sandy's place as well. That'll take a bit of time, so nae rush for you to be back."

Duncan winked at him. "Thanks, Al. You're a star."

"Aye, and not a lot of people have noticed that, so thanks very much for saying so."

ARCHIE MACKINNON'S croft out in Kensaleyre was barely a fifteen-minute drive from Portree. It was already dark despite being only half-past four when Duncan pulled onto the track leading up to Archie's cottage. Sunset was before five o'clock by this time of the year, but the heavy cloud cover and storm front made sure they lost the light even earlier this day. Snow was once again falling and Duncan shuddered at spending the coming night in his little caravan if he didn't get a chance to preheat it before bedding down for the night.

The cottage was almost in darkness but for a flicker of light emanating from one window. Duncan knew that was the one room that Archie lived in. He only used three rooms in his home, by his own admission; the kitchen, bathroom and the living room. Knowing Archie would never come to the front door, Duncan made his way to the rear and rapped his knuckles on the back door into the kitchen.

When no answer was forthcoming, and reluctant to stand outside in the gathering snow, Duncan tried the handle and found it unlocked. He entered and was met by Archie's dog who scampered up to him, tail wagging. Duncan closed the door and dropped to his haunches, scratching the dog behind the ears. It leaned into his touch affectionately.

"Hey boy... where's the big man?"

Standing up, the dog turned and ran off into the living room. Duncan felt the chill in the air despite having only just come in from the outside. He followed the dog and stopped at the threshold of the room. The flickering light from an oil-burning lamp, set on a table in the corner of the room, was all that illuminated the interior. Archie, asleep on the sofa which doubled as his bed, was snoring, one hand hanging down to the floor where it rested in an ash tray which was overflowing. The air in the room was stale and smelled bad but there didn't appear to be any indication of damp which was good. These houses were built to survive the harshest of Scottish winters.

Duncan blew out his cheeks. Archie stirred momentarily, absently scratching his upper arm and mumbling something inaudible before he settled and the snoring began once more. Duncan shook his head, returning to the kitchen where he tried the lights only to find there was no power. He opened the fridge door to be met by an overpowering smell of rotten food. There was very little inside, not surprising seeing as the appliance was off. It was the residual odour of dairy products and meat that had gone off previously. Becky was right to be concerned.

Closing the fridge, he jumped as he caught sight of a figure in the corner of his eye.

"It's customary to at least say hello before raiding a man's stores," Archie said, leaning on the door frame.

Duncan laughed, still recovering from being startled. "I thought you were asleep, man."

"Aye, I was but some fool was rifling through my things... and it woke me up."

Duncan pointed at the fridge. "Well, I'll not be taking anything from in there will I? When was the last time you went shopping?"

Archie sniffed, wiping his nose with the back of his hand. "The other day."

"Which day?"

"Ach... last week sometime. Whenever. What's it to yer?"

Duncan observed his old friend. Even by Archie's standards he was quite a state. At least six-three tall and with a power lifter's build, Archie Mackinnon had an imposing frame beneath the mass of red hair sprouting in every direction and the beard that masked his features. All Duncan could really make out were his dark eyes which even in this light looked sunken and hollow.

"What's going on with you Archie?"

He waved the question away, glancing at the clock on the wall. "Fancy a drink?"

"Aye, a cup of tea would go down well."

"Nah..." Archie said, shaking his head. "I cannae do you tea." He turned and disappeared back into the living room for a moment before returning with a bottle under his arm, a small glass in his hand and the lantern. Both bottle and glass were empty. "Come on," Archie said, setting the glass and bottle down on the counter before pulling on his wellies.

"We going somewhere?" Duncan asked.

"Aye, if you want to talk to me." Archie stood, put on a thick coat, retrieved the bottle and glass and made for the door. "Oh, and bring a glass," he said, pointing at a cupboard above the stove before striding out into the steadily falling snow. Duncan sighed, retrieved a glass from the cupboard and followed his friend, holding the door open for the dog to go in front of him.

The dog barked and took off after its owner. Archie crossed the snow-covered ground to a small barn at the back of the cottage. It was a ramshackle building, cobbled together bits of timber and corrugated sheeting but sturdy enough to withstand the stiff winds that swept across the island. Archie levered open a large door sitting on a runner above, gesturing for Duncan to hurry up. He needed no second invitation, keen to get out of the snow. He hoped Russell and the team had made it off the hillside already, otherwise they'd be in trouble. Similarly, so would he be if the intensity of the snow increased and he hadn't already set off back to Portree.

"Close that door will you, Dunc," Archie said, hanging the lamp next to them from an old nail in the frame.

Duncan did as he was asked, sliding the door closed with some difficulty. The wheels clearly hadn't been greased in a while and the door shuddered to a close. The wind continued howling about the building, whistling as it found its way between gaps in the sheeting and even reverberating as it vibrated two sheets that were not as tightly screwed into place as they should be.

Duncan turned to see his friend walk to the back of the barn as his eyes adjusted to the gloom, in spite of the light offered by the lamp. The barn felt warm or at least warmer than he'd expected which was odd. Archie opened a door at the rear and the smell of wood smoke drifted across to him. Duncan wandered across to see what Archie was up to, just as the big man returned. He tore a strip off something and held out his hand.

"Hungry?"

Duncan squinted in the gloom, accepting what was offered.

Archie put what was left in his palm into his mouth. Duncan looked at what Archie had given him; it was salmon. Freshly smoked. He sniffed it and then took a bite, seeing Archie grinning at him, the white of his teeth looming out of his beard.

"Archie... you're smoking your own salmon."

He nodded. "Aye... Archie's Smokies... I should open a stall at the market and—"

"Where are you fishing?"

Archie waved away the question, turning to the side of salmon he'd brought in from the next room. Duncan made to step past him but Archie tried to block his path only for Duncan to side step him and peer into the next room.

"Bloody hell, Archie!"

Inside the cramped room was a fire pit, roughly four-foot square. Four metal bars were suspended from the walls above a smouldering bed of wood shavings. Duncan quickly counted almost two dozen salmon, gutted and tied in pairs at the tail with hemp twine, draped over the bars. He glared at Archie who looked sheepish. Now Duncan saw a half-empty sack of salt at Archie's feet beside a plastic tub which also had salt in it.

"There's no way you caught that lot in the river, Archie."

Archie smiled nervously. "Well... there's plenty to go around. It's all fresh like... cured overnight in the salt and properly smoked. There's no yellow dye used to make my fish look traditionally cooked because it is tradition—"

"You've been poaching from the farms, haven't you?" Duncan asked. Archie shrugged and made to reply but Duncan held up a hand. "No! Don't tell me anything... don't say anything... I do not want to know."

"Ah... Dunc... a man has to eat—"

"Eat?" Duncan pointed at the fish. "That is not a personal supp... Are you selling it too?"

Archie sniffed, averting his eye from Duncan's gaze. He shuffled his feet.

"Well?" Duncan asked.

Archie scrunched up his nose, lowering his voice, "Aye... but you told me not to say anything."

"Archie!"

"I know! I know, Duncan... I'm sorry—"

"No, you're not sorry, Archie. You're not sorry at all, are you?"

Archie's brow furrowed and he thought about it for a moment and shook his head. "No... you're right. I'm not sorry."

"Bloody hell!" Duncan said.

"Well... they've got thousands of fish in them there pens of theirs," Archie said. "They're not going to miss a few fish, are they?"

"If they catch you... you'll find yourself in front of the sheriff."

"If they catch me, they'll kick ma teeth in," Archie grumbled under his breath.

"Then why—"

"Because I need to earn a few quid, Duncan!" Archie said. "You know how it is... a few quid here, a bit there... it's how you get by on the island. It's how we've always got by."

Duncan rubbed at his face with both hands, shaking his head. "Maybe once... back in the day."

"No, not back in the day, every day. Things haven't moved on around here as much as you think, Duncan."

"Maybe not for you—"

"Not for many of us!" Archie snapped. "It's how it is. It's how it's always been." He cast an eye over Duncan. "You can stand there in your suit... with your fancy brogues or whatever you call them. And I'll no' be taking moral advice from the likes of you, Duncan McAdam!"

"Shoes, Arch. I call them shoes… and they're not fancy."

"Yeah well, whatever…"

Duncan took a breath, stepping away from his old friend's homemade smoke house, folding his arms across his chest. Archie lifted his gaze to meet Duncan's eye, losing the defiance and looking rather sheepish again. He shrugged.

"Tastes good though, eh?"

Duncan laughed, trying hard to stop but failing. Archie laughed too, his lips splitting into a toothy grin.

"Aye… damn tasty, Archie."

"I've got some venison if you'd prefer?"

Duncan sighed, rolling his eyes. "And those guys will likely shoot you if they catch you on the estate."

"Aye, but they'll have to catch me," Archie said with a wink. "No one knows the land better than me."

Duncan exhaled heavily, closing his eyes.

"Drink?" Archie asked, seemingly keen to change the subject.

"Is that why we needed the glasses?"

"Aye," Archie said, clapping him on the shoulder and giving him a gentle tug forward. A gentle tug from Archie was akin to being dragged by most men and Duncan found himself off balance as Archie pulled him across the barn to where he had set up a still. A small rack was set to one side with a half dozen bottles lying on their side. Archie picked one up and unscrewed the cap, passing it to Duncan who sniffed at the contents. "Go on, have a nip," Archie said, "but… go easy."

Duncan picked up the two glasses and poured a measure in each. Archie frowned at the level and against his better judgement, Duncan added some more to the second glass. Archie smiled as he received it. Raising the glass, he tipped it towards Duncan.

"Slàinte," Archie said.

"Slàinte," Duncan repeated, sipping at the liquid. It burned his mouth and Duncan coughed involuntarily after swallowing. "Geez..."

"I know... hell of a kick, hasn't it?" Archie said in a squeaky voice.

"That'll lift paint off the car..."

"Aye, it's good though."

Duncan set his glass down, wincing at the strength of the aftertaste. He stared at his friend who seemed self-conscious under Duncan's gaze.

"What is it, Dunc?" he asked after a moment had passed with nothing said.

"What's going on with you, Archie?"

He shrugged.

"Becky is worried—"

"Ah... Bex is always worrying about something. As if she hasn't got things of her own to deal with."

"She's worried about you, Archie," Duncan said. "And so am I."

Archie looked at him glumly. "Ah... it's..."

"What is it? Talk to me," Duncan said.

Archie shrugged again. "It's Fiona. She... er... you know, wants a divorce like."

Duncan frowned. "I thought you two were already divorced."

"Nope... separated... all official and that, but not divorced."

Duncan nodded. "Well, it'll give you closure."

"Aye... closure... right," he said, bobbing his head. He took a deep breath. "She wants half of everything."

Duncan looked around. "Half your fish?"

Archie fixed him with a stern look. "Half of everything. The house, the croft... everything."

Now Duncan understood. "I don't suppose you could pay her off for her share of the house?"

Archie sniffed. "With what... half a doe that I poached at the weekend?"

Duncan shook his head. "I... don't want to hear that. Seriously though, have you spoken to anyone about it... a solicitor or something?"

"Solicitors cost money."

"Divorce costs money," Duncan countered.

"Which is why I'm no' divorced yet, Dunc." Archie pulled a small wooden stool out from beneath a workbench and sank down onto it, nursing the drink in his hand. "It'll no' be Fiona. It'll be that bastard she's shacked up with just now."

"A postman, isn't he?"

"Postmaster," Archie corrected.

"Ah..."

"Tosser."

"Probably," Duncan said, nodding.

"Still... looking at the bright side," Archie shrugged, "he has to live with Fiona every day and I don't."

Duncan laughed. "You'd like to live with her every day, let's be honest."

Archie smiled. "Aye... maybe one time that was true."

Duncan allowed the silence to grow for a few moments. "So, what are you going to do?"

Archie raised his eyebrows. "I thought..." he sighed. "I thought I'd bury my head in the sand for a few more weeks and then..."

"And then?"

Archie shrugged. "I thought then I would ask you what I should do."

Duncan laughed. "Yeah, right." Archie laughed as well. "Hey, what did you mean before…"

"Before when?"

"When you said Becky had things of her own to deal with?"

"Ah… nothing. Forget I said anything."

Duncan didn't press for an answer but Archie was ducking the question.

"I thought," Archie said, smiling, "that you were going to ask about me questioning your morality…"

"Yeah, what was that *the likes of me* comment about?"

"Ah, I was just angry," Archie said. "Think nothing of it."

The thing was, Duncan couldn't help but think about it. There was quite a lot that Archie said in their exchange and, despite his protestations to the contrary, Duncan had the sense that Archie hadn't been speaking off the cuff and had meant every word. He just didn't know why.

CHAPTER NINE

Duncan entered the ops room, spying Alistair on the other side of the room standing next to the filing cabinet where the team kept their tea and coffee-making facilities. Caitlyn was at her desk, a phone clamped to her ear, concentrating hard. He was pleased to see Russell was already back from The Storr which meant SOCO had made quick work at the scene. They had no choice what with the weather closing in as it had done. The DC nodded to Duncan as he passed him, making for Alistair.

"All good, boss?" Alistair asked as he came up to him. Duncan nodded. "I was just making a cuppa. Do you want one?"

"Aye, cheers. On both counts."

Angus Ross approached with his mug in hand, Alistair passing him the box of teabags. He thanked him with a smile. Alistair cast an appraising look over the detective constable from head to toe.

"You're looking very colour coordinated today, young Angus," he said.

Angus was sporting a brown pin-stripe suit with a

matching brown shirt and tie along with tan brogues. He smiled at the compliment.

"Thank you very much, sarge."

"Aye," Alistair said, arching his eyebrows. "You kinda look like a big jobby."

Angus flushed and both Russell and Caitlyn burst out laughing behind them. Angus put the box of teabags back on the shelf, sighed and shot Duncan a resigned smile. "Note to self; dinnae wear all brown to the office ever again." A comment that only seemed to make the situation funnier.

"Ah... sorry, wee man," Alistair said, recognising Duncan's disapproving expression, "but that is quite a stylish combo... but a word of advice?"

"Aye, go on then," Angus said, reticent.

"Never come to work in clothes you wouldn't be happy for a drunk to puke on."

Angus thought about it, nodded and made his way over to the urn where they had the hot water. Alistair turned to Duncan.

"We've made some headway with Sandy Beaton."

"Go on," Duncan said, following Angus to put hot water in his own mug.

"SOCO processed the scene quickly but they assure me they were thorough."

"Anything stand out to them?"

Alistair shook his head. "Not really. The covering of snow has made mapping the area difficult, but they think he fell from further up the slope and rolled down to where we found him."

"From atop the ridge?"

"No, they don't think so. The FME had a preliminary look at the head injury once we'd got the body down and he reckons there isn't enough damage to warrant falling from that height."

"Tripped and caught a rock during the fall then?"

"That's a possibility, aye," Alistair said, "but we'll have to wait for the pathologist to complete the autopsy for confirmation of that. That should be done by this time tomorrow, unless Craig finds anything exotic during the process."

The pathologist, Dr Craig Dunbar, was a curious little man but was also good with detail in Duncan's experience and he was looking forward to his assessment.

"Sandy's camera was found a little way away from the body, a bit further back up the slope," Alistair said, walking Duncan over to his desk. "Presumably, he was holding it when he fell and dropped it during the tumble. The lens was cracked," he said, reaching his desk where a black camera sat inside a sealed evidence bag. Alistair held the bag aloft. "It's digital, so I had wee Angus upload the pictures from the memory card."

"Good idea. Anything interesting?"

"That's what we're just about to find out," Alistair said, pointing to Angus who spun his chair to face his monitor. The DC double clicked on a file and a number of folders were displayed on the screen. Duncan and Alistair came to stand beside him.

"Well, they're all listed in date order," Angus said, looking up at Duncan. "Shall I start with the most recent?"

"Aye."

"There's nothing from yesterday," Angus said, "so does that rule out the theory that he was out there to take pictures?"

"Can't say that just yet," Duncan said. "He may not have lined one up before he fell… or perhaps he deleted some."

"Aye, well there's nothing from Friday… but Thursday…" He opened the file and there were four picture thumbnails.

Angus clicked on the first and opened it. Duncan was surprised. The image wasn't what he'd expected. Far from the stylised panorama shot that Sandy had displayed around his gallery, this one was a picture taken in the street. It looked familiar and Duncan squinted to try and recognise the shops in the background.

"Is that…"

"Bank Street," Alistair said. "That's the seating outside An Talla Mòr… opposite the Royal Oak. They do a pretty decent bagel in there at lunchtime."

"The one on the corner," Duncan asked, "in the old church?"

"Aye."

The picture was taken in the heart of Portree, on a bend where the road opened up to reveal a panoramic view of the bay. However, the shooter was looking back towards the town. Angus opened the next photo and it was almost identical. As were the following two images.

"Taken in sequence," Duncan said. The same woman was in all four shots although the vehicles on the road behind her were moving but only slightly. "Maybe that was a burst mode?" Duncan suggested. Alistair looked at him. The images were so close together it was as if they'd been taken in quick succession, almost one on top of another. He leaned in and examined the woman. "I wonder who she is then?"

"I dinnae recognise her," Angus said.

"Me neither," Alistair said with a shake of his head.

"Well, Sandy photographed her for a reason. Can you try and find a name for her, Angus?"

"Will do," Angus said.

Duncan's gaze lingered on the woman, sitting at a picnic table sipping at a cup of coffee. Perhaps the café would have a credit card receipt or some CCTV footage that might help establish whether she was local or a tourist, or maybe they'd recall a conversation with her.

"Why don't you call in and see if the staff remember her," Duncan said to Angus who nodded. Despite the photo being taken in the sunshine, likely around midday and, notably, prior to this burst of recent snowfall, it had still been cold this past week and not many people would have chosen to sit outside to drink their coffee by themselves. Maybe she stood out for a reason. Perhaps Sandy had met her. Either way, it was a curious sequence of photos to take. "When was the file previous to this one created?"

Angus's brow furrowed as he checked the dates. "The next one was three weeks ago," he said glumly, looking up at Duncan. "I doubt that's relevant to his death."

"Aye, check anyway," Duncan said, patting him on the shoulder before moving off. "How about Sandy's finances?" he asked Alistair. "Any progress on confirming his sister's view of his affairs?"

"Caitlyn has been working on it," Alistair said and at mention of her name, Caitlyn hung up the phone, smiling at them as they approached her desk.

"I got a warrant for his bank accounts," she said. "The bank has been very forthcoming, which is nice."

"That was quick," Alistair said. "Who are you sleeping with to get results so fast?"

Caitlyn laughed. "Wouldn't you like to know."

"I would, aye!"

"My dad's the branch manager which helps."

"Ah…" Alistair said, frowning. "Well, I definitely hope you're no' sleeping with him."

"What have you found out?" Duncan asked her.

"He doesn't have a business account, so all his finances pass through his personal current account. I guess he's registered as a sole trader rather than a business, but for our purposes that makes things easier. The balance on his account mirrors pretty much what his sister was telling us... always in the red for the better part of two years, adding in random payments to keep the wolf from the door, so to speak. House is rented... and the monthly rental payments appear just as random as any other. There's three hundred and odd pounds going out to a company... looks like a leasing business, I reckon, so that'll be the car I guess."

"He really does live by the hairs of his backside, doesn't he?" Alistair said quietly.

"The cash injections," Duncan said, "are they the ones his sister gave him from time to time?"

"Aye, I reckon so," Caitlyn said, nodding. "That is up until about three months back. He got a twenty-two thousand pounds payment into his account from a gallery in Edinburgh—"

"That'll be the painting he won the competition with, selling it on to a gallery," Duncan said to Alistair. "The one Erin, his assistant, told us about."

"Aye," Alistair said with a sideways grin, "*his assistant.*"

Caitlyn's brow furrowed as she studied him. Alistair angled his head.

"Good chance he was playing hide the sausage with her behind her husband's back."

"Oh right," she said. "Who's her husband, anyone we know?"

"Dougie Henderson."

"Bloody hell. Playing with fire there," Caitlyn said. "Dougie's a firecracker."

Alistair sent Duncan a knowing look. "See, what did I tell you?"

"Yeah, we'll have to pull him aside," Duncan said, turning back to Caitlyn. "What else?"

She concentrated on her screen. "He has a few transactions passing through from the gallery. I know they're from the gallery because they're Red Stripe payments – that's an online payment service – and pretty easy to manage."

"Many of those are there?"

"There do seem to be more since he got a bit of publicity surrounding that painting competition," she said with a shrug. "I guess all publicity is good publicity."

"His sister mentioned commissions, didn't she?" Duncan asked.

"Aye, there's a few random payment transfers come into the account... each is around a grand, so I guess that's his deposit."

"And what was he selling those commissions for afterwards?"

"No idea. I haven't seen any large sums come in... maybe he hasn't finished them yet?"

Duncan exhaled. "Aye, I suppose so. How long does it take to do a painting? Anyone know?"

Alistair shrugged. "Maybe we should track down his lady friend and ask her. Morag credited her with stoking that particular passion in her brother... along with him stoking something else, I should imagine."

"Well, we'll have to ask. Caitlyn," he said, turning to her, "can you find this Lorna or Laura who lives out Duntulm way?"

Caitlyn frowned. "I'm good... but I might need a bit more? The last name was sketchy as well wasn't it? Somerton or...?"

"Sutherland..."

Duncan nodded. "Aye, well, see what you can do with it. There aren't many places out there, so we can always go door to door if we have to, but…" he glanced out of the window; it was still snowing, "I'd rather not if we can avoid it."

"I found something interesting," Angus said, drawing their attention. "Sandy has someone trolling his gallery on social media… nasty comments and stuff."

"Why would someone want to post shite about a gallery?" Alistair asked. "It's not like he's a famous footballer or something."

"You're new to social media, aren't you, sarge?"

Alistair clipped him on the back of the head. "Sarky wee sod."

"He's pretty big in the art and photographic community though," Angus said, smiling from his small victory. "Usually this stuff is just a bored keyboard warrior looking for attention, posting one star reviews just for the craic… but… maybe on this occasion they went a bit further, eh?"

Duncan crossed to Angus's desk, perching on the edge and looking at his screen. "Anything threatening?"

Angus frowned. "Nothing specific, no… but I'm only just getting going."

"Right, well if there is… see if you can trace the IP and if it turns out to be local, then it'll be worth a visit."

"Aye, right you are, boss," Angus said.

Duncan turned to Alistair. "Fancy popping out with me?"

"Aye, where to? My guess, it's either tracking down this Lorna lassie or having a word with Dougie."

"Flip a coin?" Duncan asked.

"I've no' found Lorna yet," Caitlyn muttered without taking her eyes from the screen. "Sorry."

"Tails, it's Dougie then," Alistair said.

"Dougie Henderson it is," Duncan added.

CHAPTER TEN

ALISTAIR MOVED to his desk and opened up the Police National Database on the screen. "Let's run him through the system and see if he's been up to anything before we head over there." Bringing up Dougie Henderson's profile, Alistair raised his eyebrows. "Hmm..."

"Something interesting?" Duncan asked.

"Aye, it looks like Dougie had a quiet spell after his brush with the law over that red diesel business... probably trying to see out his suspended sentence before getting into anything. However..."

"I like a good however," Duncan said, his curiosity piqued.

"However, there's a report here of a public order offence... Dougie was cautioned. It was dealt with by..." Alistair's frown deepened before his eye was drawn to a figure passing the ops room, "Ronnie!" he shouted, and the rounded head of the stout PC Ronnie MacDonald peered around the door jamb into the room, searching out who'd called him. "Speak of the devil and he shall appear," Alistair said, beckoning Ronnie to come over.

The constable made his way across the room, a cup of

vending machine coffee in one hand and a half-eaten sandwich in the other, frantically chewing and swallowing before reaching Alistair's desk.

"What can I do you for?"

"Dougie Henderson... you dealt with a disturbance a while back—"

"Oh aye..." Ronnie said. "What about it?"

"Was he fighting?"

"Aye, he was... scrapping with a bloke at lunchtime. You know that wee fella from the tyre place, the one on Dunvegan Road?"

"Aye. Serious, was it?"

"Nah," Ronnie said, shaking his head and then taking a sip of his coffee. "It was a whole lot of shouting and threats... nae nice for the passers-by to see and hear like, but nothing really to worry about."

"He was cautioned though."

"Aye, they both were. Had to really... couldn't just give them a ticking off. If it'd been outside the pub late on a Friday night, I'd have sent them away home with a flea in their ear but broad daylight... on the weekend in front of bairns and all." He shook his head. "The duty sergeant was right... we had to set an example."

"You didn't actually charge him though."

"No... if I had done, he still had that diesel thing hanging over him. He would've gone down like, and well, you know... that didn't seem right. Not for a bit of aggro over a woman."

Duncan and Alistair exchanged a quick look.

"What are you asking for?" Ronnie asked, reading their expressions.

Duncan asked, "Which woman? Erin?"

"Aye," Ronnie said. "It was Erin's birthday and they'd been out for a bite to eat and I reckon Dougie had been liberally applying the drink to aid the passage of the food... you know?"

"He was blootered?" Alistair asked.

Ronnie nodded. "I think wee Kenny – from the tyre place – caught Erin's eye... or he did hers... who knows really? Anyways, Dougie took offence to it and it all went from there."

"Anything in it from the other side?" Duncan asked.

"Wee Kenny?" Ronnie shook his head. "No' really. Kenny'd no' say boo to a goose like, but he'd had a couple down him as well... the sun was shining after all, you know." Ronnie tilted his head. "Probably got caught having a glance at Erin... she's a nice-looking lass after all."

"Right. Cheers, Ronnie," Alistair said. The constable smiled and nodded to Duncan before leaving.

Duncan sucked air gently through his teeth, considering what he'd just heard. "Sounds like Dougie has a bit of a jealous streak running through him."

"Aye... and like I said, Dougie is the sort of guy you don't want to come across late at night in an alley... particularly if he's got it in for you," Alistair said.

"Capable of murder?"

Alistair frowned. "Premeditated... I'd say no... but I think he spends most days living on a short fuse and if you were to catch him at the wrong time, then..." He splayed his hands wide.

THE HENDERSON's croft lay on the north-western edge of the crofting township of Borve, roughly five miles from the island's capital, Portree. Duncan was grateful that the sprawling township was situated just off the main A87 road that ran from Portree to the Calmac ferry terminal at Uig. The road was well maintained with a decent surface, much appreciated by drivers as the snow was still falling.

"Any idea when this storm is likely to pass?" Alistair asked as he picked their way along the road. The storm front had caught the island's council off guard which was unusual. In the event of forecast snowfall, the gritters would be out to treat the main arterial routes around the island, ensuring safe passage was possible should it be needed. Obviously, the narrow township roads were secondary, but even these would be gritted and in the event of major snowfall, ploughed, to keep people moving. However, right now they were all playing catch up.

"A couple of days was the last I heard," Duncan said, his fingers curling around the door handle as Alistair took a bend a little faster than maybe he would have liked. Alistair noticed in the corner of his eye.

"Don't worry... this pick-up is the Taliban's favourite for a reason."

"I thought they all went for the Landcruiser?" Duncan said, drawing Alistair's eye to him.

"Do they? Oh well, more fool them. I could stage a coup in a central African country in this thing," Alistair said, grinning. "A little fallen snow won't stop us."

Duncan wished he shared the same levels of confidence. Heavy snow reminded him of the days the family were snowed-in back when he and Roslyn were weans; trapped out at the croft with their father, unable to make use of the freedom that came with getting out and about with his pals. This weather triggered memories long buried, but never forgotten.

"You don't like the weather?" Alistair asked, snapping Duncan back into the present.

"Not much, no."

"Well, you know what they say in these parts about that?" Alistair asked, slowing to negotiate a tricky turn off the main road and onto a single track that looped its way back towards Borve. "If you don't like the weather—"

"Aye, hang on for twenty minutes."

They both laughed.

Alistair took a turning on their left and followed the track as it snaked up the hillside to the north before angling west. They arrived at a large hangar-style barn which was covered with a corrugated metal roof that curved from one side to the other, but the front, back and sides were exposed. It was vast, so there was still plenty of respite from the elements beneath the canopy.

The track split here, continuing on to the north, or they could cross a cattle grid and head west. This was the route Alistair steered the pick-up towards, the enormous wheels drumming as they crossed the cattle grid and weaved their way up the hillside. They didn't have far to go. Around the next bend they found themselves in a natural hollow with banked moorland to the west and the north giving the inhabitants the perfect location to build a shelter. This was exactly where the old croft was located. Skye's crofters weren't daft, knowing how to give themselves not only the best chance of survival in this harsh climate, but the opportunity to thrive as well.

"Aye, aye... there's Dougie," Alistair said as they approached the property. Duncan looked beyond a red SUV, parked out front, to a man in the open garage, leaning over a quad bike with an open toolbox beside him at his feet. The seat was levered up giving him access to the engine bay beneath it. He paused what he was doing and watched them park before returning to his task.

Duncan took Dougie's measure as they got out of the pick-up. He was a big man, tall and broad shouldered with an air of strength around him. This was to be expected because these men were out on the land in all weathers and it was a tough life, one requiring a particular mindset. He was dressed for the elements, sporting a thick chequered overshirt with a padded gilet and a woollen beanie. He wore fingerless gloves enabling him to work on the engine of the quad bike. It looked like he was stripping something down, bits and pieces lay on an old tartan rug draped over the front rack.

Dougie paid them no attention as they approached. An old four-bar electric heater was belting out some warmth but all it could really achieve was to take the edge off the chill in the air.

"Having trouble with the quad eh, Dougie?" Alistair asked.

"Aye," Dougie muttered under his breath, still focussing on his task. "Air filter is knackered."

"Couldn't happen at a worse time, huh?" Duncan said. Dougie stopped and slowly turned his unkempt, bearded face towards Duncan, looking him up and down whilst absently chewing something. He sniffed and stood upright, laying the ratchet down on the rug.

"It wasn't me," he said flatly.

Duncan frowned. "What wasn't?"

Dougie took a deep breath and sighed, folding his arms across his chest. "Whatever yous are after someone for, it wasn't me."

Alistair smiled. "Come on, Dougie, don't be like that. All we want is a chat, that's it."

Dougie snorted. "Aye, right, Mr MacEachran." He eyed both of them in turn. "Come on then, out with it. What do you want?"

Duncan fixed him with a hard stare. "Have you spoken to Erin?"

At mention of her name, Dougie's expression changed

momentarily before the veil lowered once more. "Not since she left for work this morning, no. Why? Something happened?"

"No, your wife is fine," Duncan said. Dougie nodded curtly.

"So... what?"

"Sandy Beaton's been found dead," Duncan said flatly, watching him intently.

Dougie's eyes narrowed but he held Duncan's gaze. He lifted his right hand and scratched the end of his nose, sniffing again. "Is that right?"

"Aye," Alistair said. "We found him lying out in the shadow of the Old Man."

Dougie's gaze drifted over to Alistair. "Out at The Storr, was he?" He arched his eyebrows, glancing skyward. "That's a daft place to be in this kind of weather."

"It's no' the best," Alistair agreed.

Dougie inclined his head in Alistair's direction.

"You don't seem all that surprised," Duncan said.

"Surprised?" Dougie shrugged. "That man was always full of surprises... and all of them boggin'..."

"You're not a fan of his then?" Duncan asked.

Dougie chuckled drily. "Well... I'll no' be missing him, that's for certain."

"Would your good lady wife say the same?" Alistair asked.

Dougie looked at him but didn't respond.

"They seem close," Duncan said, "Erin and Sandy... she seemed almost distraught when we spoke with her about this earlier. I figured she'd have shut the gallery and come home."

"Well, you don't know her very well then, do you?" Dougie sneered. He turned and picked up the air filter he'd just removed from his quad bike, making a show of inspecting it. "So, why are you really here?"

"Why?" Duncan asked.

"Aye, you didn't come out here just to give me the good news, did you?"

"The good news? That's crass."

Dougie shrugged, holding the filter in one hand as he glanced sideways at Duncan. "Why should I care what happens to a bloke like Sandy? I guess I'm a car length up in traffic tomorrow, aye?" Duncan and Alistair looked at one another, Alistair cocking his head. "So, what happened to him? Did he fall?"

"Maybe he was pushed," Alistair said.

"Pushed, you say?" Dougie asked, nodding whilst not making eye contact with either of them. "That'd be karma for you."

"Karma?" Duncan asked.

"Aye, what comes around, goes around and all that." Dougie shrugged. "Whatever happened to him, I'll wager it's payback in one form or another. Nature has a way of asserting itself, doesn't it?"

"You know anyone with an axe to grind?" Duncan asked.

Dougie set the filter back down, meeting Duncan's eye and smiling. "Every married man on this here island, I reckon."

"Including yourself?" Alistair asked.

"Oh…" Dougie said, cocking his head in Alistair's direction, "you can definitely add me to that particular list."

"Bold statement," Duncan said.

"I'll no' mess about, it's true." Dougie fixed his gaze on Duncan. "But if you're looking for someone who did him in… then I'll tell you straight, it was nae me."

"What were you doing yesterday?" Duncan asked.

Dougie's expression was a picture of concentration. "I was here… on the croft… working."

Duncan looked around. "What were you doing?"

"I was going to be servicing this old thing," he said, tapping the handlebar of the quad bike. "But as the weather shifted… I had to get about bringing in the sheep." He gestured to a collie, sleeping on an old blanket near to the fire. The dog had paid them no attention, which Duncan saw as a sign of firm training and skill on the dog's part. It was a working animal, uninterested in their presence. "That took me well into the evening before I had to abandon it because of this damned filter. I didn't want the thing dying on me out there. I've got enough to do as it is."

"You got many still out there?" Duncan asked, looking out into the steadily falling snow.

"Aye, a fair few but they'll be right until tomorrow."

"You don't think it'll worsen?" Duncan asked, still watching the snow falling.

"It's no' too bad," he said. "There will be much worse before the spring comes calling, that's for certain. The last time we had snow like this in November, the winter was the worst in nigh on thirty years." He glanced between them. "Brace yourselves, gentlemen. This winter is going to be a doozy."

Duncan nodded. "Tell us about what happened between you and Kenny."

Dougie met Duncan's eye with an unreadable expression. "Kenny?"

"Aye, you and he had a coming together a while back… the police were called…"

"Oh… that Kenny. The wee bampot was asking for a good hiding." He glared at Duncan. "I didnae do anything though… I mean, I held back, you know?"

"So we were told," Duncan said. "What did he do to you?"

Dougie sniffed hard. "He… er… touched my missus, you know? I could nae let that pass now, could I? I had to make it right."

"Oh, did yer, aye?" Alistair asked.

Dougie looked over at him and nodded. "I did, aye."

"And… making it right was… giving him a beating?" Duncan asked.

"Except on this occasion… I was more restrained," Dougie said. "You lot turned up before anything got going." He sighed, his demeanour softening. "I suppose that was for the best, all things considered."

"Does it bother you?" Duncan asked.

"Does what bother me?"

"Erin working alongside Sandy, being so close to a man you clearly despise?"

Dougie nodded with a wry smile. "If I had my way, she'd be nowhere near the likes of him."

"Some might say there's an easy way to avoid that happening in the future," Duncan said.

"What… by seeing him off the edge of a mountain?" Dougie asked, shaking his head. "There's easier ways of getting rid of a problem than that, Detective?"

"Detective Inspector McAdam," Duncan said.

"DI… eh?" He looked at Alistair. "They're promoting the inspectors younger and younger these days. Fossils like you and me are soon to be a thing of the past, eh?"

"Speak for yourself, Dougie. I'm still in my prime," Alistair said, straight faced.

"You keep telling yourself that, Mr MacEachran… one day you might believe it!"

Alistair remained stone-faced but his eyes moved to Duncan who nodded.

"That'll do for now, Mr Henderson," Duncan said. "However, we may well be back should the situation change."

Dougie raised his chin defiantly. "If you see Morag… give her my best."

Duncan met his eye and Dougie held it. "You know Morag?"

"Aye, I do. She's all right is Morag. Having a wee shite for a brother must have been a pain in the neck. At least she'll be free of him now as well."

Duncan gestured towards the pick-up with a nod and Alistair fell into step beside him. Dougie returned to working on his quad bike.

"Nice guy," Duncan said as they walked.

"I told you. He's a cold one."

"You think he did it?"

Alistair hesitated. "I don't know. You?"

They reached the pick-up and Duncan looked back towards Dougie, still paying them no heed. He shook his head. "I think he's capable but…"

"Does nae mean he did it."

"True," Duncan said, getting into the passenger side. His mobile rang the moment he closed the door. "DI McAdam."

"Sir, it's Caitlyn. I've found Lorna."

CHAPTER ELEVEN

DUNTULM WAS a small township on the north-western edge of the Trotternish peninsula. The main coastal road running along the peninsula from the ferry terminal at Uig on the west coast passed through Duntulm before continuing on to almost as far as the northern tip, before looping around and down the east coast back to Portree.

Before entering the township from the west, they passed the viewing point that offered unparalleled views across Tulm Bay towards the islands of the Outer Hebrides. They followed the directions given to them by Caitlyn, turning left just before they reached Loch Cleat, slowing as the access track was less well maintained and, with a covering of snow, Alistair could no longer make out the hazards. Duncan was grateful for the use of the pick-up truck this day.

In the depths of winter, it would occasionally fall to locals who had access to all-terrain vehicles to become an ad hoc emergency service when required. In those events, generational storms or similar, the community would often come together, much as it always had done in the past, to get each other through.

"Caitlyn says it's the last property we come to," Duncan said, peering ahead. The snow had eased now to a light flurry, the whiteness of the covering aiding them in reading the landscape, reflecting any and all available light.

They made their way past the old coastguard cottages, now used as holiday accommodation. They were in darkness this evening. Perhaps no one was resident or if they were, maybe they called time on their break to get off the island rather than risk being cut off. When the big Atlantic storms hit, it wasn't unusual for the more remote properties to be without power until the linesmen could be deployed to reconnect them.

The last property was an old croft house. Oriented towards the west, it had a clear view towards the ruins of Duntulm Castle, occupying a prominent point on the cliff's edge. Once keeping a watchful eye over the ships passing between the inner and outer islands, it was now an unstable structure slowly collapsing into the bay. Not that this fact stopped the thousands of tourists from stopping here to catch a sunset or to pick their way down to the shore and explore the dinosaur footprints preserved in the rocky shoreline.

Alistair parked the pick-up on the gravel-lined driveway in front of the house. Lights were on inside and Duncan led the way to the front door where he rang the bell.

"The temperature's falling away, isn't it?" he said. Alistair nodded but didn't have a chance to reply as the door opened. Duncan was surprised to find a woman far older than he expected peering out at him. She seemed just as surprised when she cast an eye over them. Duncan produced his warrant card. "DI McAdam and DS MacEachran," he said, smiling. She gave the ID a cursory inspection and her expression of surprise only seemed to increase. "I'm sorry to disturb you, but we're looking for Lorna Somerton. Is she home?"

"If you mean Somerwell, then yes, I certainly am home, Detective Inspector."

"Forgive me. Our information is a little vague." He looked at her, intrigued. She wasn't what he'd expected. Lorna noticed. "I'm sorry, I was expecting someone…" He didn't wish to say younger, but that was the truth. If Sandy Beaton was in a relationship with this woman, he hadn't expected her to be perhaps two decades his senior. Lorna was in her sixties.

"Else?" she asked, finishing his sentence.

Duncan smiled sheepishly. "May we come in for a moment?"

"Of course," she said, pulling the door wider to make room for them. "We're letting all the heat out and on a night like this, that's not a good thing."

They entered, Alistair closing the door behind them, and she led them to the rear of the house where Duncan spied a picture window angled out to the right of the castle and directly over the bay towards Harris.

"This is some place you have here," Duncan said. The house itself was fairly modest but the views must be awe inspiring even during spells of inclement weather.

"Thank you," she said, smiling and offering them a seat in the living room. A wood-burning stove was roaring away, the pleasurable orange glow emanating around the room. "There's no finer place on earth."

"I have a place on the coast myself," Duncan said, his partially reconstructed house flashing to mind, "but it's not a patch on what you have here."

"I know, I'm very lucky," Lorna said.

"How long have you lived here?"

"Ooo… it must be getting on ten or so years now," she said, thinking hard. "I must admit I don't really keep track anymore."

"Just you, is it?" he asked.

"Yes, just me," she said. Duncan glanced at her left hand and she noticed, holding it up for him to see properly.

"No wedding ring, if that's what you were looking for?"

Duncan felt sheepish again, smiling. "Sorry, force of habit."

"That's okay, dear. I chose not to marry... although I have been asked a couple of times."

"Not by anyone who made the grade then?" Duncan asked.

She smiled. "Something like that, yes. I'm... an independent sort of woman... a free spirit, if you will. People like me don't tend to fare well when it comes to compromise."

She could be describing him. He could relate. "So, where are you from originally?" he asked her. "The east coast... southern?"

"The Lothians?" she asked, arching her eyebrows. "Hah! No, not me. I'm a Lang Toun girl."

"Oh... are you? Where's that, Laurencekirk?"

"More towards Kincardine way, but yes," she said, inclining her head with an accompanying smile.

"Damn... I'm usually pretty good with accents. It's always been something of a party trick that I do," Duncan said, regretting his radar being so off.

"Well, our father was employed in the servicing of the rigs, so we moved around a lot to follow the work, you know?"

"Ah, that'll be it."

"As children we were dragged around all over the place. We even had a spell abroad but my mother never took to it," she said, shrugging, "so we wound up back here; up in Nigg at that time. So... what brings you out here on such a treacherous night as this?"

Duncan met her eye. "I wish it was under better circumstances, but we understand you know Sandy Beaton. Is that correct?"

"Sandy?" she said, surprised. "Yes, we're friends."

"When did you last speak with him?"

She thought for a moment. "Early in the week, I should think. Monday or Tuesday. Why do you ask?"

"I'm sorry to be the bearer of bad news, but I'm afraid Sandy has passed away."

Lorna's hand came up to her mouth and she gasped. "Passed... but... how?"

"We are trying to figure that out at the moment. How close were the two of you, if you don't mind me asking?"

Lorna hesitated, her eyes flitting between Duncan and the silent form of Alistair who was still standing in the background. Duncan caught her eye and leaned forward.

"Were you close friends?" he asked the question again, only phrased it differently.

"We... yes, we were good friends," she said, swallowing hard and shaking her head. "I–I can't believe he's gone. Are you sure... that it's Sandy?"

"Yes, we are," Duncan said. "It's not official yet but we are positive."

"Oh my... poor Sandy." Duncan allowed her a moment to absorb the news. She had her hands in her lap, wringing them constantly. She looked up at Duncan. "How... what happened to him?"

"He was found by a passer-by," Duncan said. "He may have ventured out on The Storr, possibly on the lookout for a great camera shot."

"Oh... in this weather... yesterday?"

"We believe so, but we're still trying to figure out his movements over these last couple of days."

"Oh Sandy... that's awful," she said.

"You say you're friends. Are you... romantically linked at all?"

She laughed momentarily as he asked. "I'm sorry, I shouldn't laugh but no… I'm almost old enough to be Sandy's mother… We were friends. We have a shared interest."

"Painting?"

"Yes, that's right," Lorna said. "Sandy has recently rekindled his love of painting. It's a long-held passion of mine and so we have that in common."

"His sister credits you with the resurgence of that passion."

"Morag said that?" Lorna asked, placing a hand on her chest. "That's so sweet of her to say, but I doubt that's true. Sandy is… was… his own man. He's not the type to be easily led. He would do what he wanted to do, most of the time."

Duncan nodded. "I'm hearing that from a number of people. Did you find him a difficult man to be around?"

"I should imagine he would be an awful partner or husband…" she cocked her head, "but fortunately, for me at least, we were only friends and spoke often about painting and little else, to be honest."

Duncan looked around the room but didn't see any paintings hanging in the room which surprised him. Lorna noticed.

"I love art, Detective Inspector, but I'm more of an art historian than an artist in my own right. I doodle sometimes, but my passion lies elsewhere, more in the structure and methodology and the process rather than the physical act of painting itself. I know my limitations and I gave up trying to be a Rembrandt myself many, many years ago."

"I see," Duncan said. "And what did you make of Sandy's work?"

"Oh… he has a wonderful way of applying oil to canvas. If only he'd kept at it all those years ago when he chose his photography over his painting. I do wonder where he would be by now."

"But his paintings are generating interest now, aren't they?"

"Yes…" she said tilting her head, "but a painter is like any other artist, be they a musician or an author, the more they hone their craft, the better they become. Fine art is… something that takes time to reach your potential. Sandy, as good as he is, has left it rather late."

"I don't think he's going to improve now," Alistair said under his breath. Duncan heard but Lorna appeared not to have.

"You see, the competition Sandy won," she leaned forward. "You know of that, don't you?" Duncan nodded. "That was a beginner's competition, you see. I fear that if he was to be judged against more established painters then he'd be found wanting."

"I understand that Sandy was looking to maximise his earnings from the fame he garnered in the field with that competition win."

Lorna nodded. "So, I understand… although I did suggest to him that he may be getting a little ahead of himself."

"How did he take that?"

She frowned deeply, lowering her voice. "Not well, I have to say. Very few of us actually enjoy criticism though."

A gust of wind battered the outside of the house, rattling the windows. Lorna hunkered down into her seat, shuddering as she looked out of the oversized window towards the bay. The snow was more like sleet now, driving against the windowpane in waves.

"I fear this will be a long night," Lorna said. Her eyes widened. "I'm so sorry. Where are my manners. Would the two of you like some tea?" She made to get up, but Duncan raised a hand to stop her.

"There's no need. We'll not be stopping long."

"Oh… I'm so not used to having visitors that I completely forgot. It's very rude."

"Honestly, it's fine," Duncan said. "You don't have any family who come out here to take advantage of where you live, to see the views then?"

"No… I had a sister, but she passed away some years ago now. As did my folks."

"I'm sorry to hear that," Duncan said. "So, it's just you then?"

"Yes, it's just me, so you'll understand why I am such a… solitary person."

"Do you not get lonely?" Alistair asked.

She glanced up at him. "From time to time, yes. I mean, I'm not a robot. I have feelings, obviously, but some of us are built to… I was going to say be alone. Perhaps that is a step too far. Those of us who prefer solitude. Yes, that's a more fitting description. I avoid relationships these days."

"I must admit I've never heard anyone coin that particular phrase."

Lorna smiled. "It suits me. Like I said, I prefer my solitude."

"You'll certainly find that all the way out here," Duncan said.

"I am blessed, it's true."

Duncan looked to his right as if he could see through the walls of the house. "Do you have neighbours around?" he asked. "I'm just thinking about this storm—"

"Oh, away with you," she said, dismissing his concern with a flick of her hand. "There's been far worse than this."

"Okay, but do you have everything you need?" Duncan asked just as the lights dimmed and then flickered. All three of them looked at the ceiling pendent, waiting for the power to go off. It did so only seconds later. They were left in the flickering glow of the wood burner.

"Do you happen to have any candles with you?" she asked.

Duncan shook his head, standing and moving to join Alistair at the window.

"It looks like everyone is out," Alistair said, peering into the darkness. Things must have deteriorated significantly to have brought the power lines down. The sleet struck the window with force and both men turned back into the room. Lorna seemed unperturbed.

"I recall one time when I found myself camping out during a storm," Lorna said, "unable to go outside even for the rudimentary calls of nature. Two days hunkered down listening to nought but the wind. Once it was over we had to dig our way out." She looked at Duncan and then Alistair. "That passed in good time, and we didn't have a wood stove to keep us going."

"Where was that?" Duncan asked, intrigued. "Not Laurencekirk I suspect."

"Nepal," she said, her expression taking on a faraway look. "It was a long time ago though; another life entirely."

Duncan returned to his seat. "Lorna, may I ask what you knew about Sandy's finances?"

She expressed surprise. "I... I don't really know anything about that. Why do you ask?"

"I'm trying to understand Sandy and what his life was like at this time and in the months running up to now. Was he stressed about money? You said he was hoping to cash in on his new status."

"Sandy is a very typical Scottish man... of a sort anyway."

"Meaning?"

"Quick with a smile and a sharp retort... keen to impress any and all around him." She seemed suddenly melancholy. "I've known many of these men over the years. They present an image to anyone watching... and you rarely see what is actually going on under the surface." She sighed, looking at Duncan with a half-smile. "Until it's too late, of course."

"Sounds painful," Duncan said.

"Something else from a long time ago," Lorna said, tilting her head. "I'm sorry, Detective Inspector, but what I knew about Sandy Beaton stretches no further than what he could put down onto a canvas."

"That's okay, don't worry."

"What a tragic end to a life. He had so many more good years left in him."

Duncan nodded. He took out his mobile phone. "Tell me, Lorna. Do you happen to know this person?" He opened a picture, one of those taken from Sandy's memory card of the woman sitting outside An Talla Mòr, turning the mobile and passing it to Lorna. She accepted it, peering at the image in the flickering firelight. Her eyes narrowed as she concentrated on the image and Duncan thought they might be about to catch a break but Lorna frowned and shook her head.

"No, I'm so sorry. I don't recognise her," she said, handing the mobile back. "Who is she?"

"We don't know," Duncan said, glancing at the picture himself.

"Sorry," Lorna said, wincing.

"Never mind. It was a long shot."

"How is Morag?"

Duncan inclined his head. "Bearing up. I don't wish to speak out of turn, but she didn't seem all that surprised that something happened to her brother."

Lorna raised her eyebrows at that. "Well, Sandy was a bit of a rogue. Anyone who spent any time with him at all could see that. I suppose his sister would know better than most."

"Do you know Morag well?"

"No, I can't say I do. I think I've met her… maybe only once or twice. She seemed nice though."

CHAPTER TWELVE

LORNA SOMERWELL CLOSED the door behind them and they walked hurriedly back to Alistair's pick-up, keen to get out of the driving sleet. At least the change would likely bring about more passable roads even if did mean the chance of a greater risk of ice.

"So, do you want to head back down to Uig and stick to the A87," Alistair said, "or do you fancy continuing around the headland and coming down the east side?"

Alistair's mobile rang before Duncan could answer. It didn't matter, they needed a bit of time to heat the cabin and clear the gathered snow and ice from the windscreen before they could leave.

"Aha… right…" Alistair said, glancing sideways at Duncan and biting his bottom lip. He pursed his lips and passed the phone to Duncan. "I think you'd better take this one."

Intrigued, Duncan took the mobile. "DI McAdam."

"Hello, sir, it's Ronnie Mac—"

"Hey, Ronnie." Duncan saw Alistair look nervously towards him. "What's up?"

"There's been an RTA," Ronnie said, "on the 855 just north of Lealt Falls."

Duncan wasn't surprised. The coast road running down the east side could get pretty treacherous in bad weather and tonight certainly qualified.

"Anyone hurt?"

"Aye... only the one vehicle involved... two occupants. Both have been packed off down to the hospital. It's nae looking good for the wee lassie, but the driver should be okay."

"Right... what's this got to do with me?" Duncan asked. It wasn't for CID to investigate road traffic accidents.

"Well... I thought you'd want to know because of your connection to the family like. The car belongs to the Mcinnes wifey—"

"Becky?" Duncan asked, a stab of fear punching him in the chest.

"Aye, but she wasnae in the car, but her two bairns were. The lad, Callum, was driving," Ronnie said. "He's proper smashed up the car too. I dinnae know how he managed it... it's a straight bit of road, but it looks like he may have touched a back wheel off the tar and it's just kicked round on him... and he's managed to flip it."

"Geez..." Duncan said, sighing. "Has... er... anyone told the parents yet?"

"No, not yet," Ronnie said. "The weather's wreaking havoc across the island and we're stretched pretty thin. I was going to head over once we've swept the road clear and that, but I thought you'd want to know."

"Yeah, yeah, I do. Thanks, Ronnie." He glanced at Alistair. "Listen, we're done out here and we can come back via you and call in on the Mcinnes, save you the trip." Alistair met his eye and nodded.

"Okay, sir. I'll leave it with you then. Like I say, the lassie is in a bad way but the boy should be all right. He was still conscious when the first responders reached them. They were lucky. Even his sister."

"Okay, thanks Ronnie. We'll see you in a bit."

Duncan hung up, taking a deep breath and exhaling. He passed the mobile phone back to Alistair and reached behind for his seatbelt.

"You okay?" Alistair asked.

Duncan nodded. "I'll be grand. Thanks for this."

"For what?"

"Driving me around to Becky's place."

"No problem. They live up at Maligar, don't they?" Duncan nodded. Alistair tilted his head, patting the steering wheel before him. "You'll not get up there if you weren't in one of these."

"Aye, probably right."

Alistair put the pick-up into gear and reversed briefly before engaging first and pulling out of the driveway and making his way back to the main road. The lights were out to the entire township and Duncan would usually be wondering how much of the island was affected. However, right now, all he could think about was what he was going to say to Becky about her children.

The roads on the east side of the Trotternish peninsula weren't as badly affected as they were on the west side. The Trotternish Ridge offered some protection from the Atlantic storm but even so, Alistair had to take care. Turning off in Staffin, they made their way up into the hills. The headlights of the pick-up were all that lit their route. Every property they passed was either in darkness or had camping lights or candles, so slivers of light were all that could be seen.

Duncan directed them to the Mcinnes house, the last in a

line of crofts facing south-east towards Rona across the water of the Inner Sound. Becky must have seen their approach or heard the pick-up's massive diesel engine because she came from the front door out into the falling sleet, hope written in her expression. She was crestfallen to see Duncan get out of the passenger side.

"I'll stay here for a minute," Alistair said to him, leaning across the cabin. Duncan nodded and closed the door. He made his way to where Becky stood, waiting for him.

"What is it?" she asked. "What's happened?"

Duncan inclined his head, for once words escaped him. He'd made these calls frequently over the course of his career and he'd never struggled before. He came to stand before Becky. "There's been an accident—"

She reached out, gripping his forearms in a vice-like hold. "Are they okay? Callum and Eilidh… tell me they're all right, Duncan?"

"Their car came off the road… down by Lealt," he said, meeting her eye. She was terrified. "Apparently, Callum lost control and the car left the road—"

"Duncan! Are they okay?"

"Callum will be all right," he said and by omission, Becky realised that her daughter hadn't fared as well. She made to speak, her lips moving but no words followed. "They're both on the way to the hospital now," Duncan said as she released her hold on his arms. She visibly wilted before him and he reached out, fearing she was on the verge of collapse. At the first touch of his, she reacted by throwing her arms up, knocking him away from her. He hesitated, stunned by her action, his arms aloft as if she had drawn a gun on him. "Easy, Bex," he said, and she stared at him, wide-eyed and horrified. Duncan looked towards the house. "Is Davey inside?"

"No… Davey's… out," she said quietly, almost inaudible

above the noise of the wind and the sleet. They were both soaked now, but Becky didn't appear to have noticed. Duncan looked around and saw that Davey's truck wasn't here and he wondered how he might be getting on if he was out on the croft in this.

"I can take you to the hospital, if you like?"

Becky maintained her thousand-yard stare for a moment, looking straight through Duncan, but then her eyes focussed and she looked directly at him.

"Shall I take you to the hospital?" he asked again.

She nodded. "I'll... just get my coat."

Without another word, Becky turned and walked purposefully back into the house, returning into view a moment later, closing the front door behind her. She dragged her arms through her coat as she walked to the pick-up and Duncan held the door open for her. Climbing up into the back row of seats, she nodded to Alistair and settled in. Duncan got into the passenger seat and Alistair moved off.

No one spoke for a few minutes and Duncan could see Alistair using his rear-view mirror to see Becky. He glanced at Duncan, arching an eyebrow in query. Duncan turned in his seat to face her.

"Do you know where Callum and Eilidh were heading tonight?"

She looked at him, expressionless, and shook her head. "No, I don't."

"Not a great night to be out driving," Alistair said. Becky's eyes flicked to the mirror and the two of them made eye contact for a second, but she didn't reply. "How old is your lad?"

Duncan's head snapped back to Alistair. What with being caught up in all the drama of the event, Duncan hadn't considered that. Callum couldn't be more than sixteen years of age.

"He's fifteen," Becky said as Duncan turned back to her. She said it to him, watching for his reaction.

"Fifteen?" he said.

"Sixteen next month."

"What's he doing behind the wheel of a—"

"Leave it, Duncan for God's sake," she muttered.

Duncan stared at her but she turned her face to the window, staring out into the blackness, folding her arms defiantly across her chest. Duncan turned to face forward, catching Alistair offering him a surreptitious look. Duncan silently mouthed the words *I know* in reply.

Returning to Staffin, they turned right onto the coast road heading south towards Portree. Duncan wanted to give Becky advance warning.

"We're coming up on the accident spot soon, Becky."

She kept her gaze out of the window and said nothing, but he was sure she'd heard him. Spotting the red and blue flashing lights ahead at the end of the straight just before a sweeping left-hand bend, Alistair slowed the pick-up. They hadn't come across any other vehicles on the road since departing Becky's house in Maligar. Everyone was evidently hunkering down to see out the storm.

The patrol car was parked on the left-hand side of the road at an angle, ensuring it had the largest side profile possible to oncoming traffic. They drew alongside and an officer was standing by the side of the road between them and an upturned vehicle beyond the verge. Becky gasped behind him, and Duncan felt for her. Seeing the wreckage of the car her children were travelling in must be incredibly frightening.

The officer turned and recognising them, he walked over as Duncan wound his window down. It was Ronnie MacDonald, wrapped up as well as he could be in a full-length high-viz coat, the collars turned up to almost meet the edge of his cap which was also wrapped in a plastic cover to shield it from the steadily falling sleet. Ronnie nodded to both of them, peering into the cabin and spying Becky in the rear. He smiled at her, almost apologetically and Duncan could see that she appreciated it with a polite half-smile in return.

"Sir," Ronnie said and then looked past him to Alistair who looked at the car behind him.

"When will they retrieve it?" he asked.

Ronnie was resigned to his fate; to wait there for some time. "I'm waiting to hear. We need to chart it," Ronnie said, referring to the investigation into how the accident happened. "But there's a lot going on tonight. If I'm lucky they'll let me tape it off and go home."

"Been a long day," Alistair said.

"Aye... right enough." Ronnie looked skyward, half closing his eyes in response to the driving sleet. "And no one's going home until this lets up a bit."

"Stay safe, Ronnie," Duncan said, and the constable nodded, patting the door and giving him a thumbs-up as Alistair moved off. Duncan looked behind him to see Becky staring at the wreckage, transfixed, as they got underway.

At the front of the hospital, Alistair stopped and both Duncan and Becky got out. Duncan held the door, looking back at Alistair.

"I'll see what's what and then give you a call."

"No problem," Alistair said. "I'll head back into the station and tie everything together."

Duncan checked his watch. "Listen, send the team home for the night. There will be nothing anyone can do at this hour. We'll have a briefing first thing tomorrow morning."

"Right. If there's anything you need in the meantime, just give me a call."

Duncan looked over his shoulder. Becky was at the entrance but appeared reticent to go inside.

"I think someone needs you," Alistair said, nodding towards her.

"Aye," Duncan replied, closing the door. He heard the engine pick up as Alistair drove away. He hurried to Becky, putting an arm around her shoulder and they walked into the hospital together. He was pleased she didn't brush him off like she had done before.

Having identified themselves at the nurses' station, they were directed to the waiting area with no further information. Becky sank down onto one of the many plastic seats in the foyer. It was a busy night with over half of the available seating occupied with a mix of patients awaiting their turn for treatment or relatives of those already in triage. They were in a quiet corner, out of earshot of others provided they kept their voices down.

Becky leaned back resting her head against the wall behind them. Now they were under decent lighting, the hospital ran on back-up diesel generators and so they still had power, Duncan casually studied Becky's face. Her eyes were red-lined and the skin around them was puffy. She'd been crying, a lot by the look of it. He hadn't seen her crying since they'd reached her place at Maligar, so it must have been prior to knowing about the accident.

"So..." Duncan said quietly, scratching the corner of his eye absently and looking ahead, "do you want to talk about it?"

Becky opened her eyes, still focussed on the ceiling above though. "Yeah, what do you mean?"

"Earlier," he said, turning his head towards her. "What happened at home?"

She sniffed, glancing briefly at him before averting her eyes from his gaze straight away. "I don't know what—"

"Come on, Bex," Duncan said gently. "Remember what I do for a living."

She rubbed at her face with both hands before taking a deep breath but seemed reluctant to speak about it. Duncan theorised.

"Did you and Callum have a falling out or something?"

Becky shook her head. It was a slight gesture, her lips pursed. Duncan sat forward, resting his elbows on his knees and cradling his chin in the crook of thumb and forefinger. He waited patiently. He didn't have to wait long. Becky took a deep breath and he saw her stiffen.

"What do you think happened?" she asked.

Duncan angled his head slightly. "Driving too fast... distracted by the weather... it only takes a moment. Who taught him to drive, you?"

She shook her head. "No. It was his... dad." She exhaled. "Davey taught him."

Duncan arched his eyebrows. "Might need a refresher," he said softly.

Becky laughed, releasing some of the pent-up tension. "Aye... I guess driving instructor should be taken off his CV, eh?"

"I'd say so," Duncan said.

"Thanks, Duncan."

He looked at her. "For what?"

She half-smiled. "For being here."

"Ah..." he said, shrugging. "What's a guy to do, eh?"

"Thanks anyway," she said, reaching a hand out towards him. He took hers in his own and squeezed it gently. She smiled appreciatively.

"Mrs Mcinnes?"

Becky was on her feet in a moment, striding towards the doctor calling her name. Duncan hurried to catch up.

"I'm Becky Mcinnes," she said, drawing the man's attention. He smiled at her, doing his best to look reassuring but Duncan had seen that look many times before. He'd practised it himself on numerous occasions and now feared the worst. "How are my children?"

"Would you like to step into somewhere a bit more priv—"

"No," she said sternly. "I want you to tell me my children are okay."

The doctor held up a hand to placate her, nodding. "Okay… your son, Callum, is going to be fine. He has a mild concussion… a few scrapes and bruises, but he will be right as rain in a day or two. We'll keep him in overnight for observation—"

"Can I see him?"

"He's on his way up for a CT scan at the moment," the doctor said. "It's purely precautionary, but we want to make sure we've covered everything. After that, he'll be transferred to a ward… but…" he hesitated, glancing at Duncan and then back at Becky, "the police are waiting to speak to him."

Becky shot Duncan a dark look. As if it was his fault or something. Duncan knew it was standard procedure. They'd be taking blood samples or a breathalyser test to see if he was under the influence at the time of the accident as well, but he figured it was best not to mention that at this time.

"And Eilidh? How is she?"

The doctor seemed pensive. "I'm afraid her condition is much more serious than your son's." Becky's somewhat aggressive stance dissipated, her expression changing to one of abject terror. The doctor sought to calm her. "Eilidh… did you say?"

Becky nodded. "Yes."

"Eilidh suffered some abdominal trauma… and is in

theatre. Initial assessment suggested her spleen may have ruptured… and she has suffered a mass of internal bleeding."

Becky doubled over, one arm clamped across her stomach and other hand raised to cover her mouth as she reacted. Duncan stepped forward and caught her as she sank down, ensuring they both fell gently into a ball together on the floor, his arms around her. Becky buried herself into his chest and Duncan held her tightly, feeling tears well in his own eyes.

CHAPTER THIRTEEN

"He's in trouble, isn't he?"

"What's that you say?" Duncan asked, blinking furiously and trying to orient himself. Every other strip-light overhead was off, the lighting phase indicating to him that it was the middle of the night, as if his aching back and gritty eyes weren't enough to convey that message. He must have dozed off. He checked his watch. It was two-thirty in the morning.

"Callum," Becky said from her seat next to his, rolling her head on her shoulders to look at him with a pensive expression. "He's going to be in trouble, isn't he?"

Duncan couldn't sugarcoat it for her, but he thought better of spelling it out fully. At least, not tonight. He nodded. "Aye."

"How much trouble?"

She wasn't going to let it lie. He checked the time again and then looked down the corridor. It was empty but he did see movement from an adjoining room. Was that the staff restroom? He wasn't sure. They'd been sitting there now for hours. Callum's scan was completed and he'd been moved to a recovery ward for rest. Becky had been allowed in to see him, but only briefly and by that point her son was asleep. Now they were waiting for news on Eilidh's surgery.

Duncan looked at her. He may have slept, perhaps only for a few minutes, but she hadn't. Her legs were jigging, her hands thrust deep into the pockets of her coat in her lap. She looked lost. Looking directly at him, unlikely to accept the brush off, Duncan sniffed and sat forward, rubbing the sleep from his eyes.

"When I went off to the toilet, I dropped in on the officers waiting to see Callum," he said. Becky's eyes widened in a mixture of alarm and anger. "I wanted to find out their reading of the accident."

"And when were you going to share this with me?"

She was indignant. He could understand. He decided not to hit her head on.

"Look... they don't think he was drinking or under the influence of any drugs... which is a good thing."

"Right..." Becky glared at him. "Because my kids don't take drugs, Duncan. What kind of mam do you think I am?"

Duncan closed his eyes, taking a breath and allowing her the opportunity to rant if she chose to. She simmered down, rubbing her mouth and chin with one hand.

"That's the good news," Duncan said. "There were no other vehicles involved... and it was an accident."

"That's good, right?"

He nodded. "But... that's where the good news ends, I'm afraid."

"Go on."

Duncan exhaled, meeting her expectant eye. "He's under age, has no licence or insurance... Eilidh's injuries will count against him as well—"

"She's his sister."

Duncan shook his head. "It doesn't make a difference. He's still endangered her life… caused injury."

"Christ!" she muttered, shaking her head.

Duncan pursed his lips, allowing the information to sink in.

"Have you spoken to Davey?"

She sat back, expressionless. "I called him earlier."

Duncan nodded, glancing both ways down the corridor. "I thought he'd be here by now."

Becky didn't say anything.

"Do you want me to give him a shout, chase him up—"

"No."

He nodded. Something else was going on here, but for the life of him he had no idea what. "His daughter's in surgery. He should be—"

"I said I'd called him. He'll be here just as soon as he is, okay?"

"Yeah… of course," he said, dropping it. He stood up, keen to stretch his legs which had gone numb. It was those damned seats. They weren't designed to spend hours sitting on them.

"You don't need to stay," Becky said. He looked down at her. "What's that?"

"You can get yourself away home, if you like? You don't need to be here."

He cast an eye over her, but she didn't look up at him. He crossed the short distance between them and sat back down, reaching for her hand, he pulled it gently from her pocket and held it in his lap.

"There's nowhere else I need to be just now," he said. She half-smiled at the comment and he lifted his left arm, inviting her to lean into him. She did so and he put his arm around her shoulder, drawing her to him. She rested her head on his chest.

She wasn't a tall woman and had been a slight girl when they'd been a couple all those years ago, but now she seemed older than her years. It was as if the threat of injury and the suffering of her children had sucked the life from her. Becky felt fragile in his arms.

Duncan kissed the top of her head through the mass of blonde hair, and she put her left arm around his waist, clinging to him.

He didn't know how long they stayed like that, locked together in their embrace but neither of them saw the arrival of the surgeon. He was standing in front of them before they knew he was there. Becky sat up, rubbing at her eyes. Duncan checked the time. It was shortly after six in the morning. They both must have slept although he didn't feel well rested.

They stood, Becky's expression showing she expected the worst. The doctor did his best to reassure them with a smile.

"The surgery went well, we believe," he said. Looking between them, he went on. "Your daughter is in a stable condition. We managed to stem the blood loss, but it was as we expected; we had to remove her spleen. It had ruptured and the amount of blood lost brought on haemorrhagic shock… which can be dangerous to say the least." He held up a hand. "However, as I said, her condition is stable although she remains on the critical list."

Becky glanced at Duncan, relieved.

"What is the prognosis for her recovery?" Duncan asked.

"That's a little early to say," the doctor replied. "The next twenty-four to thirty-six hours are critical and we need to see how she recovers from the surgery as well as the trauma of her injuries."

"Can we see her?" Becky asked. The doctor looked at both of them in turn.

"She is still under from the general anaesthetic, and we will keep her sedated for the next twelve hours to give her body time to heal, but... I'm sure we can give you a little time with her." He looked at Duncan. "Are you her father?"

Duncan shook his head. "No, just a friend."

"The mother only then, I'm afraid." He looked apologetically at him, but Duncan signalled it was okay. Becky turned to him, clasping his hands in hers.

"You go and see to your daughter," he said. "Do you want me to stick around and give you a lift home?"

"We got a lift here together, remember?"

"Oh yeah," Duncan said, recalling Alistair dropped them there and he had no car. "I could arrange for someone to give you a ride home, if you like?"

She shook her head. "No, it's okay. I'll call a cab or something."

"Right."

The doctor led Becky away and Duncan watched them leave. They reached a set of secure double doors and the doctor typed a code into the pad on the wall. A click sounded and he pushed the right-hand door open. Becky reached out and touched him and the doctor stopped. Becky turned and hurried back to where Duncan waited. She slowed as she reached him, taking his hands and leaning forward she kissed him on the lips. Backing away, she held his gaze and smiled awkwardly as she let go of his hands which fell limp to his sides. A curious mixture of emotions flashed through him; fear, exhilaration and nervousness.

"Thanks, Duncan," she said, backing away before turning and hurrying to the waiting doctor. Duncan said nothing as she disappeared from view and the door swung closed behind her. The latch clicked into place and Duncan was alone in the corridor, the momentary silence punctuated by staff arriving for their shift at the far end of the corridor, but no one paid him any attention.

Duncan made his way towards the exit, stopping a pair of nurses who were wearing outdoor coats, chatting and laughing as they made their way into work.

"Excuse me, which way is the canteen?"

They pointed towards a map of the site on the far wall but also gave him directions to the staff and patient refectory, confirming it would be open for breakfast in a few minutes. Duncan figured he'd get a coffee before heading across town to the police station. He thanked the nurses and made his way through the maze of corridors, all of which looked identical. He'd easily get lost in this place.

Taking out his mobile as he walked, he scrolled through his contacts to find Becky's number. He selected the landline and dialled it, stopping in a quiet spot so as not to have to contend with numerous people coming and going when the call was picked up. However, the call rang out with no opportunity to leave a voicemail. If the power was still off, perhaps the phone had run down its battery overnight. He put his mobile back in his pocket and resumed his walk to the refectory. With a bit of luck, he'd be able to purchase some food as well.

CHAPTER FOURTEEN

DUNCAN WALKED into the ops room shortly before 7 AM. Alistair, Caitlyn and Angus, sporting a dark blue suit and a white shirt today, were already at their desks, but Russell Mclean was nowhere to be seen. No doubt he was still trying to thaw out after overseeing the scenes of crime boys up on The Storr during the snow.

Alistair eyed Duncan as he approached and he half expected a sarcastic comment regarding his appearance. He would deserve it. His skin felt clammy beneath his clothes and he had several itches that wouldn't go away.

"Everything all right at the hospital?"

Duncan nodded. "The surgery on Eilidh went well, but it's a waiting game for the next day or so."

"And wee Callum?"

"A concussion… and a bit banged up," Duncan said, scanning the information boards that had been populated with a lot of information since the previous day. "But he'll be okay, I reckon."

"Good!" Alistair said in an upbeat tone. "You'll want to

have a wee word with Fraser seeing as he went with the ambulance yesterday."

Duncan looked towards the door. "Right, I'll do that later. Where are we at?"

Alistair cleared his throat and got up from behind his desk. "Briefing, boys and girl," he said in a loud voice. Caitlyn and Angus turned to face them, both acknowledging Duncan with a nod and a smile.

"Where's Russell?" Duncan asked.

"He's running late," Alistair said. "His athlete's foot is playing him up or something."

"Gout."

Duncan looked at DC Ross and Angus cocked his head.

"It's gout Russell's suffering with," Angus said. "Standing around on the mountain didn't help."

"What is gout anyway?" Caitlyn asked.

"Good living," Alistair replied. "Or so they say... but I don't think it's true, mind."

Duncan folded his arms, feeling the first stabs of hunger at having missed dinner the previous night and breakfast was whatever he'd managed to get from the hospital vending machine to go along with his coffee. He'd been there too early for food. "So, walk me through what we've learned so far."

Alistair nodded. "Right, we've been into Sandy's bank accounts more thoroughly than the fly through Caitlyn managed yesterday. Sandy's finances make the national deficit look like a lottery win."

"That bad, huh?" Duncan asked.

"Dire... absolutely dire," Alistair said, shaking his head. "Aside from the copyrights to his photos and his paintings, the man leases everything else. The car, the gallery and his home... he owns none of them, and he's behind on his payments." Alistair frowned. "And based on what we saw out at his place last night, he's no' going to be getting his security deposit back from the landlord either."

Duncan's brow furrowed in concentration. "What about the prize money from that competition he won? I thought that was supposed to ease his worries financially."

"So his sister thought, aye," Alistair said. "Looks like her confidence was misplaced though. He didn't use that money to clear his debts. The landlord who leases him the gallery has been onto the court about evicting him."

"So, what did he spend the money on?"

"Fast women and faster cars," Alistair said drily.

Caitlyn looked up. "He definitely spent a lot in the pubs in and around the town." She shrugged. "Looking through his debit card transactions, I imagine he was throwing it around playing the big man. You know what men are like, trying to prove they're bigger than what they are... in all departments."

"Burned through it pretty quickly then?" Duncan asked.

"Aye," Caitlyn said. "You know what they say, a man and his money are soon parted."

"A fool," Angus corrected her.

"What's that, young Mr Ross?" Caitlyn asked.

"It's *a fool and his money are soon parted*."

Caitlyn looked at him, her lips curling into a knowing smile. "Aye, like I said." She winked at Angus, and he pressed his tongue into his cheek, shaking his head.

"Angus has been going through Sandy's phone records," Alistair said.

"It's made for interesting reading," Angus said, taking Alistair's cue. "I've looked at the mobile phone records and the registered landline number for the gallery. Beaton didn't have a landline at his house, only a broadband supply apparently." He shrugged. "Relying on his mobile, I guess."

"Not unusual these days," Duncan said. "What did you find out?"

"A trickle of phone calls coming into the gallery but very few outgoing, so I switched to his mobile records and that was interesting. Sandy seems to make a fair few calls locally… to fast-food places… friends and the like, you know. But there's been a number this past week from a caller over in Edinburgh. It stood out, so I looked it up to see who it's registered to."

"And?"

"It's a gallery in the old town… pretty swanky place too, from the look of the website."

"Enquiring after his paintings or photographs?" Duncan asked.

Angus shrugged. "No idea, I've just got dates and times, but it stood out because they've been calling each other this past week. So, I went back a bit further and they've been in contact for a while. The frequency hasn't been as regular, but they've been chatting for well over a month or so."

Duncan found that interesting. "Maybe he's been trying to establish a line into some upmarket clientele… or wants to run an exhibition at their place."

"Aye, that's what I thought too. Should I give them a phone?"

"Yeah, do it; see what they have to say," Duncan said. "Anything else?"

"Aye… a few calls from withheld numbers… we only have the duration of the call, date and time. I dinnae know if it's significant or not. I've asked the service provider to offer up the details of who the numbers belong to if they have it. Still waiting on them coming back to me."

"Good work, Angus," Duncan said.

"There is one other thing that's very interesting," Angus

said. "Sandy's friend, the lady you went out to see last night...
what was her name again?"

"Lorna Somerwell," Duncan said.

"Aye, she spoke to Sandy the day before yesterday on the
phone."

"What time?" Duncan asked, his forehead creased.

"Er..." Angus looked down at his notes. "Nine-thirty in the
morning, Saturday. Then again, a half hour later. And they've
spoken a couple of times earlier in the week as well."

Duncan and Alistair exchanged a look. "She didn't mention
that last night," Duncan said.

Alistair wrinkled his nose. "They're friends though, so
having spoken earlier in the week isn't particularly relevant
and she was pretty shocked to hear about Sandy's death."

"She might have mentioned speaking to him on the day he
died though. Odd." He turned back to Angus. "Was Sandy
calling her or..."

"Both ways," Angus said. "Call duration varied... from a
couple of minutes earlier in the week to fifteen and then
twenty minutes on Saturday."

"We'll have to revisit her and ask about that," Duncan said.
"Any outgoing calls that caught your eye?"

Angus shook his head. "I'm still working through them,
but he's a creature of habit, so the people he calls are quite
regular."

"Let me know if there are any repeated calls to married
women at odd times of the night, will you?"

"Will do, sir," Angus said.

Duncan smiled at him. "Good work, young man."

Angus beamed. "There's something else that's been
bugging me, sir."

"Go on," Duncan said.

"The camera, the one Sandy took out with him on the night he died."

"What about it?"

"I'm no expert... but I do like taking the odd photo here and there, and the camera itself... seems wrong."

"Wrong? In what way?"

"For someone like me, for everyday use, it's just fine but for a professional... especially one looking to take shots they would display or sell, it's not right. I looked up the model... the lens... and they aren't what a pro shooter would take out there." He shrugged. "It struck me as really odd, that's all."

"Okay, everyone bear that in mind. Now, how did you get on with the neighbour's door camera?" Duncan asked. When Alistair called on the property, no one had been home, but he was planning to follow it up.

"I spoke to the bloke. Nice guy. Because we have no idea of a time frame, he said he'd have to download all the video footage from Saturday." Alistair frowned. "Apparently, it activates every time someone passes by on foot or in a vehicle."

"It must record a lot in that case."

"Aye," Alistair said. "Which will be a significant ball ache to go through but might yield some positive results for us."

Angus chuckled. "I pity the poor numpty who has to wade through all of that."

"Excellent!" Alistair said, patting Angus on the shoulder with a firm hand. "Well done for volunteering."

Angus sighed and Caitlyn laughed. "That'll teach you to be quick with the jokes, wee man."

Angus rolled his eyes at her and then smiled. "Any idea when this guy is bringing the footage in, sarge?"

"Some time today, he said when I spoke to him on the phone."

"I'll have a word with the front desk and make sure it gets

passed straight through to me," Angus said, making a note on a post-it and sticking it to the edge of his monitor.

"What time can we anticipate hearing something from the pathologist?" Duncan asked.

"Not until the end of today," Alistair said. "At the earliest."

"Okay… what about our mystery woman?"

"The one in Sandy's photograph?" Alistair queried. Duncan nodded. Alistair shook his head. "No joy on that. Anyone who's looked doesn't recognise her. If she's a tourist passing through or just someone from off the island paying him a visit, then we're likely stuffed on that front."

"Keep at it. Circulate the photograph around uniform and see if anyone has any leads as to who she is."

Russell Mclean lumbered into the ops room, grunting and grimacing with every step. He threw his coat across his desk and sank down into his chair, which squeaked under the sudden weight. He hefted his left foot up onto the desk and blew his cheeks out.

"Nice of you to join us, Detective Constable Mclean," Alistair said, arching a solitary eyebrow in his direction.

"Ah… I'm so sorry, Al," Russell said, dispensing with the formality of rank. The two of them had joined Portree station at the same time many years before and were old friends. He was the only person Alistair allowed to be so informal. "Ma foot is playing me up something rotten. It's like walking on crushed glass… but it's inside your damned shoe." Red-faced, he winced for added emphasis. "It sucks getting old, you know." Russell's gaze shifted to Duncan and he seemed anxious. "I'm really sorry, sir. I'll try not to let it slow me down."

Alistair laughed at that. Russell threw him a finger and then dropped it when Duncan shook his head.

"Sorry, sir."

"Do the best you can, Russell," Duncan said. The DC nodded, attempting to rub his aching foot but there was no way he could reach it, such was the ample girth hanging around his midriff.

"Angus," Duncan called. The DC looked up and then rose from his desk and came over to them. "Brief Russell on what you're doing with the telephone calls. Leave that with him and then take a walk over to An Talla Mòr. See if they know who the woman is in the photograph. Cast an eye over their CCTV… credit card receipts, if she didn't pay cash… who she met, anything and everything you can find out. Yes?"

"Will do, sir. Long shot though, eh?"

"It is, but sometimes you get lucky in life," Duncan said.

"And sometimes," Alistair said, "you make your own."

Duncan stepped away and Angus pulled a chair across to sit down with Russell. Alistair came to stand with Duncan.

"What are you thinking, boss?"

Duncan took a breath. "I'd like that pathology report to come through."

"Looking for confirmation that it's a murder?"

Duncan nodded. "Aye. It might even give us a steer as to who did it. The why will likely follow." He glanced at the clock on the wall. "I think I'll borrow a pool car and head out to Duntulm."

"Apply a bit of pressure to Lorna? You could always phone. The power came back on up that way early doors."

"No, I'd rather see her face when I ask her about it."

"Fair enough. Do you want me to come?"

Duncan shook his head. "No need. It might just be exactly as you say; an oversight on her part."

"You might want to take a shower first."

"Nah… they'll have to take me as they find me today. I'll sort myself out later."

"As you wish," Alistair said. "But a word of advice?"

Duncan nodded.

"Stay downwind, aye?" Alistair said with a wink.

CHAPTER FIFTEEN

DUNCAN FOUND Fraser MacDonald in the canteen tucking into his breakfast. Just the smell lingering in the room made his mouth water. There were more officers than normal in the canteen this morning, a sign of everyone being called off their rest days and suffering extended shifts due to the storm front. It was still yet to pass, and as a result, it was a case of all hands to the pumps until further notice.

Fraser was piling a fork-full of bacon and fried egg into his mouth as Duncan sat down opposite him.

"Morning, sir," Fraser said, spraying egg yolk down his chin as he spoke. He picked up a paper napkin and wiped his mouth, still chewing. He looked dog-tired but had the same cheery disposition he always did, no matter how irritated or stressed he was, he always tried to suppress it. Duncan had him pegged as a cardiac waiting to happen, not least because his diet largely consisted of anything deep or shallow fried.

"Morning, Fraser." Duncan scratched the side of his head, enviously eyeing the square sausage on Fraser's plate. "Can I... can I pick your brains about that RTA last night?"

"Ah... the Mcinnes boy?"

"That's the one. You went with him to the hospital, right?"

"I followed on, aye," Fraser said, cutting into his sausage and first driving it through a puddle of brown sauce before putting it in his mouth. Having a mouthful of food didn't stop him talking though. "He's in a spot of bother is that young man." Fraser raised his eyebrows and nodded to labour the point.

"You breathalysed him, didn't you?"

He nodded. "Aye, it was negative. He hadn't had a drop of the drink like." Fraser scratched his ear and then inspected the end of his finger. Cocking his head at whatever was beneath his fingernail, he flicked it to his left and took a swig from a cup of tea. "I had the nurse take a blood sample though. These days the kids are more likely to be on something rather than drinking." He sighed. "Sign of the times I guess."

Duncan frowned. "So… what's he looking at?"

Fraser exhaled, setting his cup down. He glanced around to check who might overhear. No one was particularly close to them, but Fraser lowered his voice anyway. "You're friends with his mum, aren't you?"

"Aye," Duncan said, holding his hands up, "but I'm not looking for any special treatment. I'm just… you know?"

Fraser met Duncan's eye for a moment before he resumed eating his breakfast, sniffing as he took a mouthful of black pudding. Whilst chewing, he shifted the food around his plate in an almost choreographed dance with knife and fork.

"The Mcinnes boy… no licence, insurance… I'd usually be looking at a minimum of a careless driving charge, but what with the weather last night," he said, looking thoughtful, "I guess we could dispense with that one." He set his cutlery down and pitched a tent with his fingers in front of his face, still chewing. "I assume the parents won't want to report the car as stolen?"

Duncan smiled, Becky coming to mind. "I doubt it, but I've not spoken to them. As long as they don't put in an insurance claim for the damage, I guess it'll be all right."

Fraser inclined his head, swallowing. "I would say we'd go easy on him... seeing as no one was hurt aside from himself but..."

"His sister."

Fraser nodded. "Aye, the sister." he shook his head. "In a bad way, I gather."

"She'll pull through," Duncan said, "but yeah, not great."

Fraser spread his hands wide. "Let's hope the bloods come back as negative on the drugs too... and maybe he'll no' get thrown to the wolves. He's a good lad, by all accounts. I've never had anything to do with him which I cannae say for many of the teenagers in these parts."

"Problem generation, eh?"

Fraser, who'd picked up his cup of tea, holding it with both hands, pointed at Duncan with a forefinger, the hand still wrapped around the cup. "Feral is the word you're looking for, sir. Feral. If they were badgers, they'd be culled."

Duncan laughed. "They're not all bad."

"No, sir. Just the feral ones." Fraser sipped at his tea, swallowing hard. "And they're breeding like rabbits."

"Badgers and rabbits." Duncan inclined his head. "A lethal, if not magical, combination." Duncan rose.

"Not seen a badger in these parts for a while," Fraser said absently, sipping at his cup of tea. "Pine martens... a lot of those, mind."

"Thanks, Fraser."

"Oh, sir?"

Duncan looked back. "Yeah?"

Fraser's forehead creased in concentration and he licked his lips before wiping his mouth with a napkin again, then his fingers, scrunching up the paper and tossing it down onto the empty plate.

"You're pals with Archie Mackinnon, aren't you, so the keck was saying anyway?"

Duncan nodded. "Aye. We were at high school together. Why?"

Fraser's gaze narrowed. "One of the landowners spoke to me recently... reckons Archie's been on his land doing a bit of poaching."

"Right." Duncan shrugged, feeling awkward. "Did they see him?"

Fraser shook his head. "No, but they think he's been at it. I know Archie can be a funny old bugger... but any truth in it, do you think?"

Duncan exhaled, looking away. "Archie's... well, he's Archie."

Fraser nodded sagely. "I hear you."

"Catch you later, Fraser. Thanks again."

"No problem, sir." Fraser was focussing on his tea, staring at the liquid. "Anytime like."

DUNCAN WALKED out into the station's rear access yard, scanning the parked cars for the pool car he had keys to. It was gently snowing again. Portree had been spared any real depth of snow but the forecast had the volume increasing in the coming twenty-four to forty-eight hours. Spotting the burgundy saloon parked in the far corner, Duncan crossed to it and got in as quickly as he could.

The interior was cold and ice had formed on the inside of the windscreen. Looking around for a scraper, he couldn't see one. Resigned to waiting for the engine to warm up and the demister to clear the windscreen, he hunkered down in his seat to wait. His thoughts drifted to Becky and Eilidh, then to Callum and the predicament he'd put himself in. Kids could make such foolish decisions, but at the time, he must have thought all would be fine. Maybe he'd done similar before. The harshness of the weather around Skye could catch even the locals out, let alone a teenager with barely any driving experience.

He took out his mobile and looked up Becky's number. He hesitated before tapping the call button. The call connected and rang a few times before she picked up.

"Duncan," Becky said, her tone was fatigued, clearly through lack of sleep as well as emotional exhaustion.

"Hey, Bex. I was just calling…" He had a thought. Why was he calling? He took a deep breath. "How are you?"

Becky snorted. "I've been better."

"I know… stupid question. Sorry."

"No, no. Don't be… it's okay. I'm…" Words failed her.

"Tired?"

She laughed. It was a dry sound without any genuine humour. "Aye… very tired."

"How is Eilidh?"

"She's sleeping. They tell me that's a good thing but… oh, Duncan… she has so many machines rigged up to her… tubes… it's… it's horrific."

Duncan pursed his lips. He didn't know what to say. The police are trained to handle these situations but when it falls closer to home, the training doesn't seem to cut it.

"What about Callum? Have you been able to see him?"

"Yes. He's going to be okay. Physically, at least." Becky sniffed and he thought he'd heard her voice crack, but he couldn't be sure. "Worrying about his sister, you know?"

"Aye, I'm sure he is."

"Duncan… is he in serious trouble?"

"I'm afraid he is, aye." Becky was silent. "But he's a good kid… not been in trouble before, so…" She didn't respond. Becky had a lot on her mind right now. "Focus on Eilidh. The stuff with Callum will sort itself out later."

"Aye… suppose so."

"When did Davey turn up?"

"He… hasn't been here—"

"What? Where the hell is he?"

"I… I don't know," she said. "I've not spoken to him."

Duncan was puzzled. "I thought you'd called him last night?"

"I left him a message. I guess he hasn't picked it up yet."

"Right." Duncan pinched the bridge of his nose between thumb and index finger. His head was hurting. Probably an indication of lack of sleep, food and dehydration. "Listen, I'll—"

"I… have to go, Duncan. I'm not really supposed to have my phone on while I'm in here."

"Okay… I'll… um… speak to you later then."

"Okay, bye."

She hung up and Duncan stared at the screen for a moment before putting his mobile away. Irritated by the wait for the windscreen to clear, he used a credit card to scrape the ice off the interior. Weirdly, the exterior didn't have ice on it and the wipers were able to clear the powdered snow in a couple of passes. Duncan fastened his seat belt and put the car into gear, moving slowly to the gates which opened as soon as he approached.

The road north was clear. The council gritters had been out and about doing a solid night's work of keeping the main arterial routes of the island passable. However, when Duncan turned off at Staffin, things became more treacherous but still manageable. His anger continued festering as he drove up into the hills and a little voice in the back of his head told him he shouldn't be doing this, but he often failed to heed his own advice.

Becky's car was still lying on its roof by the side of the road, a layer of crisp snow insulating it from prying eyes. If not for the police tape wrapped around it, no one would know that the scene had been attended. No doubt the wreck was still there as a result of the storm and would likely be recovered once normality resumed. Duncan slowed as he passed the crash site, but he wasn't keen to linger there.

The main road through Maligar was less well travelled and Duncan found his car losing traction at several points where the previous snowfall had now frozen solid with a new layer of fresh powder on top. Here, it would only be the inhabitants of the township who would make the effort to clear the road, and no one had seen to it this morning. If this storm front didn't let up soon, someone would need to, otherwise the township would be cut off until the thaw came. For now though it seemed like everyone was willing to let nature take its course.

Pulling into the driveway of the Mcinnes' croft, a silver Mitsubishi Shogun sat in front of the house. Davey was home. Duncan got out of his car and approached the front door. He hadn't reached it before it was yanked open and a red-faced Davey Mcinnes stepped out. Duncan nodded, barely keeping himself in check.

"How's it going, Davey?"

"All good, Duncan," Davey said curtly. "A bit early for you to be calling round, isn't it?"

"Aye… well—"

"I've seen more of you since you've been back on the island than I ever did back in the day." He folded his arms across his chest, ignoring the snow settling on him. Duncan wasn't going to be invited in it seemed. "I presume it's Becky you're after… but she's already left for work."

Duncan cocked his head. Something in his expression must have registered with Davey because his open hostility shifted, if only slightly. "Becky's still at the hospital, Davey."

Davey's eyes narrowed. "What's that you're saying?"

"She's at the hospital… with your kids."

Davey studied him, scratching at the top of his head, his brow furrowing. "What… er… what's happened like?"

"There was an accident," Duncan said, choosing his words carefully, "just south of Staffin. You didn't see it?"

"No… I've… er… not been down that way."

Duncan sniffed, confused. "Well… it wasn't good, you know. You've not spoken to Becky or picked up any messages then?"

He shook his head. "No, I've been busy… with work and that."

Duncan looked around. He didn't appear to be busy. He briefly caught the whiff of alcohol on the breeze, standing downwind of Davey.

"So, you didn't wonder where your kids were when you made it home last night, eh?"

"I stayed out the night, not that it's any of your concern, Dunc."

"Stayed out?"

"Aye… busy with—"

"Work. Aye, you said. I can see you're hard at it."

"Ah… get tae fuck, Duncan."

Duncan felt the anger returning. "Are you no' even going to ask after your family?"

Davey flinched at hearing the comment. "Aye… of course… are they okay?"

"Eilidh is in a bad way, there's no easy way to put it, sorry."

Davey looked away for a second, tight-lipped.

"Callum will be all right. He's a little banged up but he'll be okay."

"Right." Davey nodded. "And... er... and Becky?"

"She wasn't in the car. Callum was driving."

"Oh aye... Callum. I see."

"You don't seem altogether surprised, Davey." He searched Davey's expression to explain his apparent belligerence, but the man's stance only appeared to harden further as the seconds passed. "What am I missing here, Davey?"

"Everything," Davey said softly before taking a step backwards, turning on his heel and striding back towards the house. "As usual," he called over his shoulder without looking round.

"Are you going to the hospit—"

Davey slammed the door, leaving Duncan alone. He shivered, suddenly more aware of the cold and the snow falling around him. Rubbing his chin with one hand, he walked back to the car and got in, pleased to be out of the elements. His gaze lingered on the house and he saw a flicker of movement through one of the forward-facing windows but nothing more. He sighed and started the car.

CHAPTER SIXTEEN

DUNCAN WAS PLEASED to find the power had been reinstated to Duntulm as he entered the scattered township. Lights were on in homes as he passed them. The old coastguard cottages near to Lorna's house were still sitting in darkness though. The tourists had either left early or decided to delay their trip or cancel it entirely, likely a result of the weather.

Lights were on in Lorna's house and Duncan knocked on the front door. He stamped his feet on the mat to clear the snow, reluctant to traipse it into the house. However, his knock went unanswered. He did so again, stepping back and craning his neck to see through the nearest window. He could see through towards the kitchen in the rear and despite lights being on, he couldn't see any sign of movement.

Making his way around the house towards the rear, he glanced out towards the ruins of Duntulm Castle and the bay beyond. The snow had eased, for now, and he could see dark patches in the sky coming towards them across the water from the Western Isles. The islands themselves were lost in thick sea mist.

"Enjoy the respite," Duncan said to himself. There was still no sign of Lorna in the house but there was another building a short distance away. It was modern but constructed in the style of a traditional àirigh, or sheiling; a hut used by crofters across the highlands to shelter from the storms while tending their livestock in the summer grazing months. This one was far more substantial, a contemporary designed, permanent structure rather than those often-temporary functional constructions of days past.

Light emanated from one facing, illuminating a block of snow-covered ground to the west and Duncan made his way over, rounding the corner to find a curtain wall of glass facing the bay. Lorna, startled by his sudden appearance at the window, almost dropped the palette in her hand, placing her free hand against her chest. She smiled a moment later and beckoned him to come inside.

The door was to Duncan's right, and he pushed it open, greeted by the sound of soft classical music as he entered, banging his feet against the exterior wall to shake off the snow before doing so. Lorna crossed to where her mobile phone lay on a nearby table and paused the music playing from speakers mounted on every wall.

"I'm sorry, I didn't realise you were here," she said, lifting the phone and tapping on the screen. She angled the phone towards him. "I have a front door camera and it's supposed to notify me when someone approaches." She smiled apologetically. "The power cut must have messed up the connection or something." She cursed softly. "I'm no good with all this technical malarkey."

Duncan smiled. "Sorry, I didn't mean to startle you."

She waved away his apology. "No matter."

Duncan looked around. The building was pretty much a cube, one room with a high ceiling and the only window was facing north-west.

"I'll bet you have a wonderful view on a clear day," Duncan said.

"I can even make out Scalpay from Harris," Lorna said, shrugging, "until my eyesight gives out anyway."

Duncan smiled. He glanced around the sheiling, spotting numerous canvases stacked against each other. Some were on the floor, others on shelving. Nothing was on display. It could have passed as a storeroom if not for the piece she was working on. Duncan came to stand at her shoulder, admiring the angry storm clouds over what he guessed was Tulm Bay; the very same view he could see in front of him. Not that the detail of the water was visible today but nestling between the white of the snow-covered landscape and the mass of swirling cloud above, he knew it was there.

"I didn't think you painted," he said absently.

"Not quite what I said," Lorna replied with a half-smile. "I said I know my limitations. I'm better at theory than I am at practice.

"Well, this is pretty impressive to me," he said, examining the detail of the painting.

"That's very sweet of you to say." Lorna set her palette down and wiped her hands on her apron before lifting it over her head and hanging it on a wall-mounted peg. "What brings you all the way back out here so soon after your last visit?"

"I just have a couple of quick questions I wanted to ask you, if you don't mind?" She shook her head, returning to stand beside him as he still observed her painting. He gestured towards it. "I really like this, and I'm not one for... is it oil?"

"Yes, I prefer oil over acrylic paint. Which puts me in the minority these days," she said. Pointing at it with a flick of her hand, she looked glum. "I'm not feeling this one to be honest. I'm considering painting over it and starting afresh on something else."

"You can't be serious?"

She laughed. "Deadly serious." She raised a hand in an arcing motion, indicating the many canvases that lay stacked all around them. "Most of these are either reused canvas or waiting to be."

"You can reuse them?" Duncan asked, embarrassed by his ignorance.

"Of course," she said, smiling. "Even the greatest painters in history reused their canvases. To think what lies beneath some of the finest artworks hanging in exhibitions all over the world…"

"Lost classics?" Duncan asked.

"Perhaps… although if the painters thought they were rubbish, then who are we to judge?"

Duncan laughed. "True." He couldn't help but think she was overly critical of her own skills though.

"So… what is it you want to ask me?" Lorna said, pulling a stool out from beneath a nearby bench and sitting down. "I would offer you a seat, but I only have the one… I'm not used to visitors to my studio."

Duncan smiled. "No need, honestly. It was a question regarding when you last spoke to Sandy."

"Oh, right," she said. "Nae bother." Her eyes narrowed. "You could have phoned? The power's been back on."

"I know but I like the drive."

She seemed unconvinced but didn't labour the point. "So, what do you want to know."

"Can you clarify the last time you spoke to Sandy for me?"

"I thought about it after we spoke last. Early last week, definitely. The Monday or the Tuesday, I'm still not sure. That is what I said, wasn't it?"

"Aye, you did. We've been going through Sandy's things, building a timeline of his movements and so on," Duncan said.

"His phone records have the two of you speaking on Saturday morning."

Lorna fixed him with her gaze, her lips parting slightly. "Yes… that's right. We did speak on the phone Saturday." She smiled awkwardly. "I… I'm so sorry. When you asked about talking to him, I thought you meant in person. Like… having seen him to talk to. I should have said."

Duncan nodded. "What did you talk about? On Saturday, specifically?"

"Oh… nothing special," she said, blowing out her cheeks. "He… er… asked about coming out this way next week to maybe do a bit of work. He can't really do much at his house. It's not really set up for painting or so he says."

"You've never been to his house then?"

She shook her head. "No. I always saw Sandy at his gallery or he came out here." She turned her head to look out at the landscape. "He always said this place was inspirational."

"I can understand that. So, the conversation was completely normal… he didn't give off any strange vibes or anything?"

Lorna was thoughtful. "No, he seemed his usual self, upbeat and quite charming."

"And the second call?"

"The second?"

"Yes," Duncan said, glancing at his pocket book, "there was a second call half an hour after the first."

"Oh yes… he asked for some career advice, as I recall."

"Regarding painting?"

She nodded. "He'd been nervous about asking. I suppose he didn't want to impose on me."

"He has had contact with a gallery in Edinburgh recently as well. Do you know anything at all about that?"

Her brow furrowed momentarily. "He did say something

about perhaps hosting an exhibition somewhere. Could it be related to that?"

"I guess so," Duncan said, but he had no idea.

"He didn't mention anything specific about any gallery though." She fixed him with an inquisitive look. "Edinburgh, you say?" He nodded and she arched her eyebrows. "He really had stoked some interest in his work then. Good for him."

"Sadly, he won't be able to enjoy it," Duncan said.

"No... such a shame. I know you have only just begun your investigation, but are you any closer to knowing what he was doing out there?"

"As you say, it's still early days," Duncan said. He took a moment to look around the space, contemplating everything she'd just said. She seemed open with him. Her body language was relaxed, her toes pointing in his direction and her hands were resting flat on her thighs; all indications that she was genuine. "You said painting was a hobby for you."

"Yes, it is."

"Some hobby," he said, smiling.

"I know, but I have a lot of free time... and always have done."

"Why is that?"

"Well... my parents were comfortable, you know, financially." She shrugged. "They passed away when I was young and I was an only child, so everything they had came to me."

"I'm sorry to hear that," Duncan said.

She shrugged. "It was all a long time ago." She drew a deep breath and smiled. "So, I've been very lucky, in one respect, in that I've never had to work in the way most people do. Fortunately, I've never had expensive tastes and I could go where I wanted, within reason."

"And you wanted to come and live all the way out here?"

She laughed. "Why ever not? It's beautiful out here and no

one bothers you if you don't want them to. And," she said, raising her eyebrows, "as long as I live frugally there's no reason why I can't just tinker with my hobbies."

"A life many of us can only dream of," Duncan said.

"Well, many dreams can become nightmares once the reality kicks in."

Duncan caught her expression, a momentarily peculiar one, before she seemed to throw it off and replace it with a broad smile. She noticed him watching her.

"Forgive me, I was away… off someplace else for a moment." She looked at him apologetically. "I don't often think about my family. It's been many years… but it is still painful."

"I'm sorry, I didn't mean to bring back bad memories."

"Oh, think nothing of it. Life has a way of throwing things at you one after another. Sometimes too much comes along at the same time, and it knocks you over."

Duncan nodded. He could relate to that thought. "All you can do is pick yourself up and go again."

Lorna smiled again, nodding. "What happened yesterday no longer matters. Today is another day."

"Profound. Who said that?"

"Someone very dear to me," she said, looking out into the darkness now enveloping the outside as the clouds Duncan spotted crossing the Minch made landfall. "But it was a long time ago." She looked at Duncan. "I'm sorry to not have mentioned the phone calls. They were so insignificant that they completely slipped my mind."

"Can you think of anything that Sandy said, or the way he spoke, that might indicate he was under stress or that something odd was going on?"

"No," she said, shaking her head. "Sandy was his usual self. I mean, he was a little flat, but it was Saturday morning and I imagine he'd been on the drink the night before." She looked glum. "That was one of Sandy's vices."

"The drink?"

"Yes. Like so many, I think he thought he needed it to be entertaining." She sighed. "Quite the opposite, if you ask me. Sandy had so much to offer. I just wish he'd have believed in himself a little more rather than giving in to his base desires."

"Alcohol and women?"

She met Duncan's eye and slowly nodded. "If I had to say, I would anticipate one, or both, of those would likely be the death of him. Not that I ever thought that would happen, mind you."

"Sadly, that might just turn out to be the case, Lorna."

CHAPTER SEVENTEEN

DUNCAN WALKED BRISKLY BACK to his car, keen to get out of the snow although it was falling more as sleet now, driving at him almost horizontally with the increase in wind speed. Remind me why I thought it'd be good to be back on this accursed island again? He slammed the car door, shaking ice and snow off his head as he rushed to get the engine started and turn on the heaters. Rubbing at his eyes he heard his mobile beep several times in quick succession. Glancing at the screen he saw messages from the station, from Angus and Alistair. They could wait a minute or two.

He dialled Becky's number, but the call cut straight to voicemail. He hesitated as the automated voice suggested leaving a message but then hung up without saying a word. Drumming his fingers on the steering wheel, the wind and sleet battering the exterior of the car, the whirring of the fans circulating air in the cabin, he pondered what to do. The earlier conversation with Davey was still playing on his mind. The whole situation was unsettling for many reasons.

A quick search on the internet, working slower than usual through his phone, produced the hospital's telephone number.

A quick call later and he was passed from the switchboard through to Eilidh's ward.

"Hello, it's Detective Inspector McAdam calling... I'm inquiring as to the wellbeing of one of your patients."

"Which patient, Detective Inspector?" the nurse replied.

"Eilidh Mcinnes."

"Ah... yes, wait a moment please."

He wasn't placed on hold, although sound became muffled, and he guessed she had the phone pressed into her shoulder or chest. He didn't have to wait long.

"Mr McAdam?"

"Yes."

"Eilidh's condition is still listed as critical, but she is stable and had a good night following the operation. Her consultant hasn't finished his morning rounds yet, but in an hour or so we should have another update for you, if you'd like to call back then."

"I'll do that, thanks."

Duncan was pensive. Should he ask or not?

"Is there anything else, Mr McAdam?"

"I... was wondering about the family."

"Ah yes... Eilidh's brother was also in overnight, wasn't he?"

"That's right. Do you know his status?"

"He's on another ward, but I can check for you." This time he was placed on hold, the telltale double beep repeating every five seconds confirming it. The nurse came back soon enough. "Callum has been discharged already," she said.

"Right, thanks. That's good news. Tell me, is Eilidh's mother with her?"

"She is. I can see her from my station. Would you like to speak to her? I could—"

"Er… no, no that won't be necessary. I was just checking," Duncan said. "Thanks very much for your help."

He hung up but remained staring at the screen for a moment. The screen lit up. Alistair was calling.

"Hey, Alistair. What's going on?"

"All good here, sir," Alistair said. "How did you get on with the good lady of Duntulm?"

"Okay," he said. "She was remarkably calm when I challenged her on her omissions yesterday."

"On the level, do you think?"

Duncan looked across to Lorna's house. "Aye, seems that way."

"You don't sound convinced."

Duncan laughed. "I'm rarely convinced… people always manage to surprise me."

"Aye, I hear you. We've got something here."

"Go on."

"You remember Sandy's neighbour talking about a proper stramash going on the other night?"

"Aye, he thought someone was going to come through the wall…"

"Yeah, well, the neighbour down the way has come through with those video files from the doorbell camera."

"Aye… and?"

"Well, as you know the camera faces the road and not Sandy's house, but it does activate when people walk or drive past. Seemingly, on Saturday evening, a red SUV came down the road, slowing as it passed this guy's place and approaching Sandy's. Who do we know who drives such a vehicle?"

Duncan exhaled heavily. "Dougie."

"Dougie Henderson, aye. Now you, much like myself, don't believe in coincidence."

"Nah... was it Dougie?"

"Hard to say. The camera is the wrong angle to pick up a number plate and the camera is motion activated, so the car was nearly past the house before it started recording... but, regardless, we can tell it's the same car."

"And there was some kind of a trouble at the house—"

"Which fits with the time stamp on the camera footage, so unless it is a coincidence... and some other bloke, who also happens to drive a red SUV, is stopping by to try and stove Sandy's head in, then I think it's reasonable to ask Dougie a couple of extra questions."

"Wait for me." Duncan checked his watch. "I'll get back into Portree as quickly as I can. We'll go out to Borve together."

"Right you are, boss."

"I asked Lorna about the gallery, you know, the phone calls between Sandy and the place in Edinburgh."

"Oh aye. What did she say?"

"Didn't know anything about it, but she said he may have been discussing setting up an exhibition. Can you look into the gallery for me or have one of the team do it."

"Aye. What do you want us to look for?"

"I don't know really," Duncan said, scratching the side of his head. "I'm just being thorough. See if we can find out who Sandy was speaking to, about what... that sort of thing."

"Angus is back from An Talla Mòr."

Duncan's curiosity piqued. "How did he get on?"

"Good and bad. Which do you want first?"

"Start with the good. I like good."

Alistair chuckled. "He couldn't get the name of the woman in the photos. No one knew her, but we know she was a tourist because her and her husband were chatting with the staff. They're Americans, from Tennessee, on a tour of the UK. They started in London, moved up through Yorkshire to Edinburgh. Then they came across to Skye for a few days and were heading on to Ireland."

"Did they have anything to do with Sandy as far as we know?"

"Still working on it, but the staff have CCTV of them inside using the facilities… and she waited outside for her husband who must be struggling with the local food offering, based on how long he spent in the gents."

Duncan laughed. "Any footage of them speaking to anyone outside?"

"No. The external cameras only cover the front entrance and another at the rear. If they were speaking to Sandy, then they did so off camera."

"Is that the bad news then?"

"Pretty much covers it, aye."

"Can we get a hold of their names?"

"They paid with a card, so young Angus is trying to get their details through the bank, but they're still asleep stateside, so it'll take a bit of time. Once we have their names, we can cross check who they are and what they do… see if Sandy crosses their path but…"

"But?"

"My gut tells me they're just ma and pa on a whirlwind tour of the old world, know what I mean?"

Duncan sighed. It looked like another dead end. "All right. Keep Angus on it. You never know where the break will come."

"True enough, but if old pops and his wifey are killers, I'll eat my hat."

"You don't own a hat," Duncan said. "While he's at it, have him run a background check on Lorna too."

"Lorna Somerwell? Aye, can do. You just being thorough again?"

"Aye, something like that... I don't know," he said, peering out into the falling sleet. "There's something about her that's..."

"Weird?"

"I'd have gone for eccentric... but we can use your word."

"Eccentric people have money," Alistair said. "Common folk are just plain weird."

Duncan smiled. "I'm on my way back."

He put his phone away and selected first gear, clearing the windscreen with the wipers so that he could see. The wheels spun momentarily as he pulled away. The snow was still settling, the sleet doing little to change things. Duncan tuned the radio in on the car and caught the local news headlines. The full force of the storm front was yet to make land but was forecast to in about twelve hours' time. If the wind increased more throughout the day as forecast, then there was every chance of more disruption and power lines coming down. Linesmen were being called in from across the highlands, which meant they expected things to get worse. Much worse.

He thought about calling Becky again but decided against it. He winced as the suspension groaned, the nearside front wheel bouncing out of a large pothole in the unadopted road. All the thoroughfares through the scattered townships of Skye were mixtures of compacted soil, gravel or slate chips and often a combination of all of these materials. Owners tended to take care of their stretch of track, often repairing them on an ad hoc basis with whatever materials were readily at hand. However, the freezing conditions and the harsh weather made quick work of patch repairs. The snow cover masked these traps and the last thing Duncan wanted was to burst a tyre out here in these conditions.

He slowed down and picked his way along the track. Passing the three terraced coastguard cottages, he drove up the slope to the main road, the car losing traction as it went up the incline. He almost didn't have enough momentum to make it, but he knew if he got to the crest, he'd be onto the main road which was clear. Once on the A855, he felt comfortable although he took it easy. It wouldn't take much to find yourself off the road in these conditions.

On the approach to Kilmaluag, he saw a black BMW saloon parked in a passing place, lights on and wipers periodically clearing the windscreen. The occupants, with the interior light on, appeared to be poring over a map. Duncan considered stopping to see if they needed assistance, but as he came alongside and slowed down, the driver glanced up, waved and the car edged forward before quickly accelerating away. They must have stopped to check their route. He had to admire holidaymakers who were still willing to continue with their plans under these circumstances. If it were him, he knew he'd stay at home and wait out the storm.

CHAPTER EIGHTEEN

It was Erin Henderson who opened the door to them, peering out, wide-eyed and fearful.

"Hello, Erin," Duncan said. "We're here to see Dougie. Is he about?"

She looked past them, her lips pursed. The red SUV was in the driveway along with a small hatchback which was likely Erin's. Despite the garage door being almost fully closed, they could also see the thick wheels of Dougie's quad bike inside.

"Come on, Mrs Henderson," Alistair said. "It's cold out here... and my patience is pretty thin when I'm cold."

Erin relented, stepping back and opening the door wide before beckoning them inside.

"Dougie... is...er..." Erin's eye flitted nervously between them. "He's not in a good place."

"Who the hell is that now?"

Duncan and Alistair exchanged a look upon hearing the shout from somewhere in the rear of the house. Erin tilted her head, gesturing for them to come with her. The woman had an odd walk, almost a shuffle as she made her way along the narrow hallway, hands clasped together in front of her. They followed and she led them into a large sitting room with French doors looking out to the south, not that any view was visible. The day remained overcast, and the steady snowfall only served to reduce visibility further.

Dougie Henderson was sitting in an armchair, slumped with his arms dangling over the sides. In his right hand was a can of beer and the television remote was in his left. The sound was muted, or turned down, and Dougie was staring at the screen. It was unclear if he was actually paying attention or if it was just the flickering images that held his attention.

"Dougie, love... it's the police."

"The fecking polis..." Dougie muttered. Alistair pointed out the collection of beer cans already on the side table next to the armchair. Duncan counted six or seven before Dougie's head turned towards them. His lips curled into a sneer. "You here for me?"

"Aye," Alistair said, "and I reckon you know why, too, eh Dougie?"

"Yer bastard," Dougie muttered.

"Dougie!" Erin said, but Duncan raised a flat hand to let her know it was okay and that they'd handle it. She lowered her eyes and moved aside as the two detectives walked over to Dougie, who watched them with wary, slightly glazed eyes.

"You've been looking forward to this, haven't you, Alistair?" he said, scowling at him.

Alistair tilted his head. "Not really, Dougie. I'd rather have nothing to do with you at all."

Dougie snorted, lifting his beer can and angling it towards them. He made to drink from it and then sat forward before hurling the half-empty can at them. It missed both Duncan and Alistair, as it was thrown with all the accuracy one might expect from a drunken man acting in the spur of the moment, but they were splashed with beer as it flew by.

Dougie attempted to get up and launch himself at them, taking a swing at Alistair who stepped to his left and gave Dougie a gentle push, all that was needed to throw him off balance, and Dougie staggered forward with his own momentum and toppled over the coffee table sending himself sprawling to the floor. Duncan arched his eyebrows and Alistair wiped his hands, as if dusting them off.

"It's been a while since I've had to manage a drunkard… but it's like riding a bike."

Duncan turned to Erin who was horrified. "How much has he had?"

"Enough for him to keep his hands to himself but not enough to silence him."

That was a telling answer.

"When did he start drinking?"

She inclined her head, looking into the kitchen. "He finished the bottle of whisky that he cracked the seal on last night, and the beer was this afternoon's efforts. I suppose it was you two who spoke to him earlier?"

"It was. Did he talk to you about it?" Duncan asked.

"Talked?" She shook her head. "Shouted at me… from the minute I walked through the door… aye, that was Dougie. I don't think he cared for your visit earlier."

"People rarely do," Duncan said, "particularly if you have form for being aggressive."

"Especially," Alistair added, moving to stand over the stricken form of Dougie who was now groaning and barely awake, "if said individual has an issue with a dead fella."

Erin looked at Alistair as if she had no idea what he was referring to. Alistair smiled at her and dropped to his haunches to take a closer look at Dougie.

"He'll be fine… but he's had a skinful. I doubt we'll get a lot of sense out of him for a while yet." He arched his eyebrows. "As much sense as we get out of him at the best of times."

"You think Dougie had something to do with… with what happened to Sandy?" Erin asked.

Duncan fixed his gaze on her. "It stands to reason. He didn't appreciate your relationship with Sandy."

She scoffed. "My relationship? We were colleagues—"

Alistair laughed and she glared at him. "Come off it, Erin. We're detectives… no' muppets."

Her defiance wilted and she averted her eyes from Alistair's gaze, shaking her head.

"Are you annoyed because we're pointing out the obvious," Duncan asked, "or because you thought you and Sandy were better at seeing one another under the radar?"

She looked at her husband. He was snoring now; great rasping intakes of breath. She momentarily shut her eyes, taking a deep breath to settle herself.

"Are you going to fill in the gaps for us?" Duncan asked. "Or do we have to do it ourselves?"

She sighed. "I suppose it doesn't matter now," she said, crossing the room and sinking down onto the sofa. "That great lump doesn't care… despite what he might say. He hasn't cared for a long while."

Alistair made sure that Dougie wasn't likely to choke on his own vomit, should he be sick, and that his airways were unobstructed. Once he was happy, he signalled to Duncan. They'd let Dougie sleep for a while before transporting him back to the station. Duncan sat down on a chair opposite Erin whereas Alistair perched on the arm of the sofa, keeping a watchful eye on the sleeping Dougie at his feet.

Erin took another deep breath, steadying herself.

"So, how long have you and Sandy been seeing one another?" Duncan asked.

She shrugged. "I wouldn't say we were seeing one another exactly."

"Then what would you say?"

"We've been... in a relationship, off and on for about a year—"

"A bloody year?" Alistair said. Duncan shot him a look and he raised a hand by way of apology. "A year?" he repeated quietly.

Erin nodded glumly. "I always liked Sandy. He's such a fascinating man... so interesting... daring."

Alistair silently mouthed the word *daring* to Duncan, careful to ensure Erin didn't see. Duncan smiled internally. Of all the things they could describe Sandy Beaton as, daring would also be very low on Duncan's list.

"Please go on," Duncan said.

"Well...there's not much to say. We didn't plan for anything to happen," she said, looking over at Duncan, smiling awkwardly. "It just... sort of did."

"Aye," Alistair said, "seemingly these unfortunate intimate accidents appear to happen to Sandy a lot."

Erin ignored him. "Sandy has many flaws... I know. I can see them. I'm not blind. And, yes, you are right," she said, looking at Alistair, "he is something of a... a... lady's man."

"Do you think it was different with you?" Duncan asked.

She looked at him, any awkwardness gone from her expression to be replaced with acceptance. "No. Not for Sandy... although it was for me, and I managed to kid myself for a long time that he felt for me in the same way as I did for him."

"But he didn't?" Duncan asked and she shook her head. "Did he know that you..."

"That I knew he was using me?" she asked. Duncan nodded. "Probably. Sandy didn't really care for anyone else bar himself. It is part of his appeal. At least it was to me," she said, her eyes drifting to her husband lying prostrate on the floor. "I know I was just one of many who Sandy would pick up and put down when it suited him."

Alistair looked at Duncan, evidently questioning the woman's sanity. Duncan was more forgiving. Erin wouldn't be the first woman, or man for that matter, who found themselves hopelessly attracted to someone their rational mind knew was wholly unsuitable, only to continue with the dalliance in the slim hope that they could alter that person's make up. They seldom could though. In reality, it was their own patterns of behaviour that drew them towards these types of individual, rather than an unstoppable magnetic force that compelled them. If they looked hard enough, they'd likely find an individual in Erin's past who was emotionally unavailable, selfish and probably narcissistic.

It was likely this familiarity that made Sandy attractive to her. People are drawn to familiarity, both good and bad, almost doomed to repeat the cycle time and again without ever understanding why they keep doing it to themselves. Duncan thought about Dougie. He didn't seem all that dissimilar to Sandy, beyond the outward appearance.

"Dougie confronted Sandy, didn't he?"

She nodded. "Yes, some time ago. He was arrested for it. They both were."

"What about more recently?"

She looked at Duncan inquisitively, her eyes narrowing. "When do you mean?"

"This past weekend perhaps? Saturday?"

She held Duncan's eye for a moment then shook her head. "No... I would know if he'd been to see Sandy." Duncan arched his eyebrows. "I would!" She pointed at her husband. "You've seen what he's like after you came around today. Can you imagine how much he would be drinking if he and Sandy had a coming together? Let alone if he'd…"

"If he'd killed him?" Duncan said.

"Aye… but Dougie wouldn't do that. He's many things… but not that."

"Who said anything about Sandy being killed, Erin?" Duncan asked.

Her eyes darted towards him and away again just as quickly. She shrugged. "I… I… don't know. It's just that people are talking. You know how things get here on the island. Everyone wants to be in everyone else's business."

"That's what the gossip is saying, is it?" Alistair asked.

She angled her head. "Aye. That's what they're saying. Why would Sandy go out there with that weather forecast? I mean, it was said it'd be bad enough and it was far worse than they said on the TV… and Sandy isn't daft. Besides…"

"Besides?"

She met Duncan's eye. "One of the men who went up the mountain spoke to… well, someone I know. And they said you thought it was… suspicious."

Duncan and Alistair looked at one another. It would appear that the mountain rescue team were not as discreet as they'd hoped. Duncan figured Alistair would be having a quiet word with his old friend, Willie Maciver, about this lapse in discretion. It might be fun to be a fly on the wall during that conversation.

"Is there anyone you can think of who might have it in for Sandy?" Duncan asked her.

She cocked her head. "You mean aside from half the married men on the island?"

Duncan sighed. "How about jilted lovers?"

She stared at him but said nothing.

CHAPTER NINETEEN

DUNCAN CAST one last look over the sleeping form of Dougie Henderson before the custody sergeant closed the door. The closing of a cast-iron cell door echoed through the cell block but as Duncan peered through the viewing slot, Dougie hadn't stirred. He'd woken briefly in the car on the way back from Borve, but only to mumble incoherently before fading out and back into a restless, drunken sleep.

"You'll no' get anything useful out of him until the morning," the sergeant said. "He might be fit for interview around two or three in the morning."

Duncan snorted. "I'll be in ma bed by then, I can assure you. He can sleep it off on a plastic mattress. An uncomfortable night might make him more accurate in his explanation tomorrow."

"Keen to be away home, you reckon?"

"Aye, that's the plan," Duncan said. "Keep an eye on him though. His life, what it is, is falling apart around him, so..."

"Right you are, sir. I'll have him checked every half hour."

Duncan left the custody suite and made his way back up to the ops room. He'd sent everyone home to get some rest. It'd been a long couple of days. He felt a little guilty though. Most of uniform were still on duty; a result of the storm. There were multiple accidents across the island, vulnerable people cut off due to fallen power lines and everyone was needed. However, he needed his team to be focussed. Tiredness led to mistakes and in a murder inquiry, mistakes could leave a killer on the streets.

Alistair was still in ops, reading through the updated information boards populated by Angus, Caitlyn and Russell with what they'd learned during the day.

"Is our boy tucked in for the night?" he asked.

Duncan nodded. "We'll interview him tomorrow morning, see what he has to say for himself."

"Did you see the grazes on his knuckles?"

"Aye. Could have got them working on that quad—"

"Could have got them pummelling Sandy Beaton and pushing him down a mountain too."

Duncan smiled. "I know. Fighting with him doesn't necessarily make him a killer though. Keep an open mind."

"Craig has been in touch with his autopsy report," Alistair said.

"And?"

"Well, long story short, you were right to be suspicious," Alistair said, pointing at the boards. Duncan moved closer to see Alistair had already updated the detail surrounding Sandy's wounds.

"Straight edged implement caused the head wound?" he asked quietly.

"I know basalt can have a sharp edge to it, but those rocks he fell upon didn't have right angles to them," Alistair said.

"He was struck… and then fell?"

"Aye, looks that way. And those markings you spotted, at the wrists?"

"Yeah?"

"Cable ties… Craig reckons. Removed pre or post mortem, but I guess it does nae matter which."

"No, not really. Someone's gone to great lengths to make this look like a tragic accident."

"Aye… even laying out a camera for us too."

Duncan looked at him. "You think Angus was right? That camera was just for show?"

"Well, if it was nae suited for the task… and the shots on the memory card were of old Wilma and Huckleberry touring the UK… Sandy was probably just pressing buttons to make sure the damn thing was working."

"You don't think they're related to any of this then?"

"Pah! Angus got the names earlier… they are nobodies, just over here on holiday."

"So we have a good old-fashioned homespun murder to deal with after all."

"Aye, looks that way, right enough." Alistair stretched, stifling a yawn. "Right… I'm heading home. How about you?"

Duncan was looking at the photograph of Sandy pinned to the information board. He nodded. "Aye. Let's call it a day and go home."

"Do you want me to drop you off?"

Duncan's car was still at the croft. "Bit out of your way."

"How else are you going to get home? Fly?"

"Ros is over visiting our mum, so I messaged her and said I'd call in. I reckon she'll be good to drop me back."

"Suit yourself," Alistair said, switching off his computer and rising from his seat. He slipped his right arm through his coat as he passed Duncan. "I'll see you in the morning."

"Aye, goodnight, Alistair."

Duncan yawned, checked he had his keys, wallet and mobile before switching the lights off as left the ops room.

Much of the station was already in darkness. Those officers on standby for deployment were gathered in the refectory where food had been provided to see them through. He could hear chatter, laughing as he passed the room, acknowledging several uniformed constables as they passed him in the corridor.

Stepping outside into Somerled Square, Duncan zipped up his coat and turned the collar up as well. Although the snow-fall had eased, it was only a temporary respite based on the forecast for the next twenty-four hours. After that, the storm's intensity should be on the wane, but he was sceptical. After all, they'd failed to predict the course of it once already. He'd caught a national weather report and they were saying some-thing about the oscillating wind pattern across the Atlantic had shifted at the last moment. It sounded like bollocks to him, but nevertheless it didn't change the fact they were going to have to deal with it.

His mother's residential care home was on the outskirts of Portree, so Duncan made the walk as quickly as he could, keen not to be caught outside when things took a turn for the worse. His mother's condition appeared to have stabilised in recent weeks. Her mental capacity didn't seem to be deteriorating, but her lucid moments were few and far between as it was.

The receptionist welcomed him as he entered the lobby, shaking the snow from his coat and stamping his feet before walking in.

"Good evening, Mr McAdam."

He smiled. "Duncan. How many times?"

She smiled. "Sorry, it's habit. Roslyn is already upstairs with your mum."

He thanked her and made his way up to his mother's room. The door was ajar, and he knocked gently before enter-ing. Roslyn was sitting in a chair beside their mum who had her seat in her favoured position by the window looking out over Portree's bay. In the darkness he could just make out the outline of the hills on Raasay, illuminated by the light reflecting from their covering of snow. Roslyn smiled as he approached, leaning over to kiss his mum on the forehead.

"Hello, Mum. How are you?"

She didn't acknowledge his affectionate kiss. Her expression remained impassive, her eyes staring out over the bay. He looked from his mum to his sister.

"Hi, Ros," he said, leaning over and kissing her on the cheek. She rested a hand on his forearm and squeezed gently.

"Mum's not having the best of days."

Duncan observed their mother. She always looked frail these days, a far cry from the firebrand he remembered from his youth, but tonight she seemed paler than normal.

"Is she okay? She looks—"

"Pale, aye. That's what I thought too." Roslyn seemed concerned. "I spoke to the nurses, and they said she's okay in herself. It might just be the time of year."

Duncan reached out and placed his hand gently over his mother's. Her skin felt cold. He could feel the warmth coming from the radiator mounted on the wall beneath the window. She had a tartan blanket draped across her legs and Duncan found another on the far side of the room. He folded that and laid it across her lap as well. Still, his mum didn't seem to notice.

Duncan picked up another chair, brought it across the room and sat down next to Roslyn. "So, how are things?" he asked.

"Same as usual, Duncan." She looked at him. "How about with you?"

The question was asked with a searching look which he was perturbed by. "Meaning?"

She shook her head ever so slightly. "Just asking."

"When you say it like that, you're never just asking."

Roslyn smiled. "I heard about young Callum Mcinnes."

"Ah… right."

"I presume you've spoken to Becky?"

"Aye… I was with her at the hospital."

Roslyn looked at him. There was that same expression.

"What?" he asked.

"What, what?" she replied, the smile dissipating. "I'm sure you have it under control."

"I have what under control, exactly?"

Roslyn turned the corners of her mouth down and shook her head. Not for the first time recently, Duncan felt that everyone seemed to know more about a situation than he did.

"Is Becky okay?" Roslyn asked in a rare show of empathy. Duncan knew they didn't get on, but he'd never quite put his finger on why. Becky always suspected that Roslyn never thought she was good enough for Duncan when they were dating, but he didn't buy that. Becky was a decent person. If anything, he thought it was the other way around.

"The last I spoke with her…" He remembered her kissing him in the corridor. "She… was upset but coping."

"She has shown remarkable resolve," Roslyn said, following her mum's gaze out of the window, "over the years."

Duncan studied her face, looking for the cutting sarcasm that was something of a family trait; certainly in the women folk of the McAdam family anyway. He didn't see any sign of it though. Roslyn caught him watching her and smiled.

"I don't hate her, you know—"

"You do!" Duncan said, smirking.

"No… I dislike her intensely. But that doesn't stretch to hating her."

"Oh, well that's okay then."

She laughed.

Once visiting hours were over, Duncan walked downstairs with his sister beside him.

"Any chance of a lift home?" he asked.

"You'll have to get around Ronnie," she said, gesturing to their car in the car park. The daytime running lights were on, Ronnie MacDougall sitting in the driver's seat watching them from across the car park.

"Ah… that'll go well," he said absently.

Roslyn slapped him playfully on the arm. "You speak to him while I nip to the ladies. It's a bit of a drive home."

"That'll be your oversized prostate," Duncan said to her. She looked over her shoulder at him, grinning as she ducked back into the building. Duncan drew his coat about him and thrust his hands deep into his pockets as he crossed the short distance between the building and where Ronnie was parked up.

"Hi, Ronnie. How's it going?" Duncan asked as Ronnie wound his window down.

"Duncan." He looked past him. "Where's Ros off to?"

"Call of nature."

"Oh aye."

Ronnie was staring straight ahead. He couldn't make it any clearer that he wasn't keen to engage Duncan in conversation.

"So, what's the craic, Ronnie?"

He looked up at Duncan. "With what?"

"Why are you always so off with me?"

Ronnie's eyes narrowed. "Am I always off with you?"

Duncan smiled bitterly. "Come on, man. If you've got something to say, then spit—"

"Why did you come back here, Duncan?" Ronnie said. "Back to the island?"

"It's my home... why shouldn't I come back?"

"It's a place you could nae wait to leave... so why come back?"

Duncan's back was up. "What's it got to do with you what I do with my life?"

Ronnie's gaze drifted to him. "If only your decisions didn't impact others, eh?"

Confused now, Duncan frowned. "What did I ever do to you?"

"The same as you did to everyone, Dunc," Ronnie said, cracking open his door and getting out. He stood before Duncan, hands on his hips. "It's always about you, isn't it?" he said, jabbing a finger in the air towards him.

"What's that supposed to mean?"

"It means drama follows you everywhere you go, Duncan. It always has and it always will." Ronnie puffed out his chest. "And I for one, am sick and tired of dealing with the fallout from your shite."

"My..."

"You've never taken responsibility for anything in your life... ever, and somehow, I doubt you're ever going to. You'd be doing everyone a favour by getting off the island and staying the hell away."

Duncan's mouth was open, and he saw an intensity in Ronnie's expression, let alone his words, that he'd never seen before.

"What have I missed?" Roslyn asked, coming to stand with them.

Duncan, locked in a death stare with his brother-in-law, shrugged, breaking the eye contact. "Nothing." He stepped back, kissed his sister on the cheek and walked away.

"I thought you needed a lift home?"

"I've got other plans," he called over his shoulder and he heard an accusatory tone in his sister's voice.

"What did you say to him?"

And Ronnie's defensive reply.

"I didnae say anything that shouldna be said."

"Oh… you bloody men."

Duncan increased his pace, the snow falling steadily once more. It wasn't long before he was back in Portree centre and he ducked into McNabs. The bar was pretty empty. Most people weren't venturing out, but it was still open and that was all Duncan cared about.

He approached the bar and the woman serving crossed to him.

"Quiet tonight," he said, ordering a pint of Belhaven.

"That's off, I'm afraid. But I can do you McEwans if that's okay?"

"Aye, that's braw, cheers."

She poured his pint, watching him from the corner of her eye. She set the pint down and he passed her a fiver as she rang it up.

"So, what brings wee Duncan McAdam into town on a night like this?" she asked. He looked at her, accepting his change. He didn't know her, or at least he didn't think so.

"Do we… know each other?"

She laughed. He had to know her, although he was sure they'd never met and he had a memory for faces. It was part of his job, after all. She was perhaps five or six years younger than him but no more. It was unlikely they'd been at high school together. She had red hair which hung loose to her shoulders. He could see tattoos visible on her arms beneath her shirt and she had a stud to the left side of her nose. She was familiar but he couldn't place her and looking at her now, he knew he wouldn't forget her.

"You were at school with my sister, although she was a few years below you."

"Oh aye? What's your sister's name?"

"Orla," she said, watching for Duncan's reaction. "McFadyen. Our mum was pals with yours. You remember?"

"Aye... Orla... I mind her." Duncan smiled, recalling the family. "That makes you..."

"Grace," she said, smiling.

Duncan couldn't believe it. He looked her up and down momentarily. "I cannae... you're wee Gracey?" She nodded, her smile broadening. She was the youngest of the family, if he remembered rightly, so maybe she was more than six years his junior. "Mind that I used to babysit you, and your sisters, on occasion? You... Orla and... er..." He snapped his fingers, searching his memory.

"Leah."

"That's right, Leah!" He smiled at her. "Leah, yeah... how is she... and Orla these days?"

"Aye, they're grand," Grace said. "Leah lives over in Glasgow now... married, a couple of kids of her own."

"Never... and Orla?"

"Moved to Vancouver. She went to Canada for a ski season, three months working in a resort..." she shrugged, "and never came back."

"Damn," Duncan said, "nice place."

"You've been?"

"Ah... no," Duncan said, his face reddening. "But I've seen pictures... on the telly and that."

Grace laughed, resting her elbows on the bar and leaning into him. "So, back to my original question; what's wee Duncan doing back on Skye?"

"Oh… you know, a bit of work—"

"Hold that thought," she said, raising a pointed finger as another customer caught her attention from the far side of the bar. "I'll be back in a minute," she said as she walked away, but glanced back at him, seemingly pleased to see him watching her. She smiled at him and he returned it.

CHAPTER TWENTY

DUNCAN WOKE WITH A START. It was still dark, and it took a moment for his eyes to adjust. Had he imagined it? The sudden movement brought forth a stabbing pain in his head. His eyes felt gritty. He coughed. Reaching to the little shelf next to the bed, he managed to knock his watch off onto the floor. It clunked as it hit the carpet and he heard a murmur beside him as she stirred.

He looked at Grace, her chest rising and falling as she breathed in and out, still asleep despite his best efforts at making enough noise to raise the dead. He must have been dreaming.

The knock came again, only this time more forceful. He hadn't imagined it after all. He swung his legs out from beneath the duvet and instantly regretted it as he felt the cold night air strike his bare skin. The movement shook the caravan slightly and the movement was enough for his mobile to register it, the screen illuminating as if he'd reached for it.

He picked it up, the glare of the screen hurting his eyes despite the auto-dimming feature. It was a little after one o'clock in the morning. He had two missed calls, the last was only twenty minutes previously. Someone knocked on the caravan door again. Duncan hurriedly pulled on his trousers and grabbed a jumper laying nearby, looping it over his head as he went through the kitchen area to the door.

Grace stirred again and he figured it would be a miracle if she didn't wake the next time someone knocked. He put his mobile into his pocket as he moved the lock aside on the door and opened it. The door opened outwards and Becky side-stepped it, so it didn't hit her as a gust of wind tore it from Duncan's grasp and slammed against the exterior.

Becky stepped up into the caravan.

"Take your time, Duncan," she said, running a hand through her wet hair. "It's not like I'm standing in the rain or anything." The forecast for the night had been more or less correct. The snowfall was now a mix of snow and sleet, driving hard from the west.

Duncan, half asleep and caught off guard, leaned out of the caravan and grasped the door, pulling it back and closing it as quietly as he could.

"Becky… do you know what time it is?" he asked quietly.

"Yes, of course I do," she said, sweeping damp hair away from her face, a few strands sticking to her forehead just above her right eye. "But I need to speak to you."

"And it couldn't wait?"

"Well obviously not, Duncan…"

He frowned. It was a perfectly reasonable question bearing in mind it was approaching the middle of the night. He glanced at the bed. Grace had rolled over and hauled the duvet atop her, burying herself from view. Duncan felt guilty, as if he was about to be caught doing something he shouldn't be doing, which he immediately thought was ridiculous.

"Um…" he shrugged. "What's… going on?"

Becky exhaled deeply, avoiding meeting his eye. She was

nervous, shifting her weight between her feet. "Listen... I know..." she hesitated.

"What is it?" he asked, placing a supportive hand on her forearm. She met his eye now, her brow furrowing.

"Why are you whispering?"

"I'm not whispering."

"You are... you just whispered then, like before."

He winced, searching for the right words. Grace stirred and the rustle of the duvet saw them both look her way.

"Ah... I see," Becky said, surprise turning to anger as she glared at Duncan. "Sorry to interrupt."

Grace opened her eyes, staring straight at the two of them. Awake quite quickly, she lifted her head and propped herself up on one arm.

"Hi," she said, smiling.

Becky returned her smile with an artificial one of her own. "Hello. Sorry to disturb..." she looked at Duncan, "you."

"That's okay," Grace said cheerfully. "I'm a great sleeper. Not a problem."

Becky inclined her head. "Oh, is that right? Good to know."

Duncan cleared his throat. "Um... Becky... Grace... Grace, Becky."

Grace waved, still smiling and Becky offered her a curt nod before turning back to Duncan.

"Don't mind me," Grace said. "Crack on. I need to use the bathroom anyway." She looked around, spotting Duncan's shirt laying across the dining table next to Duncan. She pointed at it and he picked it up and threw it over to her. She slipped it on, Becky looking away from Grace and awkwardly at Duncan. Grace cast off the duvet, and with only her shirt on, buttoned halfway up, slipped by them to get to the bathroom.

"Excuse me," she said as she slipped between them, deliberately brushing against Duncan as she passed him. He smiled, Grace grinned. Once he heard the latch on the bath-room door click into place, he looked apologetically at Becky.

"I'm sorry, I obviously—"

Becky raised a hand to silence him. "It doesn't matter, Duncan. It's none of my business."

"No, you're right. It isn't—"

"Exactly," she said, turning and making for the door. He hurried to stop her, gripping her arm. She flinched, and he immediately released his grip.

"Sorry... I didn't mean to hurt you."

"N–No... it's my fault... don't worry." She reached for the door handle and this time Duncan grasped it, keeping it closed. "Duncan, let me out."

He sighed. "Look... whatever brought you here must be important... right?" She pursed her lips, staring straight ahead at the door. "So, what is it?"

"Duncan, please let go of the door."

She looked up at him, pleading rather than angry like she was before.

"What is it?" he asked.

She inclined her head, gesturing to the door and he removed his hand. She immediately opened it and stepped out into the sleet. He followed, despite being barefoot.

"Becky!"

She spun around to face him, her gaze drifting past him and into the caravan, the door hanging open and banging against the exterior in the wind. The fire in her eyes was back. He'd seen that look many times before, but not since they'd split years ago.

"What are you playing at Duncan?"

The question threw him, and he stammered a reply. "I–I'm not playing at anything..."

Becky was seething, but for the life of him he couldn't understand why.

"What's with you?" he asked, feeling his own anger building.

"I'll tell you this, Duncan," Becky said, glaring at him. "If you treat someone like they're second best, don't expect them to be your first priority!"

She turned and stalked back to the car parked alongside his. It wasn't a car he recognised, so he assumed it was a hire car. Becky's was still on its roof south of Staffin as far as Duncan knew. She got into the car without another word and slammed the door shut, glaring at him as she fired up the engine. She struggled to start it and then ground the gears as she sought first before the engine revved far too high and she spun the wheels as the car lurched forward. Duncan backed away towards the caravan as she turned the car around and drove away into the night.

"What the fuck was that about?"

The realisation he was barefoot came to him and he hurried back to the caravan, climbing up into it and pulling the door closed behind him. He looked at the bed, but Grace wasn't there. He heard the bathroom door unlock and it opened slowly, the hinges creaking. Grace peered through the gap at him.

"Is it safe to come out?"

He smiled and nodded. Grace left the bathroom, quickly making her way past him and getting back under the duvet, shuffling under it to get snuggled in.

"It's amazing how quickly they lose the heat isn't it?" she said.

"Aye," he said quietly, standing in the middle of the living space.

"I thought," Grace said, inclining her head and drawing the duvet up to just beneath her chin, "that you were single."

He looked at her. "I am single."

"You sure?"

He nodded.

"Well, you might want to tell that firebrand wifey, who just shot daggers at me for being in your bed, that you're single."

"Oh no... she's... we're just old friends."

"Aye, you might want to tell her that as well while you're at it."

Duncan frowned. Why did he feel guilty? He hadn't done anything wrong.

"Aye... she has a lot on her mind, that's all. Her bairns are sick."

Grace wrinkled her nose. "I think she has a bit more on her mind now."

Duncan nodded. Remembering the missed calls, he took his mobile from his pocket.

"Are you... coming back to bed?" Grace asked, sliding the duvet away from her upper body. Duncan smiled. She was still wearing his shirt, although she'd already undone all but two of the buttons.

"One moment," he said, unlocking his screen and tapping the missed call notification. He thought it might be work, but it was his friend, Archie. He pressed the call back option and raised the mobile to his ear, holding a forefinger in the air at Grace.

"Duncan! Ah man... I'm so glad you called me back like..."

Duncan could hear the wind through the mouthpiece, Archie's voice was raised to be heard above it. "Arch? Where are you?" He was hit in the side of the head by Grace's shirt which wrapped around his face. He pulled it away and looked back at her. She lay naked on the bed, the duvet pulled aside completely, enticing him back to bed. "Er... Archie, this had better be good. I have... something on here."

"Dunc... I've got myself into a bit of a clusterbùrach and I kinda need your help."

Duncan frowned. "Now?"

"Aye... I'm having a bit of car trouble... a flat tyre and I dinnae have a jack. I've got the spare wheel off the back of the Landy like, but... Duncan... I really need your help, man. I'll be out here all night otherwise and the snow... it's a bit frightening like, you know?"

Duncan sighed, glancing at Grace who pulled the duvet back over herself and rolled onto her side. His face must have said it all.

"Where are you?"

"Ah, Duncan, you're a scholar and a gentleman. I owe you one."

Duncan nodded. "Aye, and you've no idea how much."

CHAPTER TWENTY-ONE

GLENUACHDARACH WAS a little north of the forested area of Keistle, central on the Trotternish peninsula. Duncan was struggling to get his little car along the track once clear of the township. The road wound its way through a wide valley with cloud-draped hills to either side. The going was slow, and Duncan almost found himself sliding off the road on several occasions, cursing Archie for putting this on him.

The track bore left and as he eased the car up a slight incline a figure stepped from the shadows into his path, and he hit the brakes. Immediately, the car went sideways and he slid off the road into a bank of snow to his right. Duncan cursed. The engine had stalled, the dashboard lit up with red and amber warning lights. He cursed again.

A gloved hand knocked the window and Duncan turned to see Archie's bearded face staring at him, offering him either a toothy grin or a grimace. He was unsure which. Archie gave him a thumbs-up and Duncan nodded. He turned the key and the engine started first time. Putting the car into reverse, he attempted to back away from the verge and line himself up on the track again. The car, however, didn't move. He could feel the wheels straining, the engine picked up as he increased the revs but the car didn't move.

Archie's face appeared out of the gloom once more, and Duncan cracked his window, keen to keep the elements at bay for as long as possible.

"I think you've got yourself hung up on something," he said.

"Oh, do you think so, Archie?"

Archie smiled, appreciating the sarcasm. "Hold on a moment and I'll be right back."

Duncan turned to look as Archie hurried away into the dark. "Arch! Where are you going? Where's your…"

He sighed. Looking ahead, he couldn't try moving forward. the car was raised on the verge and buried into a snowbank as high as the bonnet. All he could hope was he hadn't done any damage to the front wing or suspension. he hadn't been driving quickly, so he hoped for the best. Where Archie had left his Land Rover was anyone's guess.

A scrabbling sound came from outside and Duncan saw a shadow moving at the rear of the car. He unclipped his seat belt and cracked open the door, leaning out and looking to the back.

"Archie!" he called over the sound of the wind, but it was whipping through the valley. His friend was upwind, so there was no way he could hear him. It didn't matter. Archie appeared soon enough, coming to the open door, hand on the hood of his coat, stopping it from being blown back.

Archie bent down, peering in at him. "Leave it in neutral and loose the hand brake, all right?" He gave Duncan another thumbs-up signal and scurried away into the darkness. Duncan grumbled but did as he was bid. A moment later the car moved ever so slightly. The vehicle protested, a strained shriek sounding within the cabin but then it was yanked back as if being hauled over a lump in the road. The car rolled freely and came to a stop a couple of metres from the verge.

Using the headlight beams, Duncan examined the snowbank. He'd managed to mount the verge and if he'd gone another metre then he'd have been through the fence and into the field beyond. He would never have got himself out of the there. The car lurched backward again, and then settled in place. Duncan pulled the handbrake on and got out. Moving to the back of the car, he found a thick metal cable, roughly eight millimetres in diameter, attached to the rear, now showing a little slack.

Archie came back to him, clapping him on the shoulder. "Thanks for coming, Duncan." He grinned at him.

Duncan followed the cable across the road and into the next field. The gate was open, and he could make out Archie's old Defender.

"Archie, what are you doing out here?"

He shrugged. "Ah... you know? The storm and that brings the herd down from the hills and into the forest, you know?"

Duncan's eyebrows knitted. "You're out poaching—"

"No!" Archie said defensively. "I'm out stalking... and that's different."

"Stalking whose deer?"

Archie tapped his nose with one finger, grinning. "Come on, I need your jack," he said, looking at Duncan's car. "Unless you think your car can pull me out of the field and then we can do it on the harder ground. What do you reckon?"

"The ground will be frozen solid, Archie. I'll get the jack."

"Aye, probably right."

Duncan popped the boot lid and lifted the floor mat. He

had to unscrew the bracket holding the spare wheel in place before he could access the jack. The metal contraption felt cold to the touch and Duncan was already keen to get this out of the way as quickly as possible so he could get back indoors. The thought of Becky being there came to mind and he quickly admonished himself, forcing an image of Grace to mind instead.

He followed Archie's path into the field, where he found him already loosening the wheel nuts of the offside rear wheel. Duncan set the jack down, hoping he was right and that the vehicle's weight wouldn't sink the jack into the ground. He needn't have worried. The earth here wasn't marshy and it appeared as if the landowner had previously dumped some form of hardcore beyond the gate, presumably in an effort to make it easier to maintain the ground around the entrance and exit to the smallholding. Nature had already begun reseeding this area, but the jack held firm as Duncan cranked the vehicle into the air.

Archie, impressively by himself, removed the wheel and set it aside behind him and then hefted the spare into place soon after. Duncan cast a glance over the flat. The rubber of the side wall was shredded. he had never seen a flat like it. Punctures were common enough around here, even a blowout wasn't unheard of but this looked different although familiar.

He turned back to Archie, already tightening the nuts with the wheel brace. Duncan saw his left cheek. It was bleeding in several places, the blood trickling down and becoming lost in his beard.

"Archie… you're bleeding."

Archie stopped, glancing sideways at him and smiling. He let go of the brace and wiped the side of his face, staring into his palm. Whether he saw blood in this light, Duncan couldn't tell but his friend turned back to the wheel, tightening the nuts.

"All good!" he announced triumphantly, turning to Duncan and smiling. Duncan glanced at the shredded tyre again, reality dawning.

"Archie, tell me again how you got stuck out here."

He smiled awkwardly. "Aye, well I was out this way… ken?"

"Poaching, aye."

"Aye… well, they leave food out for the herd on the tracks, ken?"

"Stalking?" Duncan asked, shaking his head. "You were staking out the oasis, basically, weren't you? You knew where the herd would be."

Archie nodded. "Aye. It's just a matter of waiting. It gets a bit cold like… but it's easier than being out for hours from dusk till dawn."

"And who was there?"

"What's that you say?" Archie asked innocently, avoiding Duncan's gaze.

"They were waiting for you, weren't they?" Archie pretended not to hear. "Archie, what happened?"

He glanced sideways, appearing bashful and shrugged. "Who'd be crazy enough to be out on a night like this, eh?"

"Gamekeepers… groundsmen…"

"Aye," Archie said, a half-smile dissipating as he nodded. "They kinda ambushed me."

"Ambushed you? And then what… chased you down this way?" Duncan asked, looking around them.

"Aye… crafty bastards were lying in wait. They're smarter than I gave them credit for."

"And you've just involved me… a serving polisman in your escape!"

Archie waved his concern aside. "Ah, they'll no' be reporting anything," he said, pointing at the pellet wounds to his cheek. "They let rip when I came out of the woods..." He shrugged. "It's only birdshot mind. They didnae want to do any real damage."

Duncan pointed at the tyre. "And did they do this as you arrived or when you legged it?"

"I turned and high-tailed it back into the woods, obviously. I wasnae gonna stick around to face the music like, you know?" His brow furrowed. "But... unless you have a rocket pack, the only way in or out of this area is..." he pointed to the track Duncan's car was parked on."

"They shot out your tyre?"

Archie pointed to the rear quarter panel of his Defender. "And took a bit of my paintwork too, so it seems. It's just a bit of banter."

Duncan approached and could make out some damage just above the wheel arch. "Banter? The damn fools could have killed you!"

"Nah, away with you, man. They were only trying to scare me."

"And did they?"

Archie grinned. "Beats dying in your bed of boredom, eh?"

Duncan shook his head. "Come on, let's get you home before someone decides to teach you another lesson... and me along with you."

"Aye, sounds good," Archie said, raising his voice to be heard above the increasing wind. "I'm sorry to drag you out here Dunc."

"Ah forget it."

"If there's any damage to your car... when it got hung up, I'll see you right."

Duncan laughed as Archie dropped to his haunches to pull

the jack from beneath the car. "And how are you going to do that exactly?"

"Oh… I have something in the pipeline, don't you worry."

"Which is?"

Archie stood up, the jack wedged under his arm. "Rich folks coming to the island for a guided tour… and I'm going to show 'em around."

"Rich folks, eh?"

"Aye, gentrified folk. More money than sense… and after all, no one knows this island better than I do, right?"

Duncan nodded, taking the jack from his friend. "But tonight… it's get yourself away home."

Archie saluted. "Yes, boss."

Archie carried the jack back to Duncan's car, putting it back in its place before putting the spare wheel over it and closing the boot. Duncan was already in the driver's seat and Archie leaned in with one hand on the door and the other on the roof.

"Hey, is it true what people are saying?"

Duncan looked up at him. "That depends… what are people saying?"

"About Sandy, that someone killed him?"

"Is that what people are saying?" Duncan shook his head. "Some people talk too much right enough."

"Ah…" Archie said, nodding, "so it's true like?"

Duncan sighed. "We're looking into it and I can't say more than that."

"Disnae surprise me."

"Why is that?" Duncan asked, genuinely curious. Archie shook his head, glumly. "Come on, Archie. Out with it, man."

He shrugged. "Well… all that stuff with him selling paintings and the like."

"What about it?"

Archie grinned. "That competition he won... no one's goin' to tell me he painted that. No chance."

Duncan's curiosity was piqued. "And what would you know about fine art?"

"More than you, I'm sure about that."

Duncan laughed, considering Archie's comment. He was intrigued. Thinking back to their high school days, Archie had always been one of the best, if not the best, student in almost every subject. Their teachers considered it something of a travesty when he announced he wasn't continuing with his studies beyond sitting the highers. Despite his clear intelligence, Archie struggled with authority figures; an attitude he carried with him into adulthood.

"All right, I'm listening." Duncan fixed Archie with a keen look. "Why don't you think Sandy painted it?"

"The man had an eye for a photograph, right enough... but painting like he supposedly did... takes years of practice, study... plus an inherent talent Sandy just didnae have."

"In your opinion," Duncan said.

"Aye... it's my opinion," Archie said defensively. "And what he's been knocking out of that gallery of his in the last few years..." Archie snorted a laugh.

"What about it?"

Archie shook his head, grinning. "Do you think Sandy Beaton has the look of a man who understands art dealing?"

"No, not as far as I know."

"Then how come he manages to have a fair turnover of collectables passing through that jumped-up market stall of his? A five grand picture here... a thirteen-hundred one there... he must have the magic touch when it comes to stumbling across a bargain."

Duncan's forehead creased. "Just what are you saying exactly?"

Archie chuckled and closed the driver's door before hurrying through the falling snow back to his Defender. Duncan could see the whites of his teeth through his beard as he waved before driving away. Archie found something incredibly amusing but was unwilling to share the joke with him.

CHAPTER TWENTY-TWO

DUNCAN SET the cup of coffee down on the table and gently moved it across to Dougie, whose eyes lifted from his hands cradled in his lap, settling on the takeaway cup. Duncan nodded at it.

"Help yourself, big man."

"Does it have milk and sugar?" Dougie asked, looking up at Duncan as he sat down opposite him. Alistair MacEachran was already seated, silent, arms folded across his chest, staring at Dougie.

"Do you want it to have milk and sugar?" Duncan asked.

"No, not particularly."

Dougie scooped up the cup and sipped at it. The liquid was cool by now, Duncan having picked it up on his way into the station. Dougie frowned as he tasted the drink, putting the cup down but keeping his fingers curled around it.

Duncan lay a folder on the table before him, opening it and taking out the top sheet of paper, an image lifted from Sandy Beaton's neighbour's door camera, and then laid it down in front of Dougie whose face dropped as he stared at it.

"I was going to ask you whether you went to Sandy's

house on Saturday evening," Duncan said, "but I'm a bit tired this morning and I don't want to dance around it. You went there, right?"

Dougie sniffed, rolled his tongue along the edge of his lower lip, his eyes flitting first to Duncan and then Alistair. He nodded.

"Mind telling us what your intention was?"

Dougie pursed his lips, turning the coffee cup in his hand, averting his eyes from them. "I thought I'd stop by for a chat."

"Oh, did yer, aye?" Alistair said, arching his eyebrows. Dougie glared at him but didn't reply. Instead, he took a mouthful of coffee.

Duncan sat forward, resting his elbows on the table. "We know about Erin and Sandy." Dougie's eyes raised to meet his, eyeing him warily. "And we know," Duncan said, "that you have confronted Sandy in the past. You were arrested and ultimately cautioned due to an altercation between you."

Dougie sat back, folding his arms. "If you know I was there, why do you need to ask why? Isn't it obvious?"

Duncan glanced sideways at Alistair, who remained straight faced.

"We've had a chat with the pathologist, Dougie," Alistair said.

"That's great. Pleased for you," Dougie replied, but his bravado was contrived.

"And he says," Alistair continued, "that Sandy likely walked up The Storr before he had the back of his head stoved in… and rolled to his death. It's likely he bled to death before succumbing to the elements."

Dougie took a deep breath, licked his lips and arched his eyebrows. Alistair, his eye fixed on him, maintained his gaze until Dougie looked away. A hint of a smile momentarily passed Alistair's lips.

"What do you have to say about that?" Duncan asked.

Dougie's gaze met Duncan's and he shrugged. "That's not a nice way to leave this world, is it?" Duncan asked.

Dougie smiled. "Is there ever a nice way?"

"You don't seem too upset."

Dougie scoffed. "Why would I be? The man made a prize fool out of me... time and time again." He sat forward, his expression hardening. "And you think I should have some measure of sympathy for the bloke? Good riddance, I say."

"How about some sympathy for his family, his sister?"

Dougie nodded. "Aye, I feel for Morag all right. She's not at fault for her brother's behaviour." He sniffed, picked up his coffee and casually drank from it. "I doubt she'll miss him all that much though."

"No?" Duncan asked.

"I shouldn't have thought so, no. The man was trouble, through and through. A proper wrong-un, you might say."

"You'll not be missing him then?" Duncan asked. It was rhetorical. Dougie smiled.

Alistair uncrossed his arms, staring hard at their suspect.

"You're quite... bold, for a man who had an axe to grind with someone who wound up dead a little way after you paid him a visit. Especially when you're bearing those cuts and grazes to your hands. How'd you get those?"

Dougie laughed. He extended his hands across the table and then turned them, palms up. He nodded at the outstretched hands. "Cuts and grazes?" He stared at Alistair and then lifted his hands in the air, fluttering his fingers as if his hands were flying away. "They're the hands of a man who works for a living. A proper job, not swanning around the island giving grief to decent folk. Do you reckon Sandy would have taken a scenic walk with me of his own free will? If he was feeling threatened by me, a few scrapes of my knuckles would be the bare minimum. Where Sandy and me are concerned, he could hold his own. I might come out on top but toe to toe, I'd be black and blue." His eyes narrowed. "What do you say, Keck? You're the big man on the island, or so you think you are anyways. You really think it's me, huh? Get over yourself man."

If Alistair was offended or triggered by Dougie's remarks, then he didn't show it. He sat impassively, holding Dougie's gaze. Failing to get a rise out of him, Dougie looked to Duncan.

"I'm not your man," he said softly and sat back with a smug, satisfied smile on his face.

"I wonder if Erin will say the same?" Duncan asked. Dougie's smile faded. "Maybe she will see this as the perfect time to cut ties with you. You go down for a long time and she is free to live her life without you, without having to wrestle half the house off you, plus get you to cough up maintenance."

"Aye, and what do you know about it?" Dougie retorted.

"Enough to know a happy marriage doesn't have three people in it. You see, Erin even knew she was just one of many dalliances that Sandy had across the island." Duncan looked up at the ceiling thoughtfully. "And yet, she was still willing to go with him... rather than settle for you."

Dougie's nose twitched, his expression darkening as Duncan eyed him.

"How little you know about my wife... about how manipulative she is..."

"So, tell me," Duncan replied. "what's your side of it?"

Dougie chuckled, shaking his head. "You have no idea about Sandy and what he was up to... and what he had Erin involved in."

"Care to share that with us?" Alistair asked.

Dougie shot him a knowing look. "Wouldn't you like to know…"

"What happened when you confronted Sandy at his home on Saturday night?" Duncan asked.

Dougie smiled and it soon broadened into a grin. "All right," he said, sitting forward, "I'll tell you something. Aye," he nodded, "I was at Sandy's Saturday night. I'd had a few… so I was the worse for drink, right enough." He shook his head, inhaling through gritted teeth. "And… I shouldn't have been there. I was nae in the right frame of mind, but if I had been, then I wouldn't have been there, would I?"

"So," Duncan said, spreading his hands wide, "what happened?"

"Nothing."

"Nothing?"

Dougie nodded. "Aye, nothing. I parked outside his house right enough. I wanted to have it out with him once and for all. I wanted him to stay away from my wife… but as I sat there, I sobered up. I knew I shouldn't call him out… in case of what it might lead to."

"What might it lead to?"

He fixed Duncan with an ice-cold stare. "Because I'd likely have killed him."

"That doesn't put you in a positive light, Dougie," Duncan said. "And do I need to remind you that a man is dead."

"Aye, well I didnae kill him. If I had, I would nae be going to all the bother of trekking up a mountain first. I'd have done him on his doorstep."

"So, where did you go when you left Sandy's house?"

"Home."

"And Erin will confirm this?"

"She was nae there when I got in."

"Where was she?"

He shrugged. "How should I know?" Dougie sat back in his seat. "And I'll be saying nothing further without first speaking to a solicitor."

He folded his arms defiantly across his chest. Duncan and Alistair exchanged a glance, Alistair raised his eyebrows and tilted his head to one side. Duncan gestured towards the recording machine and Alistair concluded the interview.

Dougie looked at Duncan. "So, what happens now?"

"We'd better call you a solicitor, Dougie, because you're not going anywhere—"

"Och come on, man! I told you what happened. It was nae me. I would nae say all this if it weren't true, would I?"

"And if that's true," Duncan said, standing up, "then you have nothing to fear. Just to advise you from the outset, we will be comparing your DNA with any we find on Sandy's body or in his house. We will also be applying for a search warrant for your home."

"Ah... you're wasting your time!"

"And we will be seizing any clothing that you were wearing last weekend, or perhaps all of your clothing if we can't be sure what you were wearing that day, and sending it all to the lab for analysis. Should we find anything that links you to Sandy's murder," Duncan said, leaning on the table and towering above Dougie, "then I will see to it that you don't breathe free air for a very, very long time."

Duncan left the interview room, closing the door behind him. He put his back against the wall on the other side of the corridor and pressed the heels of his palms into his temples. He had a headache. Lack of sleep and dehydration following the drinks he'd had with Grace at the pub the previous night were all catching up on him. His mobile beeped and he took it out of his pocket. It was a text message from Becky. It said simply, *I need to see you.*

Duncan frowned. He hadn't expected to hear from her anytime soon after the events of the previous night. Grace came to mind. She'd been gone by the time he got back to the caravan which was something of a blessing. It'd been a surreal night and had she stayed then he figured it would have made for an awkward morning. His finger hovered over the call button. What did Becky want from him? This was a question that stretched beyond the text message; the reason behind her late-night visit playing over in his mind.

"Sir?"

Duncan looked down the corridor to see Fraser MacDonald standing at the end.

"Yes, Fraser. What is it?"

"I thought you'd want to know... there's a fire burning out at Duntulm. That wifey's place..."

"Lorna Somerwell's house?"

"Aye, Sandy Beaton's pal, so I'm told. It's proper raging too."

Duncan put his phone away, beckoning Fraser along the corridor to him. Fraser ambled towards him in his usual casual manner. Duncan opened the door to the interview room. Alistair looked up. "Fraser can take Dougie back to custody. You and I have somewhere we need to be."

"Oh aye, where's that then?" Alistair asked, getting up from his seat and nodding to Fraser as they passed one another in the doorway.

"Duntulm. Lorna's place is on fire."

"Ah... pish."

CHAPTER TWENTY-THREE

The drive out to Duntulm from Portree, under normal conditions, would take three quarters of an hour but with the snow and ice, they needed to take their time. Even with Alistair's pick-up on its winter tyres, the journey still took an hour and Duncan thought they'd made good time. A liveried patrol car was parked beside the approach road in front of the coastguard cottages. Ronnie MacDonald, recognising Alistair's vehicle, flagged them down as they approached. His all-weather high visibility coat was done up to the top, and pretty much all that could be seen of his face were the bridge of his nose and his eyes, peering out at them.

The intense orange glow had been visible from several miles away on their approach up the west side of the peninsula. Now they were but a stone's throw away from Lorna's house with two Fire Brigade appliances visible at the end of the track. Duncan lowered his window. Ronnie nodded, a gesture almost lost beneath his thick clothing.

"Hello, sir." Ronnie looked past Duncan and tilted his head towards Alistair alongside him. "The Staffin boys did what they could," he said, referring to the small crew based around the headland at Staffin on the east side of the Trotternish, "but the fire was so intense, there was no way they could contain it, let alone bring it under control until the Portree boys got here."

The Staffin crew were a quick response station, one of several located in the more remote reaches of the island, who were equipped to deal with situations, car crashes, emergency call-outs and indeed house fires, but the equipment and apparatus required to tackle major incidents were still based in Portree.

"Is it under control now?" Duncan asked.

"Aye, I reckon so," Ronnie said, "but probably best to speak with the station officer himself." Ronnie waved a hand towards the blaze.

"Seen anything untoward while you've been here, Ronnie?" Alistair asked, leaning over so he could be heard above the wind.

Ronnie shook his head. "I've not seen a soul beyond the fire crews."

Duncan nodded to Ronnie who stepped back as Duncan wound his window up. Alistair edged forward, parking the pick-up a short way away from the two appliances. Firemen were moving around the building. One pair were hosing down the outside, seemingly cooling the parts of the building that either hadn't caught yet or had been doused and they were ensuring there was no flare up. Others, fully equipped with breathing apparatus, were heading into the building. Two other firemen, their gear blackened with soot, appeared to have just returned from the inside.

Duncan knew they had strict timescales in which they could be inside before they needed to return and switch with another pairing. He imagined they were exploring the property in search of residents; otherwise they would control the blaze without risking lives by entering.

They both got out and exchanged a quick glance at one another. The house was in a right state. The exterior harling, painted white, was blackened by smoke escaping through windows and doors. The roof had collapsed in on the western end of the single-storey dwelling, flames still visible leaping from within. Duncan looked around and saw the station officer, identifiable by his white helmet, standing beside the larger of the two appliances.

The station officer noticed their arrival, offering them a brief glance as they approached. He held a large clipboard in his hands, on it Duncan could see several columns detailing names along with handwritten times and numbers. He was deep in concentration and cut Duncan off before he could identify himself.

"Whatever it is, you can wait until my team are through."

He didn't even make eye contact and Duncan knew better than to get in the way of the commander in such an emergency response. The station officer was in charge until the emergency was over, in this case, when the fire was out and the scene contained. Duncan looked at Alistair and shrugged. The two of them returned to the relative comfort of the pick-up until they were told otherwise.

It was another half hour before Duncan counted the fire crew who were outside. No one was inside the building and the flames had been put out. The crews were still dousing the building with water but only from the exterior now, ensuring both the safety of the crew and that the heat wouldn't allow the fire to flare up once again. The station officer ticked off the last pairing who'd returned from inside. An ambulance had arrived a few minutes previously, but the paramedic and the driver were still sitting in their cabin too. Clearly, no one had been recovered from the interior of the building. At least, not alive.

Duncan saw the station officer look their way, beckoning them over.

"About time," Alistair grumbled as they got out. Duncan was first across to meet the commander, showing him his warrant card and introducing himself.

"I know who you are," the station officer said, looking at Alistair. "I'd recognise this one even if I went blind."

Alistair smiled. "How are you doing, Ian?" He looked past him at the burnt-out shell of Lorna's house. He nodded towards it. "You do know you're supposed to put the fire out before it burns everything to the ground, aye?" Alistair's smile broadened into a grin, and he looked at Duncan. "Ian Nelson. Former blanket stacker turned fireman."

Duncan frowned, but Ian didn't seem to mind the jibe at having served in the Royal Logistics Corps. He merely laughed.

"Aye, and you made a career out of falling out of a plane on a length of rope. Somehow you got a medal for that."

Alistair nodded proudly, puffing out his chest. "Aye, several in fact."

"Long service medals, weren't they?" Ian asked, smiling.

Alistair's grin dissipated. "Long service... you cheeky sod."

Nelson turned to Duncan, removed his glove and offered him his hand. "Ian Nelson."

"Duncan McAdam."

"Oh, Big Duncan's lad?"

Duncan was confident he'd never met the man before, but it was possible he knew his father from years back. "Aye, he was my father."

Nelson nodded slowly, inclining his head. "Duncan was... a character."

That was the nicest thing most people would say about the

man. If they knew what happened behind closed doors, he was sure they'd have something else to say.

"How is your mother?" Nelson asked.

"Ah, she's been better, but thanks for asking."

"Aye, remember me to her, would you?"

Duncan nodded. He'd be very lucky if she'd be able to recall him though, unless he mentioned it in one of his mum's more lucid moments, but they were getting fewer and fewer these days. Mind you, the older the memory the more likely she was to recall it. Duncan looked at the house. The fire had gutted it almost in its entirety. Where the roof was still present, it looked somewhat precarious.

"That's a fair bit of damage," Duncan said.

"Aye, that'd be something of an understatement," Nelson said solemnly. "It looks like it started in the kitchen at the rear of the property and then spread throughout the building, gathering pace."

"How long had it been burning before you arrived?"

Nelson thought about it for a moment. "Obviously, the Staffin crew attended first. They got the call from operations just after six this morning and were on the scene within twenty-five minutes. By then the property was almost completely engulfed in flame. There was no way they could make entrance at that point. We arrived from Portree a half hour beyond that... established an entry point and began a search."

"Did you find anyone inside?"

Nelson frowned. "The intensity of the blaze was such that we couldn't progress through the entire building. The initial sweep turned up nothing, but..."

"You found someone later?" Duncan asked.

"Yes, I'm afraid so. Just the one. Once the fire was under control we were able to venture deeper. The search pairing found a body to the rear of the property but I'm afraid they'd long since passed away."

Duncan looked around, searching for signs of a body bag.

"I'm afraid we left the body in situ for your forensic team." Nelson looked towards the house. "It is charred beyond recognition. The poor soul was likely deceased well before the Staffin crew made it to the scene."

"She lived alone... and you're sure there's no other body present?"

Nelson shook his head. "If there was, we'd have found it. My boys have picked through every room in that building. We only found the one."

"Who made the 999 call?" Duncan asked.

Nelson shook his head. "I have no idea. You'll need to check with the call handler. There's no one here that we've seen since we arrived. It could have been a passing motorist or one of the residents in Duntulm, I suppose. The fire would have been visible for miles to the south-west."

"We'll check, thank you. Any idea how it started? You said it began in the kitchen, right?"

"I reckon so, aye. The most damage appears to be in the kitchen and to the rear of the property. The stone walls funnelled the fire through the property, aided by it leaping through the roof timbers and sarking." He shook his head. "My guess is the property runs off gas canisters... and there was probably a leak in the pipework. That will have led to an explosion, perhaps small but certainly enough to ignite the kitchen area."

"What could cause that? The leak, I mean?"

Nelson shrugged. "A faulty connection... perhaps the owner switched from one canister to the next without realising there was a leak. Hell, I've even seen people using rubber or plastic pipes to run as gas lines... and all you'll need is a rodent to sharpen their teeth on it."

"Really?" Duncan asked. "Who'd be that daft?"

Nelson shot him a wry smile. "You'd be surprised. When it comes to gas and electrics... I've lived in the highlands for a long time, and I've learned one thing if nothing else..."

"Which is?"

"That a lot of people just don't give a shite about the regulations."

Duncan was thoughtful. "Any suggestion of foul play?" Alistair offered him a quizzical look but said nothing. Nelson considered the question.

"I suppose we can't rule anything out until the brigade investigator has taken a look. Why? Do you think it might be?" He fixed Duncan with a stern look. "Come to think of it, what are you doing out here anyway? Something we should know about?"

Duncan shrugged. "The resident here... she's a friend of someone else who recently passed away. We need to make sure they're unrelated—"

"Oh, are you talking about that guy out on The Storr?"

Duncan didn't wish to fuel any rumours, and so he didn't answer the question. "But there's no indication from your part about how the fire got underway?"

Nelson appeared reticent. "Well, I think we need to reserve judgement until such time as all the facts are known. I'd advise staying out of the building until such time as it is declared safe."

A hint of a smile appeared on Alistair's lips. Duncan thanked Ian Nelson, who left them to return to his team.

"Something amusing you?" Duncan asked.

Alistair inclined his head towards the fire crew. "Arse protection."

"Say again?"

"He was cock-sure until you asked the question and then he backtracked; doesn't want to be wrong, so he hedged his bets."

"Aye, but who wouldn't under the same circumstances?"

Alistair nodded slowly, but Duncan had the sense that his DS wasn't the kind of man to be influenced by that sort of thing. If he had an opinion, he was more than willing to share it, whether the recipient wanted to hear it or not.

"What do you think then?" Alistair asked.

"About the fire starting?"

"Aye... damn shame for two friends to die within days of one another."

Duncan nodded. He indicated for them to make their way around the building. Smoke was still drifting up from where the flames were extinguished, threatening to reignite despite the steady snow that had started falling once again. Two hoses were at work spraying the building, methodically moving from one section to the next and damping down the area.

They kept their distance from the house, looking inside where they could. Many of the windows had popped, the plastic frames melting in the heat whereas others were blackened by the spread of smoke, making viewing the interior difficult. If the station officer was correct about where the seat of the blaze began, then there was little they could see once they were at the back of the property. The roof above the kitchen had collapsed into the interior and it was no longer recognisable as a kitchen, such was the ferocity of the blaze. Had there also been an explosion of the gas canisters, then there would be precious little evidence for the investigator to recover.

The properties that used gas in these parts did so for cooking with, and less so for heating. Obviously there was no mains gas piped to the island and heating was either by way of oil, biomass or in the case of more modern properties, air source heat pumps. However, if gas canisters were present then there would be two. When one ran out, the occupants could switch to the second and then refill or replace the first. It is conceivable that there could be an issue with the second canister. However, accidents like this were rare.

For such an unfortunate accident to occur to Sandy Beaton's friend within days of his death, was coincidental.

Duncan turned his attention to the nearby sheiling Lorna used as an art studio. It was detached from the main house and, thankfully, the wind would have carried the blaze away from it. Timber clad as the sheiling was, the flames would have gutted it too, had they leaped across to it. Duncan crossed to it and found the building unlocked. Having lived in Glasgow for years it still struck him as odd when he found people were so trusting, but in this community, everyone knew everyone and it didn't surprise him that Lorna hadn't bothered locking up.

Once inside, Duncan allowed Alistair to close the door. The sound of the wind virtually ceased as the latch dropped into place. The wind buffeted the wall of glass but the insulation on offer in the sheiling was impressive. It was probably more airtight than the croft cottage itself. He looked around, paying closer attention to Lorna's work.

"Are we looking for anything in particular, boss?" Alistair asked.

"No… just looking, Alistair. Just looking."

Duncan found the body of work to be quite impressive. Many of the canvases he'd seen stacked on his previous visit were actual works rather than blank. There were several racks where canvases were stacked against each other and Duncan carefully flicked through them, admiring the landscapes. He recognised many. In fact, multiple pictures were painted of the same locations but at different times of the year and in varying conditions. Lorna really had captured the very essence of the island. Dependent on the lighting, cloud cover and the time of day, one location could produce multiple moods.

"She must have loved this place?" he said quietly.

"Who?"

He looked over at Alistair who was leaning back whilst examining a particular piece of her work.

"Lorna. She must have loved painting the island."

"Aye, this place in particular," Alistair said. "She's done a lot here of the Western Isles... I reckon this is Harris, wouldn't you say?"

Duncan crossed to where Alistair was admiring a canvas. It was good. He pulled that one forward and behind it was another four-foot-wide canvas depicting the same scene, but as Duncan found with other works, the sky and the pitch of the waves had altered the landscape depiction entirely.

"Aye, that's Harris all right... looking north-west from here, I think."

"Up high... right on the coast. She cannae see Point from here."

"What's that?" Duncan asked, momentarily lost in admiration of the scene.

"Point... the Eye Peninsula there..." Alistair pointed to an outcropping in the painting. "It's connected to Lewis by an isthmus. You cannae see that from this vantage point. She'd have to go north of here."

"Aye, not much north of here though is there?"

Alistair smiled. "No... tough walk as well. I wonder if she just took photos and then painted from that or did she cart her gear up that way?"

"On foot?" Duncan asked. He blew out his cheeks. "She's a hardier sort than most if she did."

"Aye, maybe she got Sandy to photograph it?"

Duncan nodded. "Not a bad shout. Maybe he did."

Looking briefly at the next couple of paintings, Duncan sighed.

"What do you want to do?" Alistair asked.

"Head back to Portree, I guess. There's not a lot we can do here until the fire investigator pays us a visit. We'll need to keep Ronnie here until we can get forensics out here to remove the body, but I doubt we'll get anyone rooting through the ashes in this weather."

"Right. I'll make some calls," Alistair said.

"And then we'd better look into Lorna a bit deeper…"

"Just in case?" Alistair asked, his mobile against his ear.

He nodded. "Aye," he said quietly, "just in case."

CHAPTER TWENTY-FOUR

THE TEAM ASSEMBLED in the ops room for the briefing. Duncan glanced up at the clock and it was just after two o'clock. He cleared his throat and everyone took their seats. It had been quite a manic morning once they'd returned to Portree from Lorna's fire-ravaged house in Duntulm.

"Someone give me a rundown on Lorna Somerwell please," Duncan asked.

Angus raised his hand and Duncan gestured for him to continue. Angus flicked through his notepad, nodding to himself as he turned to face the others in the room.

"I've been looking into her background," Angus said. "I briefly did so the other day, once we knew she was pals with Sandy, so it made sense for me to revisit her." He read from his notes. "Lorna Somerwell, aged sixty-two. Unmarried, no children... has lived on Skye for over a decade now, in the same house in Duntulm."

"Does she own it?" Duncan asked.

Angus nodded. "Aye, she does."

"Family? She said they'd passed away, as I recall."

Angus checked his notes again. "Mother... and father...

yeah, both deceased. Lorna was raised by her maternal grand-mother until she also died... but by that time Lorna was of adult age."

Duncan nodded slowly. "Okay, not a lot in there. What about the sister?"

Angus shot him an inquisitive look that morphed into a nervous smile as he turned a page in his notebook before flicking through several more. He frowned.

"Sorry... I don't have anything about a sister." He looked at Duncan and then followed Duncan's glance towards Alistair. "Is there a sister?"

"That's what she told us," Alistair said, confirming Duncan's memory wasn't playing tricks on him. "She said her sister passed away, but didn't say what from."

"I'll... um... I'll have to check again," Angus said, his face reddening. "The parents died in a tenement fire in Glasgow. Lorna was seven at the time."

"Glasgow?" Duncan asked.

"Lorna said she was a... what was it again?" Alistair asked.

"A Lang Toun girl," Duncan said. "Which is what the locals call Laurencekirk but she said she was more from Kincardine, but it's in the same neck of the woods."

"Aye, that was it," Alistair agreed. "She never mentioned Glasgow to us. Is that where her grandmother lived then, Kincardine?"

Angus shook his head. "No, she stayed in Glasgow, had a house in Cambuslang. There's no connection to the east coast at all that I'm aware of."

Duncan and Alistair exchanged another glance and Alistair poked his tongue into his cheek. "Maybe there's a bit more to our Lorna than she let on."

"But why lie?" Duncan asked.

Alistair shrugged. "Some people lie just for the practice."

"If they have the need to hone their skills, aye." Turning back to Angus, Duncan asked, "What did the parents do?"

"Er… yes… the father worked in the public sector for Glasgow Council," Angus said, finding the relevant page in his notebook. "He worked on the bins as far as I can tell."

"So, nothing on the rigs then?" Duncan asked.

Angus' brow furrowed. "No, not on the rigs."

Alistair shook his head, smiling. "Do you think she told us the truth about anything?"

Duncan clamped a hand across his mouth and chin, thinking hard. "All right… what do we know about Lorna? Work history, tax affairs, travel… we need it all."

Angus scribbled in his pad, nodding as fast as he was writing. Duncan looked at Caitlyn.

"I had Lorna pegged as being from the Lothians before she claimed to be from further north. Do we have any connections between Sandy Beaton and that way?"

Caitlyn thought hard. "The only thing I can think of is the Edinburgh gallery."

"And where did we get to with that?"

Caitlyn wrinkled her nose. "I gave them a phone and the person I spoke to didn't know Sandy." She shrugged. "Had never heard of him or had any idea about them hosting an exhibition or the like. She did admit that she wasn't really the right person to speak to, but the manager was away on holiday and she wasn't sure when he's due back. Seemingly, it's not like a shop on Prince's Street or anything. It's a… what did she call it now… a *boutique* gallery. That was it. They host exhibitions… auctions and the like, but it is only open to a select clientele and they don't have a high street presence."

"Ah… the elites," Russell said, absently rummaging into a bag in his lap and producing sliced rounds of raw carrot which he put into his mouth, speaking as he chewed, "got to keep out the riff-raff, eh?"

"Aye," Caitlyn said, smiling, "something like that. How's it going with the healthy eating?"

"Miserable," Russell replied.

"Well, if they're not hosting or selling Sandy's work… what was he discussing with them over the phone?" Duncan asked no one in particular. "And somehow I don't see a bin man leaving a financial legacy large enough for his surviving daughter to live off into her sixties, let alone for the rest of her life. Something's not right here with either case. It doesn't add up."

Someone rapped their knuckles on the door frame at the far end of the room. It was Fraser.

"What is it, Fraser?" Duncan asked.

"Apparently Dougie Henderson wants a word."

"With me, specifically?" Duncan asked.

"Aye… that it be you and not…" Fraser glanced at Alistair. "Yes, you and no one else."

Alistair smiled. He knew.

"I'm a little busy just now, Fraser—"

"He is pretty insistent, sir," Fraser said. "And his solicitor has already been speaking to him, so I think it's on the level like, you know?"

Duncan checked his watch. "Okay, I'll be right down." Fraser nodded and left. Duncan turned to Alistair. "Get this breakdown of Lorna's life squared away. I need to know what she told us is true and what isn't. If she's hiding something, then we need to know about it."

Alistair nodded. "We'll figure it out, don't worry."

"Likewise, I want to know what the story is between Sandy Beaton and this gallery in Edinburgh. Maybe give the local police a call and see if they have anything to throw our way that might help." Alistair frowned. "I know, I know. It's a long shot but something has to start making sense sooner or later."

Duncan headed for the exit.

"Say hello to Dougie for me!" Alistair called.

Duncan didn't look back, but he guessed Alistair was quite enjoying Dougie being in custody. It was clear the two men disliked one another. How far back that mutual dislike went, along with what brought it about, Duncan was curious to know. One day, he might even ask the question. Making his way downstairs, his mobile rang and he saw it was Roslyn. He hadn't spoken with her since he'd had cross words with her husband, Ronnie. Although she'd dropped him a text and tried to call the previous night, he'd ignored them. He did so again now, rejecting the call and putting his phone back into his pocket.

Fraser was hovering around the custody sergeant's desk as Duncan entered the suite. He pointed towards the interview rooms. "Your man is in room three."

Duncan thanked him and walked along the corridor to the interview room, knocking on the door out of courtesy, but entering straightaway. Conversation between Dougie and his solicitor, a slightly built man in his fifties, ceased as they moved away from each other. Duncan walked up to the table and leaned on it.

"I'm a busy man, Dougie. Whatever it is you want to say to me, make it quick, aye?"

Dougie glanced nervously at the man beside him, offering Duncan an awkward smile. The solicitor inclined his head earnestly towards his client and Dougie almost scowled as he spoke.

"I... I wasn't completely honest with yous earlier."

Duncan sighed, arching his eyebrows. "Which part?" He could still smell the alcohol practically oozing from Dougie's pores and hanging in the air like the smell of an overripe piece of fruit.

"Er…" Dougie glanced at his solicitor, "when I said I went home… after leaving Sandy's."

"After you sat outside in the car, not speaking to him or confronting him. That part?"

"That bit… aye."

Duncan exhaled heavily and pulled out a chair. "Go on then, Dougie. I haven't got all day."

"Well… it is true that I didnae speak to Sandy, and I wanted to… to hurt him, you know? I said that and I wasnae lying."

"So?"

Dougie took a deep breath. "Okay… I was in my car… outside," he said, holding his hands up in front of him, "and I was thinking about what I should do." He looked skyward. "What… I might do, if I knocked on the door. And… er… I was drinking. I shouldna drink and drive, I get it, but… while I was sitting there—"

"Really, Dougie…" Duncan rolled his eyes. "I don't have all day."

"Okay, okay," Dougie said nodding furiously and waving his hands. "I look to the house and the door opens… and these blokes come out."

"Which blokes?"

He shook his head. "I don't know… just blokes. Men… not wee bams or anything. They were dressed properly, you know; shirts, shiny shoes and that."

Duncan sat forward. He glanced at Dougie's solicitor who maintained a stern poker face. "Right, and what happened next?"

Dougie shrugged. "They got into a car and left."

"Sandy with them?"

He shook his head. "No, I didna see Sandy… not till a few minutes later when he came out."

"Alone?"

"Oh, aye. Sandy was alone. he looked around when he left the house and I had to scooch down in my seat so he would nae see me."

"Did he seem all right?"

Dougie turned the corners of his mouth down and shrugged. "He seemed… like Sandy, I guess. Nervous… no, not nervous. He was agitated."

"Any idea why?"

"No. Maybe he'd been caught shagging someone else's wifey." His solicitor shot him a dark look and Dougie softened, turning back to Duncan. "Anyway… Sandy got in his car and drove away." Dougie appeared reticent but his solicitor urged him to continue. "Really?" Dougie asked him and the solicitor nodded.

"What is it, Dougie?"

"I… followed him, discreetly, at a distance."

Duncan was intrigued. "Where did he go?"

"He drove out to Duntulm," Dougie said. "You know, around the—"

"Aye, of course I know where Duntulm is, Dougie. Where did Sandy go?"

He shook his head. "I don't know."

Duncan inclined his head, but Dougie was insistent.

"I swear, I don't know. He turned off and I knew if I followed him… he'd see me. It was then that I made the decision to go home."

"Just like that?"

"Aye, just like that, I swear as God is my witness. I had all that time following him to think about what I was doing and when he turned off… out there, it was dark and almost no one lives around there at this time of the year. If I'd wanted to confront him, I could have done so there and then. No one woulda seen me!" He shook his head, then met Duncan's gaze. "No one. But I didn't. I went home, just like I said."

Duncan sat back, taking it all in. He glanced at the solicitor sitting beside his client. The man nodded his approval, signifying that was the end of Dougie's admission.

"And you didn't see where he went?" Duncan asked. Dougie shook his head. And did you see anyone else there at the same time? Another car, people... anything that stood out to you as unusual?"

"No. It was dead quiet."

"You're sure?"

"Aye, I'm sure. He turned off and I kept on the main road. I pulled in at a stopping place, you know the one where the road comes around by the sea? The tourists often stop there to catch the view. Anyway, I thought about it... and then carried on all the way round to Uig and then headed back to Borve." He sat forward, staring at Duncan, wide-eyed. "I swear that's all I did. I went home... and I slept it off. Whatever happened to Sandy that night... it had nothing to do with me."

Duncan took a deep breath. The solicitor looked him in the eye.

"I think you'll agree that my client has been cooperative."

Duncan angled his head and then nodded. "If it pans out, then yes, I'd agree."

"Then I would like to make a case for releasing him as soon as—"

"Aye, let's just hold on a minute," Duncan said, raising a hand. "I still have a search warrant to execute on Dougie's house."

"Which we are more than willing to comply with. When will this be taking place?"

Duncan had no answer to that. They were stretched thin at the moment with what was happening out at Duntulm. "We'll be underway as soon as possible," Duncan said. "However, I'd like everything that Dougie's just said to be repeated for a recording and I want a signed statement to confirm it."

"Then can I go home?" Dougie asked.

"Then, I'll think about letting you go home—"

"DI McAdam," the solicitor said. "Is it necessary for Mr Henderson to languish in a police station—"

"Aye," Duncan said, standing up. "It is." He pointed at Dougie. "Next time, tell the truth when I ask you and we can avoid all of this pantomime, yes?"

Dougie nodded, averting his eyes from Duncan's scrutiny.

"I'll have one of my detectives come down and take a statement."

Duncan left the interview room, closing the door behind him. His mobile beeped and he figured it was Roslyn again. He was wrong. It was another text message from Becky. He didn't read it. Whatever she was playing at, he had too much on his plate to consider it. Passing through the custody suite, Fraser called after him.

"The sarge wants to know if we can let Dougie go home now?"

"Not yet," Duncan said over his shoulder.

Back in the ops room, everyone was busy. Alistair, a phone tucked between the side of his head and his shoulder, saw him enter and beckoned him over.

"Aye... well, you'd better tell him that yourself," Alistair said, passing Duncan the phone.

"Who is it?"

"Pathologist," Alistair said.

"Craig," Duncan said, "I didn't expect to hear from you so soon."

"No, I shouldn't imagine you would, Duncan. I'm only just getting started with the package you've sent me, but this is rather significant and so I thought you'd want to know immediately."

"You have my attention."

"Well, this lady you've sent me, Lorna Somerwell?"

"Aye?"

"It's not Lorna Somerwell."

"Excuse me?"

"Well, I know it is sometimes difficult to tell in this day and age, society moving on and all, but I can assure you of one thing which is an absolute," Dr Dunbar said. "Lorna Somerwell is a woman... and the poor soul I have lying in my mortuary most certainly is not."

"It's a man?"

"Very astute, Duncan. In due course, we shall undoubtedly make a formidable detective out of you, I'm sure."

Duncan glanced at Alistair who arched his eyebrows. Dr Dunbar had already given him the news.

"Have we any idea who the body is?" Duncan asked.

"No, I'm afraid I left my crystal ball at home."

"Fair enough, Craig," Duncan said. "I was only asking."

"I'll get back to it, Duncan. As soon as I have any answers for you, then I'll be in touch."

"Thank you."

Duncan hung up and looked at Alistair.

"Looks like we have a missing person as well then?" Alistair asked.

Duncan nodded. "Round up some uniform and get them out to Duntulm. We need to make sure she's not still there lying in the snow and we missed her."

"I'll get on it. I'm not sure how many bodies we'll have for the search though. Things are stretched thin across the island just now."

"As many as we can pull together will have to do," Duncan said.

"I'll send Russell out with them to coordinate things." He nodded towards the forlorn-looking DC, working but keeping a watchful eye on Angus who was eating a packet of crisps at his desk while he worked. "It'll keep him away from the vending machines. I reckon he's about to crack."

Russell caught Alistair looking at him, smiling. Glumly, he popped another round of raw carrot into his mouth, frowning as he started chewing.

CHAPTER TWENTY-FIVE

DUNCAN STOOD from his elevated vantage point at the back of the smouldering ruins of what was Lorna Somerwell's home watching the small group of constables searching the snow-covered ground for any sign of her. His hands were thrust deep into his pockets and his collar turned up against the wind but for the moment at least, Mother Nature had seen fit to pause her punishing assault on the island. The Met Office forecast stated that this break in the weather would be short lived.

The storm that had battered the island since the weekend was the remnants of that which had wrought a devastating ice storm across Canada and the north-eastern United States less than ten days ago. Seemingly, Scotland was the last of her victims before fizzling out over Scandinavia. This offered the islanders scant comfort, however it was far from the worst storm to strike them and there would be more.

Alistair trudged through the snow towards him, Caitlyn a half step behind.

"No sign of her," Alistair said, drawing breath. His exhalations produced large clouds of vapour. They had begun their search near to the property and then spread the small party wider in extending circles away from the property. The snow fall had covered any potential tracks and it was likely that if there was a sign to be found, a dropped item of clothing or similar, then it was currently covered under a blanket of powder. The temperatures were already plummeting and were set to fall further throughout the remainder of the day, thereby freezing what fell in the previous twelve hours.

More snow was expected that night and in this event it might be days or perhaps a week or more before the ice beneath would melt. There was every possibility that Lorna herself may not be revealed until the thaw, if she'd escaped the blaze injured or without adequate clothing and not managed to find shelter that is. He was purely speculating though. At this point, they had no idea where Lorna was or what had befallen her or the deceased man found in her home.

Duncan looked to their left, beyond Lorna's house. The coastal road, the A855, was barely a couple of hundred metres from where they were. It wrapped around the headland close to the water before moving inland and south down the west side of the peninsula. She could have headed east across the Trotternish and then gone down the east coast road back to Portree. Turning, he looked north. There was nothing there aside from boggy hillside rising to the high point. A wonderful view could be had from up there but it was only reachable on foot and in these conditions, with no shelter, it was a death sentence.

"What car does Lorna drive?" he asked.

Caitlyn answered. "She doesn't have a vehicle registered to her."

Duncan looked at his DC. The pale skin of her complexion was whiter than normal, her blood vessels contracting as a result of the wind chill no doubt, apart from her nose which was glowing with a red and pink tinge.

"She must have a car," Duncan said. "No one can live all the way out here without some form of transport. I know the bus service is good, but you can't live here and rely purely on that."

Caitlyn shrugged. "I can only tell you what the database tells me."

"Shall we put a car or two on the bridge to Kyle?" Alistair asked, suggesting a presence on the one route off the island by vehicle, across the Skye Bridge to Lochalsh.

"And do what?" Duncan asked. "Stop every car, van and lorry crossing it? We don't even know what we're looking for." Alistair nodded, accepting the point. "Besides, if she was planning to drive off the island then she'd be long gone by now."

Alistair winced as a blast of cold air struck them. "So, what do you want us to do?"

"Go door to door," Duncan said, waving a hand in the direction of nearby Duntulm. "Maybe she's sheltering with neighbours or... someone has seen her since the fire. She can't have gone far. Can the mountain search team make a search of the headland to the north?"

Alistair shook his head. "I thought of that, so I primed Willie Mac. They're already preparing to go out on Sgùrr nan Gillean... a party of climbers were reported late after attempting the peak yesterday."

"Damn fools," Duncan said. "Can they not see what's going on on the island just now?"

Alistair cocked his head. "Aye, wiser on the hills eating grass."

Both Alistair and Caitlyn left him, calling instructions to the search team to gather. Duncan's mobile rang and he answered it, pressing it close to his ear and turning his back to the wind to reduce the noise.

"Duncan McAdam."

"Hello, Duncan, it's Craig. Can I presume you are out in the field someplace?"

"You can, Craig, aye. Can you speak up, because I cannae hear you very well."

The pathologist did as he was asked, raising his voice. "I thought you'd want to know about your man's cause of death. Often with these burns victims, it is difficult to tell unless they pass away through smoke inhalation that is. However, in this particular case, the cause of death is quite emphatic. Despite the body having suffered extreme damage to the exterior tissue, there was no indication of smoke damage to either the oesophagus or the lungs."

"He was dead before the fire took hold," Duncan said.

"Precisely. More than that, I have the cause of death."

"Which is?"

"The shotgun wound to the chest would have done it. A fairly heavy gauge judging from the shot recovered from within the chest cavity. The shot was likely taken at close range too."

"How close?"

"Less than six feet, I should imagine based on the spread. Your ballistic chaps will have a better view on that than I do, I'm sure. I took the liberty of weighing the shot recovered from the body. It is possible that some of it missed its target, but what I found lodged in the body weighed in just shy of twenty-seven grams or approximately one ounce in old money. This suggests somewhere in the mid range… perhaps a sixteen gauge cartridge but please don't quote me because it has been quite some time since I was last shooting. I'll parcel up what I have and send it across to your forensic chaps for analysis, but my brief take, for what it's worth, reveals a mixed-shot cartridge; lead, steel and probably tungsten or bismuth, I suspect."

"Moved on from pure lead, have they?"

"There are restrictions on the use of lead these days, Duncan. Lead is harmful, after all."

"Certainly is if you're shot with it." Duncan was disturbed by this news. "Is there anything else you can tell me, Craig?"

"Your victim was a young man, or young by my definition anyway. Circa early thirties… white… and in very good shape, aside from being shot to death and set on fire."

"You think he was set on fire?"

"Oh, I believe so, yes. The nature of the burns, the intensity of the blaze and the differentiation of the damage to bodily tissue at the front compared with that of the back… suggests the poor chap was doused with an accelerant, likely common old garden petrol or diesel, and then set alight."

Duncan closed his eyes, thinking. "Can we identify the body?"

"Now that… will not be easy. I have enough material to extract a DNA sample from the internal organs… and if that proves negative then we can always try to find a dental match. His teeth were in remarkably good condition and do show signs of work having been done in the recent past. He was a man to floss by all accounts. It'll take time, but I'm confident we will match him to someone, somewhere, eventually."

"Thanks, Craig. I appreciate you putting this together so quickly."

"You are welcome, Duncan. Can I take it that you've no likely candidates for who this fellow is?"

"Nope. None at all."

"Oh dear. Well… I can only do my part, Duncan."

"Thanks, Craig. We'll figure it out."

Putting his phone into his pocket, Duncan made the short walk across to Lorna's studio in the sheiling. Now aware that Lorna's home was a crime scene, he donned a pair of nitrile gloves before entering the building. The sheiling was the only part of the property undamaged by the fire. Duncan had seen enough burned buildings to know that almost all trace evidence in the house would have been consumed by the fire. The investigation team would likely determine both the cause of the blaze along with the location of where it began, but they would never be able to answer the question of who or why.

Pleased to be indoors, Duncan walked around the interior, scanning the studio for anything that stood out to him as unusual. Dougie's words came to mind, and he wondered what part Lorna had, if any, in Sandy's affairs, notably whatever it was Dougie was hinting at earlier.

The numerous paintings of the local landscape caught his eye once more, much as they had done the last time he was here. One rack featured the ruined Duntulm Castle with the bay beyond, painted in a mix of different light sources from clear days to stormy clouds or muted sunsets. Another rack had the depictions of the Western Isles across the Minch, Duncan noting the outcropping of the Eye Peninsula on Lewis which Alistair had identified. Maybe she didn't need a car. She had some of the most dramatic landscapes for inspiration right here on her doorstep.

He was still moving through the paintings, gently moving each one to see the one behind when his phone rang. He answered it without looking at the screen.

"DI McAdam," he said, his gaze lingering on one painting in particular. Lorna had truly captured the detail of the mountains of Harris. To his untrained eye, she was talented. He realised he'd answered but no one had said anything. "Hello?"

"Duncan... it's me."

He let go of the canvas, glancing around to check he was alone in the sheiling. "Becky? How are you?"

"I'm okay. Listen, I'm really sorry about last night—"

"Ah… forget about it."

"No, no… I am. I had no business just showing up at your door so late and… interrupting you."

Duncan's thoughts flashed briefly to Grace lying asleep in his bed, but he pushed them from his mind. He took a breath, gathering his thoughts.

"Are you okay? How is Eilidh?"

"She's stable… and she's doing well. The doctors think she'll make a full recovery but… losing her spleen will have implications."

"What does that mean?"

She snorted. "I don't really know. They say a lot and they talk a little too quickly for me to keep up."

"I'm sure you'll all have time to work through it."

"Yes, she'll be in hospital for a while yet."

"And Callum?"

Becky drew a sharp intake of breath, hesitating. "I… I need to speak to you about Callum."

"Sure, what can I do to help?" he asked. "You know I won't be able to influence his case—"

"No, no… I understand that," she said. "I just need to speak to you."

"Okay, no problem. I have a few minutes now—"

"No, not over the phone," she said, lowering her voice as if fearful of being overheard. "Can I see you?"

"Um… yes, of course. When?"

"When are you free?"

There was an urgency in her tone, he could sense it. He looked at his watch.

"I'm up on the north of the island… I'll be coming past you a bit later. Do you want me to stop in—"

"No!"

Taken aback by her emphatic answer, Duncan was reticent to suggest another time and waited for her to speak.

"Can we meet… perhaps at Kilt Rock?"

"Mealt Falls?" Duncan asked. "In this weather?"

"You can't come to the house just now, that's all."

"Aye, it does seem like I'm not in Davey's good books at the moment."

"Please, Duncan. I wouldn't ask if it wasn't important—"

"Yes, of course," he said. "No problem. We can meet there."

"Say… in an hour?"

"Sure. An hour."

"Thanks, Duncan. Bye."

The call ended before he could say anything and he was left with an odd feeling. Snapped from his reverie by a knock on the door frame, he glanced over to see a scenes of crime officer standing under the cover of the porch at the entrance to the sheiling.

"We're done over at the main house, sir. We were going to head across here and get underway."

Duncan nodded, slipping his phone into his pocket, still perturbed by Becky's call.

CHAPTER TWENTY-SIX

DUNCAN PASSED the right-hand turn into Elishader, a small crofting community located on the banks of the north shore of the freshwater Loch Mealt. A little way further along the coast road the main body of the loch itself was visible beside the road to Duncan's right but he took the next left into the car park and the tourist viewing platform.

The road doubled back in a loop and he found there was only one other car parked up. It was Becky's hire car. He pulled in alongside it but there was no sign of Becky. He got out and was immediately struck by the wind gusting from the west and threatening to knock him off his feet. He zipped up his coat and looked around. The coming snow had held off, which he was grateful for, but the overcast sky dampened any light and nightfall was coming early this day. The old snack van, usually serving tea and coffee to passing tourists was all locked up. There would be little passing trade today.

A solitary figure was leaning against the railings on the viewing platform. It was a large, solid concrete construction projecting out from the cliff face to enable views of both Kilt Rock and the flow of water down from Loch Mealt over the cliff and the fifty-metre drop to the sea below. Duncan went through the gate, careful to close it behind him and walked towards her, thrusting his hands deep into his pockets and elevating his shoulders to offer his neck as much protection from the elements as he could.

Although Becky was standing downwind, she didn't hear his approach. Wearing a long waterproof coat with her hood up, Becky Mcinnes stood facing out across the water, looking towards Rona. On a clear day you could see Gairloch from this vantage point as well as the west coast of the mainland. Today though, the storm clouds cloaked the Scottish coastline, shrouding it from prying eyes.

"Becky?" Duncan called as he approached, not wanting to startle her. She turned her head, the trace of a smile crossing her lips.

"Hello, Duncan. Thanks for coming."

That was an odd comment. He came alongside her, leaning on the metal railings and matching her gaze out over the water. Sleet was falling now, the first of the next wave clearly making landfall as forecast.

"What's going on, Becky?"

She turned to face him, her lips pursed. Those big blue eyes of hers stared onto his and whereas the previous night he'd seen a mixture of anger, frustration and more than a little disappointment in them, today he only saw anguish. He reached out to her and gripped her arm, concerned. She flinched at his touch, wincing at the same time. He released her, unaware of his grip being so strong.

"What is it, Bex? What's all this about."

She closed her eyes, and he could see her draw a large breath. Opening her eyes again, she looked upwards and exhaled, steadying herself.

"You remember this place," she said, casting an eye around them, "from back in the day?"

Duncan smiled. "Yes, of course. We'd all gather here... have the occasional beer and a few smokes." He also looked around. "It was all loose wire-fencing and overgrown grass though, as I recall. None of this viewing platform and whatnot."

She smiled too. "Simpler times, eh?"

"Much simpler. Adulting is hard, isn't it?" he said with a sideways grin. "No one said anything about that when we were weans, huh?"

"No," she said, shaking her head. "No, they didn't." She looked away again, staring out to sea but at nothing in particular. There was nothing out there, just a vast grey mass of cold air and even colder water.

"Becky?"

She looked at him, stone-faced. "You have to help Callum, Duncan."

He shook his head. "Bex, I've told you. If there was something I could do, then I'd happily help but I cannae interfere—"

"He's your son, Duncan."

He heard the words, but it must have been the wind because there's no way she'd just told him Callum was his son.

"Sorry... what?"

"Callum. He's your son."

It couldn't be true. Becky had a termination. He'd taken her to the clinic himself, and she'd gone through with it, too, because they'd been together for another six months afterwards. He missed a lot of things in relationships, but he wouldn't have missed that. He shook his head.

"No, that can't be possible..."

She shrugged. "Except that it is."

Her tone, her expression... both told him she meant what she was saying. He shook his head again, feeling a flutter of anger or was it anxiety welling in his chest.

"Duncan... I didn't leave you in Glasgow because I'd stopped loving you..." she took a step towards him, reaching out but he recoiled from her touch. "I... I left because I had to... because I was pregnant... and I didn't want..."

"You didn't want what?" he asked accusingly.

"I didn't want you to take it away from me... like you had the last one—"

"Now that's not fair," he said, pointing a finger at her. "That's not how it happened... at all! We talked about it."

"No, Duncan. You talked about it... about what it would mean for your life—"

"For us! What it would mean *for us* and *our lives*... that's what we talked about." He ran a hand through his hair, looking skyward. The sleet had ceased, and the snow was falling steadily again. He spun on her, grasping her arm and pulling her to him. She yelped only this time he didn't let go. "So... what, you just ran off... carrying my child and... and... you didn't say a bloody thing to me? You let me think I'd fucked up or something..."

"Duncan... you're hurting me," she said, tears welling and he realised how he was holding her and immediately let go, backing off, and raising his hands in apology.

"I–I'm sorry... I didn't mean to hurt you."

"No... no... you blokes never do, do you?" she whispered, barely audible above the wind.

"I'm sorry," he repeated, unsure of what else to say. He felt shame in that moment. Shame for hurting her now and shame for making her feel she couldn't speak her mind to him sixteen years ago. "And... please don't take this the wrong way but are you—"

"Yes, Duncan. I'm sure." She glared at him for doubting her and he felt his face redden.

"I'm…"

"Sorry?"

He nodded, averting his eyes from her gaze.

She sighed, shaking her head. "I don't blame you for being angry, Duncan. You have every right."

"Would you ever have told me… if I hadn't come back to the island, I mean?"

She snorted a laugh and he felt that familiar flutter in his chest.

"What… call you up out of the blue and say *hey, Duncan, long time no see. Oh, and by the way… here's your son?*"

He sighed. "Well, I wouldn't advise phrasing it quite like that… but…"

"I wanted to, Duncan. I really did." She rubbed her cheeks with her palms, as if she was trying to get warmth into them but he knew she was battling her emotions, trying not to cry. "When I got home… I so very nearly picked up the phone many times. I wanted to hear your voice. I wanted to be with you." She looked at him warmly. "I did phone once… but you weren't there, and I left a message. You remember?"

He remembered it well. It had been three months after he'd got back to their shared flat and found she'd packed her things and left without a word. A simple handwritten note left in an envelope on the small table they ate from every night in the kitchen.

"I didn't phone you back," he said, biting his bottom lip and lifting his eyes to meet hers.

"No, you didn't," she said quietly. "And I never called you again."

Duncan frowned, his thoughts a confused jumble of old

memories, questions and feelings he thought he'd discarded long since.

"Does… does Callum know?"

She shook her head. "No, no he doesn't. He thinks Davey is his father… and he is." Those words cut deep but Duncan didn't understand why. "He was there when Callum was born… and at his first parents' evening at the school… sports days. Davey is Callum's father."

Duncan did a brief bit of maths in his head. "If you were pregnant when you left for Skye… and Callum thinks Davey is his father, then you and he…"

"We were seeing each other, yes… at that time when I phoned you," she said, turning away from him and resting her hands on the metal railing, staring down at the frothing sea battering the cliff face below them. "Davey asked me to marry him that day."

Duncan moved to stand next to her but said nothing. This was his time to listen. Perhaps sixteen years too late, but he owed her that. If not much, much more.

"I knew I shouldn't marry him. I didn't love him," she said, stumbling over her words as emotion almost got the better of her. She shook her head. "I still loved you." She turned to face him. She was crying now, unable to stop herself. "And Davey knew it too."

"But you still married him?"

She nodded. "He was a good man, Davey Mcinnes. He loved me for who I was. He knew I would never feel the same way about him as I did about you, but he didn't care. I was fond of him… and that was enough… for both of us."

Duncan was silent for a time, listening to the howling wind and the sound of the waves crashing against the rocks beneath them.

"I always thought that you blamed me for forcing the issue

when you fell pregnant," Duncan said. She glanced at him. "You are right... I did push it."

"It was all such a long time ago," Becky said. "It doesn't matter anymore. Not really. It was another life."

"Only it's not, is it?"

"What?"

"It's this life... it's the here and now."

She nodded. "I'm sorry for dumping all this on you... now of all times. I know what you have going on with your family; with your mum." He looked away but she craned her neck to ensure he saw her. "I wanted to talk to you about it a few times, once I knew you were back on the island for good. It just," she exhaled heavily, "never seemed like a good time."

Duncan laughed. "I think we can agree on that."

She smiled then but it faded when Duncan asked his next question.

"Does Davey know?"

"Yes, of course. I would never have lied to him about that but... I didn't have to."

"How do you mean?"

She laughed. It was a genuine sound. "Davey's not daft, Dunc. He did well in his maths higher, remember?"

Duncan nodded. "Aye right. So, he always knew."

"Yes. Not that you'd know it. He always treated Callum like he was his own. There wasn't a better dad on the island."

Duncan felt a jealousy pang.

"At least... he was in the early days."

"What do you mean?"

"Ah... nothing. Forget it." She turned away from him, but Duncan persisted.

"What? He doesn't treat him right now?"

She was reticent to speak, reluctant to meet Duncan's eye.

"I shouldn't have said anything."

"But you did say something. I'm the polis, remember? We're trained to listen."

"Well, better late than never, huh, Duncan?"

Duncan closed his eyes. He probably deserved at least that. Although Becky was conciliatory.

"I'm sorry, Duncan. That was unfair."

He cocked his head. "You're probably entitled to be bit unfair around all of this. I've never been much of a catch when it comes to relationships, let's be honest."

Becky checked the time. "Damn! I have to make a move."

"What? Now?"

"Yes, Davey... he'll be back home soon, and I need to be there—"

"Why?"

"Why what?" she asked, making to go past him but he stepped across her.

"Why do you *need to be there* when he gets back?"

"Oh... leave it, Duncan."

She tried to walk by him again, but he reached out and grasped her arm, she flinched and yelped. This time, Duncan knew he hadn't taken all that strong a hold of her and her reaction was over the top. She looked down as he released her, but she didn't pull her arm away. Taking her hand gently in his, he moved the sleeve of her coat aside and saw her wrist. He took a deep breath and let go of her hand. She lowered it, clasping both hands together at her stomach.

"How long?"

She looked into his face, tears welling.

"Please, Becky. How long has Davey been doing this to you?"

She wiped her eyes, looking away. "It started soon after Eilidh was born. Up until then... he'd been the perfect father for Callum; attentive, loving. He was all that a woman would want from a father to her child. Maybe not the best of husbands, but he made an effort most of the time." She drew breath, inhaling in staggered gasps. "But all that started to change when he had a child… of his own."

Duncan held his tongue, although he could feel something brewing inside him.

"It was only harsh words to begin with," Becky said, staring into space. "I wasn't looking after the baby well enough or keeping the house tidy enough. My cooking was awful… Then he would attack me verbally… and then one day…"

"One day?" Duncan asked, trying to keep his tone measured.

"One day he hit me." She spoke so matter-of-factly that Duncan was caught by surprise. "He split my lip and – not that I knew it at the time – I suffered an orbital fracture of my left eye socket." She smiled but it was an expression of pain and anguish, not humour. "The pain was so intense… it lasted for days, but I had to stay inside the house to allow the bruising to go down before he would let me go out again."

"Did you get it checked?"

She nodded. "I did. I went to the hospital. Luckily I didn't need surgery… and it healed itself."

"How did you explain it?"

She smiled. Her eyes still had that faraway look, as if she was haunted by her memories.

"I told them I fell…" She looked straight at Duncan. "I know, lame, isn't it?"

"They'll hear it a lot."

"Yes, I learned after that what to say and what not to say… to avoid more questions. And Davey learned too." She looked up at Duncan. "He never hit my face again."

Duncan's heart sank.

"He focussed on my back from then on... the tops of the legs. The places that won't be seen." She laughed but it was a hollow, dry sound. "After all, you won't be wearing a bikini too often around these parts."

"Why didn't you leave?" he asked, immediately realising it was the most insensitive and ridiculous thing to say. If it was that easy, women the world over would never stay with their abusive partners.

"Where would I go?" she said to him plainly. "And besides... if I'm there, then he doesn't touch the children."

Duncan scowled, then forced himself to look away, taking two steps to the railings and curling his fingers around the balustrade, closing his eyes.

"I'll kill him."

"No, Duncan. You won't!" She hurried to his side and pulled him around, forcing him to face her. "You'll do nothing of the sort. This *isn't* your problem to solve. It's not about you—"

"No, it's about my son!" Duncan hissed. Becky recoiled from him, pulling her hands away from his body. He forced himself to soften his stance. "And it's about you."

She shook her head, tears falling. "And you lost me a long time ago, Duncan. I don't need a white knight to save me." She tilted her head. "Especially one dressed in rusty armour... It's too late for you to help me—"

"No, I—"

She held up her hand to stop him. "This isn't your fight, Duncan. Promise me you'll stay out of it."

He looked into her eyes, knowing his instinct was to do the exact opposite of what she was asking of him. He slowly nodded.

"But it's not too late for you to do right by Callum. Will you help him?"

Duncan had no idea what he could do, but he nodded. "Yes, of course. I'll do whatever I can."

She smiled through her tears, backing away as she clasped her hands together in prayer.

"Thank you," she mouthed before turning and walking briskly back towards the car park. Duncan wanted to go after her, sweep her into his arms and tell her that he'd take care of it. That he'd take care of all of it, her and the children. He didn't though. He stood there in silence, watching her leave.

Becky didn't look back. He heard her car's engine start and the headlights cast their beams across the viewing platform as she turned her car around and made off towards the exit.

Alone now, he turned to face the sea, grasping the balustrade again with both hands. He squeezed the smooth, freezing metal, tensing the muscles in his arms with every ounce of strength, rocking back and forth, and let out a guttural roar to the heavens.

CHAPTER TWENTY-SEVEN

DUNCAN ENTERED THE OPS ROOM. Caitlyn, Russell and Alistair were still up at Duntulm and only Angus was at his desk. He saw Duncan and rose to speak with him but Duncan waved him away, barely making eye contact, heading straight into his office in the adjoining room and closing the door. He sank into the chair behind his desk feeling the tension in his shoulders and the early signs of a headache.

There was a knock on the door and he wanted to ignore it. Obviously, he couldn't.

"Come."

Angus opened the door, peering around it to look at him. "Sorry, sir. Do you have a moment?"

Duncan nodded and beckoned him in. Angus smiled, entered, notebook in hand, and closed the door behind him before coming to stand before the desk.

"What is it, Angus?" he asked, massaging his left temple.

"You wanted us to check out the Edinburgh gallery; see if there was anything weird associated with it."

"Yes. Do you have something linking it to Sandy or Lorna?"

Angus frowned, standing awkwardly. "No... but also yes... maybe."

Duncan sighed. "Go on then, what have you got?"

Angus smiled, sitting down and opening up his notebook. "It goes back a bit, so please do bear with me." Duncan felt his head pulse, and he tried to remember if he'd left a box of paracetamol lying around somewhere. Angus was still talking. "Anyway, this gallery. It's owned by a guy called Tomlinson. Michael Tomlinson. Have you heard of him?"

Duncan shook his head. "Should I have?"

"No, I suppose not," Angus said. "If you worked in Edinburgh ten to twelve years ago then you probably would have done though. He was arrested as part of a large-scale fraud involving stolen and counterfeit artworks. The investigation was sparked by a tip from a London-based auction house who were selling something he'd previously sold to one of their clients."

"What was it?"

"Um... it was an Italian fresco... but I don't really know what that is though."

"It's a style of painting where they apply the paint directly to a wall; a plastered one, I think," Duncan said. "Presumably, the wall section was removed at some point, I suppose."

"Ah... right," Angus said, thoughtful for a moment. "Kinda... like a Banksy then?"

"Aye, I suppose so."

Duncan gestured for him to continue.

"Anyway, a joint investigation began—"

"Hang on... how much was this... this fresco valued at?"

Angus checked his notes. "The auction guide price was ten to fifteen thousand pounds."

"Not an insignificant sum."

"Aye, but that's why it was so interesting," Angus said.

"The global art market is worth around fifty billion pounds per year, and so, as we might expect there will be people who try to capitalise on that by shifting dodgy stuff. With art it's the provenance and the credibility of the seller which will determine the value of an item."

"Aye, stands to reason," Duncan said. "If the experts rubber stamp something as authentic, then you're more likely to get the best price for it."

"That's right which is why dealers and auction houses sell the higher-end items, but that's also why the higher-end items tend not to be the target of counterfeiters."

Duncan nodded. "Because it's much harder to get the fakes through the system undetected."

"Yeah, yeah, that's it exactly," Angus said. "It's not unheard of... I read earlier that it is conceivable that there are a number of artworks hanging in galleries and almost certainly held in private collections that are counterfeit."

Duncan sighed and checked his watch. Becky's face came to his mind and he forced himself to focus on Angus. "Is this going anywhere, anytime soon, Angus?"

"Like I said, bear with me. This investigation concluded that there was a criminal enterprise specialising in passing off fakes as genuine works of art, but they were operating below a certain price point so as—"

"Not to raise suspicion, aye."

"It was clever," Angus said. "Even though we're only talking about a decade or so ago, the systems in place to detect fakes were nowhere near as effective as they are presently. Now they have scanners to age the oil paints and the canvas... really high-tech stuff. Back then, apparently you could fake it much more easily. Especially if you were good with the old swagger too."

Duncan pinched the bridge of his nose. "And this relates to our case in what way?"

"The owner of our gallery in Edinburgh, Michael Tomlinson, was suspected of heading up a conspiracy to defraud auction houses and galleries by handling, if not commissioning, counterfeit artworks. I read about the case on a web search. The gallery, which had been highly regarded and in business for a hundred years until that point, closed but soon after changed hands and name... and evolved into this current incarnation of a boutique hybrid dealer cum auction house that it is now."

"And what happened to Tomlinson?"

"The case collapsed. The procurator fiscal had to halt all proceedings and on the first day of the trial, it was all shut down. It was all a bit messy from what I can gather. The team had been expecting the ringleaders to get fifteen to twenty years for what they'd been up to. It was a massive scandal when the case was dropped at the beginning of the trial."

Duncan frowned. "So, what happened?"

"It all got a bit vague at that point; sources said... all that type of thing in the reporting of the case. I tried contacting the lead detective in the case—"

"How did you get on?"

Angus looked glum. "Apparently, he's long since retired, but I spoke with someone familiar with the case. Seemingly the case made it to court because they had an internal conspirator who was willing to testify against the ringleaders. That person disappeared the night before the case opened, hence it falling apart."

"Disappeared?"

"Aye," Angus said, nodding. "Couldn't be found... despite an extensive search. The team thought they'd likely been dropped off Leith Dock or something, sporting a pair of concrete slippers." He shrugged. "Whatever happened; no witness… no case. Without that testimony they couldn't prove the conspiracy. They couldn't prove the gallery wasn't just as much a victim of the same crime as so many other dealers and auction houses."

Duncan was interested now. He sat forward in his chair and rested his hands on the desk. "Who was this insider?"

"Ah… that's where I've drawn a blank. The contact I spoke to knew the case but it was before their time. I could find out the details if you think it'd be useful?"

Duncan considered it. There was no reason to conclude that past case had any bearing on what they were doing now, but in the absence of anything else related to the business in Edinburgh, they may as well look into it.

"Aye, find out what you can. It can't hurt to check."

He picked up his mobile and called Alistair.

"Are you psychic or something?" Alistair said as soon as he answered.

"What's that?"

"I was just about to give you a phone. You won't believe what the boys and girls of SOCO have found in Lorna's studio. I don't want to spoil the surprise so I think you should see it for yourself."

Duncan looked at the time. "Is that really necessary?"

"I think you'll want to be here."

That was enough to sway him. "I'm on my way." Duncan hung up. He looked at Angus. "I'm heading back out to Duntulm."

"Okay… and what should I do?"

Duncan stood and pulled on his coat. "Do as I said. Find out everything you can about this Michael Tomlinson; where he lives, known associates… anything and everything."

"Aye, of course."

Duncan reached the door and glanced back. "As soon as you have anything of note, give me a phone."

Angus nodded and Duncan left; leaving Angus sitting alone in his office for a moment before he too got up and followed him out of the door.

THE DRIVE OUT to Duntulm gave him time to think. This was not necessarily a good thing. Passing the signpost to Maligar, knowing Becky was at home with Davey and knowing what he was willing and capable of doing to her made the bile rise in the back of his throat. Everything made so much sense to him now, but he was bothered by how he'd missed the signs. Davey's weird reaction to his children being in hospital, his lack of concern for their wellbeing and for that of his wife had been odd... more than odd, but somehow Duncan had missed those indicators which was justifiable for a civilian but for him? He was trained in spotting signs of domestic violence.

Back in Glasgow, where he'd cut his teeth, Duncan had been the man; the one person who saw the details that others missed. That was why he'd made detective inspector by such a young age. Was it the move home? Coming back to Skye, meeting the demons head on that he'd been running away from for the better part of fifteen years... had it skewed his antennae somehow or was it just another indication of his increasingly maligned moral compass? It wasn't like he'd been making good choices when he was last in Glasgow either.

He passed the Kilt Rock viewpoint, keeping his focus on the road ahead as if not looking at it would nullify the thoughts churning over in his mind. Lorna Somerwell was who he needed to focus on, and he silently, and forcefully, told himself that. His phone rang as he approached Staffin, the call coming through the speakers of the car.

"Sir, it's Angus."

"What have you got for me?"

"It appears that Michael Tomlinson is still on our radar or on our colleagues' radar on the east coast anyway. He's suspected of being deep inside a money-laundering ring. He was arrested last week and held for a couple of days over the weekend for questioning. Released on bail, mind you. His known associates have extensive criminal records and, when it comes to our case, although Tomlinson is no longer considered to be active in the art world, he is still a director of the Edinburgh gallery. The competition that Sandy Beaton won... you know, with that painting he did—"

"What about it?"

"They'd never run any such competition prior to the one Sandy successfully won. That strikes me as odd. Nothing from previous years, zero marketing around it. The only reference I found was in the print media after the winner was announced."

"That is odd," Duncan said. "It's almost as if..."

"As if what, sir?"

"As if it was fabricated."

"Why would anyone do that, sir?" Angus asked.

"Good question. I've no idea. Anything else?"

"Aye, just one thing. Probably nothing mind, but Michael Tomlinson has... or should I say, his business has a number of cars registered to it. One of which is a black BMW. I have the licence plate number."

"And that's significant why?"

"Oh, right, yeah... sorry. I'm looking at a photograph of the car just now... and it looks like Michael is driving it. It's from a mobile camera on the M90 just south of Bridge of Earn. It's a great shot of him at the wheel. I think it's him anyway. He still has the same haircut as he had back in the trial days I was telling you about. It's a lot more grey in it now though, quite distinctive. Very stylish… if you like that sort of thing, eh?"

"Speed camera?"

"Aye," Angus said and chuckled. "I reckon I'm seeing it before he is. It was only taken yesterday."

"Can you ping all the details across to my phone, Angus."

"Aye, will do."

CHAPTER TWENTY-EIGHT

ALISTAIR MUST HAVE BEEN KEEPING an eye out for Duncan because as he approached Lorna's house, the detective sergeant appeared in the doorway of the studio. It was snowing again now and it seemed to be falling heavier and faster than it had been over the course of the previous few days.

Getting out of his car, Alistair beckoned him over to the studio and Duncan didn't need a second invitation. He hurried through the snow, turning his collar up and hunching his shoulders as he felt flakes of snow slip down his neck, causing him to shiver. Once inside the studio, he closed the door, pleased to be inside.

"This had better be good, Alistair."

DS MacEachran laughed, turning and striding towards the rear. He followed him. On one side of the studio was a small toilet and utility room for cleaning up by the look of it. At the rear, open plan to the studio, was a two-metre length of worktop offering kitchenette facilities. Here there was the only other window in the sheiling-inspired building; a rectangular window laid horizontally, two metres wide and barely half a metre tall. This overlooked the approach to the main property whereas the glass curtain wall opposite faced Tulm Bay.

Duncan watched Alistair approach the cabinetry, presenting it to him much as a magician's assistant would with a giant box she was about to climb into. Duncan looked at the set up. The inset sink with tea and coffee-making facilities to the right-hand side. There was a slimline dishwasher built in underneath alongside cabinet doors and one unit with four drawers set into it. He was at loss to see what he was supposed to notice.

"I appreciate you making this theatrical, Alistair, but—"

Alistair held up a hand to silence him. "What do you see?"

Duncan shrugged. "Kitchen cabinets. What do you see?"

"I see," Alistair said walking along the length of units and stopping at the last. He pointed at a section of filler to the right of the final cabinet. That wasn't unusual. Seldom did the available space match perfectly with the cabinetry. Duncan shrugged. Alistair smiled and rapped his knuckles on the filler piece and Duncan was surprised to see it move. Alistair's smile broadened as he carefully grasped the edge of the filler piece with the neighbouring cabinet door open. Reaching for the bottom where it overhangs the kick board, he lifted it and the piece popped off into his hand and he took it away. There were two catches fitted to the rear of the piece. It pushed into them and could be easily removed rather than being firmly fixed in place as filler sections usually were. Alistair nodded towards the gap. "Ingenious, really. We found it by accident."

Duncan arched his eyebrows. "Presumably there was something in there?"

"You presume correctly," Alistair said, smiling. He nodded to Caitlyn and she produced two black briefcases, lifting them up and setting them down on the counter side by side. The gap was barely wide enough to fit them both in and they would have needed to be stacked on top of one another. It was almost as if the space had been made to measure. Duncan looked around. Considering how the studio was an architectural design statement, a black-clad exterior with birch-faced interior floors and walls, it was quite conceivable that what he'd thought was unfortunate was in fact deliberate.

"Have you opened them?" he asked.

Alistair nodded. "Photographed in situ and then we had them out."

Judging from the expression on his face, Alistair must have reached the same conclusion as he had. This little glory hole was by design. Having donned a pair of gloves, Alistair opened the first briefcase. The locks hadn't been forced so Duncan figured they couldn't have been locked. Maybe there was no point seeing as no one was likely to discover them.

The case was packed full of used bank notes, wrapped in neat bundles side by side. Duncan looked closer. The bundles were not only in pounds but also US dollars and euros. Each bundle was in large denominations. He glanced sideways at Alistair.

"How much do you reckon?"

Alistair shrugged. "More disposable income than I'll ever see in this job. Thousands… tens of thousands, maybe, if you consider both cases."

He opened the second briefcase, and it was also full. Inside the pouch of this one, Duncan spied another bundle but this time it wasn't money but passports. Laying them out on the counter, Duncan counted seven of various colours and registered several countries. The first he picked up was from the Dominican Republic and opening it to the identification page he saw Lorna Somerwell's picture, but the name was different.

"They are all hers," Alistair said before Duncan could

check. "She's either a full-on schizophrenic with a multiple personality disorder or… she's a wrong-un."

Duncan cocked his head. "Since when do schizophrenics have multiple nationalities to go alongside the personalities?"

"Aye, fair point." Alistair frowned. "Why didn't she take all of this with her if she's running?"

Duncan met his eye. "Maybe she couldn't. Who the hell is she?"

His mobile rang and he saw Angus' name flash up on the screen.

"Angus?"

"Hello, sir. I managed to get hold of a detective who was on the original investigation into Michael Tomlinson's fraud investigation. Decent bloke. I've just come off the phone with him and he's sent us some details through."

"Good. What did you find out?"

"The case collapsed because they lost their main witness the night before the trial was due to begin. The witness was the forger. A woman named… Amelie Bilodeau."

"A poetic name," Duncan said, nodding to Alistair and setting his mobile down. "I've put you on speaker, Angus."

"Oh, okay. Hi everyone."

Alistair and Caitlyn said hello.

"What do you know about her?" Duncan asked.

"A French father, Thomas Bilodeau, was a second-generation immigrant to Scotland but held dual citizenship with his native country… as did his daughters. He married a local lassie, Hilary McArdle. They had two children, the daughters I mentioned there, and one of them passed away in a climbing accident in her early thirties."

Duncan exchanged a glance with Alistair.

"And what happened to Amelie's parents?"

"Um… the father died in the late nineties… of natural

causes and the mother more recently, three years ago. She'd been living near the family hometown of Bonnyrigg."

"Midlothian," Duncan whispered quietly.

"Aye. You know it?" Angus asked.

"I know the bloody accent," Duncan said, internally chastising himself. "The investigation team thought Amelie had been murdered?"

"Aye, that's the assumption. They never found any evidence of what happened to her or what became of her if she left of her own accord. The case is still considered active but there's been no progression on it recently."

"Amelie... what if she wasn't murdered prior to the trial as the investigating officers assumed?" Duncan closed his eyes. "I can't believe I missed it."

"Missed what?" Alistair asked, offering him an inquisitive glance.

"Do you remember she told us she had a sister?"

Alistair nodded. "Lorna? Aye, she did."

"Well, she also told us she was an only child... orphaned and supposedly raised by her maternal grandmother."

"You're bloody right too," Alistair said.

"She must have stolen the identity of Lorna Somerwell..." Duncan nodded towards the passports. "And who knows how many others."

"What's that?" a confused sounding Angus asked.

Duncan shook his head. "I cannot believe she managed to throw us off so easily."

"At the time, we weren't looking at her though," Alistair countered.

"Even so, I should have stuck with my instincts."

"Sir, I haven't given you the best bit yet," Angus said excitedly. "I've got photos from the case file of Amelie Bilodeau and she is—"

"Lorna Somerwell," Duncan said. "Aye, we know."

"How did…"

"We're always a step ahead, young man," Alistair said, smiling.

"Never mind, Angus," Duncan told him. "Good work and thanks for the update."

Duncan hung up. He was thoughtful for a moment, then cast an eye around the studio in search of anything he may have missed on his previous visits. "We've still no sign of her?"

Alistair shook his head. "Do you think she's taken off?"

Duncan looked at the briefcases. "I doubt it. Not without all of this."

"Then where is she?" Alistair asked. "And if she is running… who from and why?"

"That gallery in Edinburgh, the one Sandy had that competition win through? The owner was facing some serious prison time for fraud. A big counterfeit art scam. It would appear Lorna, or Amelie… or whoever she is, was the one who'd see him go down for a long stretch. Fifteen to twenty years."

"That's fifteen to twenty reasons to want her gone," Alistair said. "Are we too late do you think?"

Duncan frowned. "Let's hope not."

"So, where do we start looking?" Alistair asked.

Duncan had no idea. His eye was drawn to the multitude of paintings of similar landscapes; the ruined castle of Duntulm and the bay beyond. To the right he saw the painting of the Minch and across to the Western Isles.

"Where would you go… if you had to go somewhere in a hurry?" Duncan asked.

"Somewhere I knew well," Alistair said.

"Somewhere safe," Caitlyn added.

Duncan thought hard. "As far as we know, Lorna doesn't

have a car. Although, we can't be sure seeing as we've no clue as to who or what she's really like."

"How far could she realistically get on foot?" Alistair asked, looking out through the glazed wall at the heavily falling snow. "Particularly in that."

Duncan looked at the paintings again and reached for his mobile. Alistair exchanged a look with Caitlyn but neither of them spoke. The call was answered, and Duncan spoke. "I'm up the way, at Duntulm. Any chance you can meet me there?" He looked at Alistair and smiled. "Aye, I can see the weather, but I need your help." Duncan smiled. "Good man. Just past the old coastguard cottages, okay?"

CHAPTER TWENTY-NINE

ARCHIE MACKINNON STOOD beside Duncan in the studio, fresh snow visible in his beard, collected from his walk between his Defender and the studio. He was concentrating as he stared at the paintings. Alistair and Caitlyn were in the background, looking on. Alistair sported a doubtful expression, but Duncan ignored his scepticism.

"Any idea?"

Archie frowned. "Well, there's only one place I can think of that anyone could stay at long enough to take in that scene."

"Where is that?" Duncan asked.

"Rubha Hunish," Archie said. "On a clear day, from there, you can see most of the Outer Isles of Lewis, Harris and Uist. It's a bit of a hike out that way but the views are stunning." Archie looked at Duncan, his eyes narrowing. "And there's the old coastguard lookout there too, just in case you need a wee bit of shelter."

"Of course. That's used as a bothy now, isn't it?"

"Aye, well maintained too. You could sleep out there if you got stuck."

Duncan looked at Alistair and he nodded, taking his

mobile phone from his pocket and stepping away to make a call. Archie shot Duncan an awkward glance and it piqued his curiosity.

"What is it, Arch?"

He shrugged and shook his head. "Nothing."

"It doesn't look like nothing."

Archie looked at Caitlyn and in turn, she looked at Duncan who tilted his head ever so slightly and Caitlyn took the hint, moving away from them to give them some privacy.

"Now," Duncan said, "what is it?"

Archie lowered his voice, evidently keen not to be overheard. "What's all this about?"

Duncan smiled. "What does it matter to you?"

"Oh... it doesn't... but..."

"But?"

"Humour me, okay?"

"A missing person," Duncan said, keen to keep the details private. "We're trying to find her."

"Oh, right. Is that all it is?" Archie smacked his lips, nodding and avoiding Duncan's gaze.

"Archie. What aren't you telling me?"

Alistair returned from where he'd made his call, staring out over the bay. What could be seen of it anyway. He looked glum.

"What is it?" Duncan asked.

"It's a no go. Willie and his team are still searching for that climbing party. Who knows when they'll be back down off the mountain."

"Maciver?" Archie asked. Alistair nodded and Archie smiled. "The amount of equipment those boys and girls cart up and down mountains... it's a wonder they can carry anyone off it as well."

"I suppose you'd go up in sandals?" Alistair asked with a wry grin.

"I might do, aye."

Alistair turned to Duncan. "We could wait until the resources, Willie and his team are free, or wait out the storm and head up there as soon as we can. They are our options."

"You want to go up to the lookout?" Archie asked.

"Aye," Duncan said. "Why?"

Archie shook his head but was less than convincing. Duncan took him by the arm and guided him away from the others.

"Archie, what aren't you telling me?"

Archie frowned. "Well... you know I said I had that little earner coming up?"

"The rich guys coming onto the island?"

"Aye, that's it. Well... I had a plan of all the hot spots to show them... around the island, you know? The timings were all a bit vague... and then I got a call..."

He looked away, reticent.

"You got a call... and what?" Duncan asked.

"They were already on the island and... er... as coincidence would have it... were asking about..." He lifted his gaze to meet Duncan's curious expression. "About... about Rubha Hunish." He wrinkled his nose and immediately looked away.

"What about it?"

"Well, they didn't ask about it specifically, but they were really keen to head out that way... which makes them proper numpties if you ask me." He leaned into Duncan. "Which is exactly what I said to them, by the way."

"How many of them were in the party?"

Archie thought hard, his brow furrowing. "Two... that I actually met... and I think there was another bloke in the car."

"Where did you meet them?"

Archie smiled nervously. "That was weird right enough. They were waiting for me at the museum."

"Of island life?" Duncan asked and Archie nodded. "When was this?"

"Last night," Archie said. He laughed nervously. "Small world, eh? Full of coincidences."

Duncan took a deep breath while giving Archie a look of consternation. "Did you take them out there?"

"Nah, did I feck! In this weather? Death on a stick," he said, eyes wide. "Especially for city folk like them."

"Where were they from?"

"Ah... how should I ken? Like I said, city folk. Proper crabbit that I wouldn't take them up there though."

"They were?"

"Aye, the big man was in the car and by the look on his face he was greetin when they told him I wasnae gonna take them up."

Duncan beckoned Alistair over to them. "This is important, Archie. What car were they in?"

"Oh, it was a big dark thing. German... a saloon. Right flash, too."

"And how did you leave it with them?"

He chuckled. "They were adamant they still wanted to go, but I told them they'd be asking fer trouble to head up there. I think they were funny in the head, to be honest with you. One of them had an OS map... and I roughly pointed out the route up. I mean... the path is well maintained. At least one of them is—"

"In this weather?" Alistair asked.

Archie cocked his head. "None of my business if some daft city blokes want to die on a mountain." he shrugged. "I told them. I swear I did."

Duncan met Alistair's gaze. "She took off in that direction…"

"And they torched the house to do what… hide the evidence of the murder?" Alistair asked.

"Whoa there… what murder?" Archie asked. Both men ignored the question.

"To conceal the death of whoever was shot in the house," Duncan theorised, "and maybe to give them cover with which to track her down?"

Alistair nodded. "We should look for the car. There can't be many places around here they would leave it."

Duncan turned to Archie. "Where exactly did you tell them to start their climb?"

"Shulista," Archie said. "It's the best route up, about two and a half kilometres from there."

Duncan took Alistair aside, lowering his voice. "If we assume these are the people looking for Lorna – or Amelie, whoever – then we have to assume they came to the house looking for her."

"You think she'd head out to the lookout at Rubha Hunish?"

Duncan arched his eyebrows. "She knows the lay of the land. She's lived here for over a decade."

"Aye, that's true enough…" Alistair turned his head to look out at the falling snow. "Could she have made it out there in this?"

"Remember those pictures she had of her in her youth?"

"The Alps," Alistair said.

"And her sister died climbing," Duncan said. "She's no stranger to these conditions. In fact, she could be more experienced in winter climbing than anyone else on the island. She could make it."

Alistair was thoughtful. "And who but the locals would know about the bothy?"

"That might be what she's counting on."

They both looked at Archie who, despite trying to look as if he wasn't, clearly had been listening in on their conversation. He spread his hands wide apologetically. "How was I to ken, huh?"

Alistair scowled at him, but it wasn't Archie's fault.

"The thing is," Alistair said, "we have a body in the morgue who... died of a shotgun wound."

"I know," Duncan said. "And I don't fancy going up there either."

"This was last night though," Alistair argued. "Surely... they'd have been and gone by now. We're probably too late as it is."

Duncan considered the point. "All right. Here's what we'll do. If the car is still parked in Shulista, we'll call in an armed response unit—"

"Which will be here immediately... tomorrow morning," Alistair said with his tongue firmly in his cheek.

"Then we go with what we have here, but we go as cautiously as possible."

Alistair was unhappy but he nodded. Archie stepped forward.

"And I'll take you there," he said.

"Archie... I can't—"

"And you're not," Archie said. "I'm putting myself there... of my own free will. If I've played a part in putting some wifey in danger, then I should help to put it right."

"It could be dangerous, Archie."

"Pah! No one knows this island—"

"Better than you do, aye," Duncan said. Alistair caught his eye. He didn't think it was a good idea but Archie was right. If anyone could lead them up there and back down again safely, then it was him. "Okay, Archie. If we go, you can lead the way."

Archie grinned. Alistair clapped him on the shoulder. "And if the shooting starts, big man, you can just stand in front of me, okay?"

Archie nodded and as the words sank in, his smile faded. "Did you just say—"

"You can ride with me, big man," Alistair said, holding the door open, the snow blowing in on the wind. Archie frowned as he passed Alistair who winked at him, his smile broadening once Archie couldn't see it.

THE TURN-OFF for Shulista was only a couple of minutes' drive away from Duntulm. Archie indicated they should take the left beside the old red phone box before they reached Kilmaluag; the phone box, a solitary piece of colour in what was now an all-white landscape. The road climbed up at a steady incline, bearing first right and then into a sweeping left bend before they came across a small car park before crossing a cattle grid. The road stretched away from them towards the north, disappearing over a crest a hundred metres away.

Duncan was disappointed to see a black BMW parked in the car park. They pulled up short of the parking area to survey the vehicle. The single patrol car accompanying them with Ronnie MacDonald and Russell Mclean inside, stopped behind them. As far as Duncan could tell, there was no one inside the BMW. A two-inch thick layer of snow lay on top of it, shrouding the interior from prying eyes. There were no impressions in the snow around the car, either made by wheel or foot, although they could have been covered by more recent snowfall. The car had clearly been there for some time.

Alistair looked across at Duncan in the passenger seat. He nodded and they got out.

"You stay here," Duncan said to Archie who had no objection to the instruction. Caitlyn got out too, Ronnie and Russell also got out of their car. Ronnie held a torch and the small group fanned out as they walked over to the vehicle. Despite the storm swirling overhead, the snow appeared to have ceased falling for a while. Duncan had checked the Met Office site prior to leaving the studio and they were forecast a brief break in the weather. What was driving at them presently was freshly laid powder drifting towards them on the strong wind. The fresh snow reflected any and all available light and where usually at this time of the evening they'd be in darkness, they could at least determine the lie of the land.

The route out to Rubha Hunish was a steady climb but to the rear and to either side of them was boggy moorland, a harsh and unforgiving landscape to traverse in normal conditions and only the foolish would attempt it in this weather.

The car was empty, the doors locked. Peering into the interior with the aid of the beam from Ronnie's torch, Duncan thought he could see a red smear on the edge of the leather upholstery on the rear seat. He pointed it out to Alistair.

"Any word on the armed response unit?"

Alistair arched his eyebrows. "Still waiting on an ETA. I wouldn't hold your breath."

"As I thought." Duncan beckoned to Archie and his friend got out, his boots crunching in the snow as he ambled towards them pulling a woollen beanie down over his head and flapping his arms as he walked, presumably to get some warmth into his upper body. "All right, Archie. You're up."

Caitlyn swept an armful of snow off the bonnet of the

BMW so that Alistair could lay out a map of the area. The two of them had to pin the edges down with two hands to stop the wind from hurling it across the moor. Archie leaned over, finding their location and under the light of Ronnie's torch, he traced their route with his gloved forefinger.

"We take this path," Archie said, "heading north, north-west keeping pretty much to the top of the low escarpment. The path is well maintained here, although it'll be quite tricky to navigate in this weather. We'll be exposed." He looked around the group, Duncan figured he was assessing their respective clothing as well as their abilities. His gaze settled on Duncan. "Are you sure you want to do this?"

Duncan didn't feel like he had much of a choice. "How long will it take us to reach the bothy?"

Archie pondered it for a moment. "In these conditions... I could do it in less than an hour but with all of you in tow, it might be a bit longer. The route is easy going for much of it and we will only ascend about three hundred and fifty metres or so, but we will be crossing some streams and boggy land. With a bit of luck much of that is frozen just now."

"That doesn't sound too bad," Duncan said hopefully.

"Aye but take care when we're crossing the cliffs. With the ice and snow, we could slip and... the wind is such that any of us could be blown off them in the blink of an eye."

Alistair nodded enthusiastically. "Piece of cake, aye?"

Archie laughed. "Well, if it makes anyone feel any better, the fall will likely kill you before your brain has worked out what just happened."

"No, that doesn't make me feel any better at all," Alistair said with a dry laugh.

Archie grinned. "Just take a hold of me as you go and the big man can break yer fall fer yer. How about that?"

Alistair cocked his head. "Sounds good to me. I'd appreciate your sacrifice."

"Right, everyone, check your kit," Duncan said. "As a minimum, we need to make the bothy and we can always shelter there until the morning if needs be."

"Aye," Ronnie said, "and what if we come up against someone who does nae want to share the aforementioned bothy?"

Duncan smiled. "We'll cross that bridge if and when we come to it." He looked around the group, reading their expressions. Everyone was nervous, although few would voice it. "Listen, I know it's a big ask. We don't know what we are walking into. Support is coming our way, but the longer we wait, the more danger I think Lorna will be in. These guys haven't come back, so it stands to reason they're still out there. Aye, it stands to reason they'll be waiting out the storm in the bothy. It's what I'd do, but we do have something on our side in all of this."

"Which is?" Alistair asked.

"They have no idea we're coming."

"Is that all?" Archie asked.

"What were you hoping for?"

Archie shrugged. "What do the Americans call it... a SWAT team or something."

A ripple of laughter passed through the group, lightening the mood. Duncan shook his head. "Sorry, Archie, but this is Skye. You'll have to make do with us."

"Aye, that's what I was afraid of," Archie mumbled, eliciting more laughter.

"Come on, let's get going," Duncan said. Alistair folded up the map, tucking it into an exterior pocket of his coat and zipping it up.

"What a way to earn a living," Alistair said, winking at Duncan.

CHAPTER THIRTY

THE PATH LED them across the heather moorland. Beneath the layer of snow was largely mud and scraggy stones interspersed with large flags to set the route apart from the wild moorland. However, in this weather the stones were invisible leaving them to rely heavily on Archie's knowledge. If the team were concerned, they didn't show it and Duncan had absolute faith in the man he'd been friends with since childhood.

Occasionally they passed large posts, set into the ground periodically to assist walkers in keeping to the trail. These too were difficult to spot, painted white and thereby blending in with the snowy landscape. The path wasn't clear and as Archie led them up a grassy embankment, the full force of the wind battered them, howling as it raced through the valley ahead. It was at this point Duncan had his first serious doubts about his decision to bring them out here. He kept those thoughts to himself and pressed on, feeling the strain in his legs as they ascended into the wind.

Conversation was kept to a minimum, partly to keep their approach as quiet as possible, although their voices would be carried by the wind far away from their destination, but predominantly because they would only be able to hear the person directly in front of them, and any reply would never be heard. The going was tough, and everyone had their heads down, trying to match Archie's pace which was far from sedate.

Duncan passed Caitlyn, seeing the group beginning to stretch out, and came alongside Archie indicating for him to ease off. He nodded, stopping for a moment to allow everyone to catch their breath and for the stragglers to join them.

"How much further is it?" Duncan asked. Archie looked around, then pointed towards some stone ruins below the escarpment to their left.

"That's Erisco down there," he said. "The old township the crofters built for the displaced during the clearances. The path will drop down from here, take us out of the wind a little. It'll get grassy underfoot and we'll need to cross a river before we start climbing again."

"How big is the river?" Duncan asked, hearing the nervousness in his own voice.

Archie smiled. "It's nae too big. Easily passable most of the time."

"Under normal circumstances," Alistair said.

"Aye," Archie replied, "but it'll still be okay just noo. We only need to worry when it's been hammering it down for days and the flood water flows off the hills. Trust me, it'll be fine."

Alistair flicked his eyes towards Duncan but didn't comment.

"Ready to make a move?" Duncan asked and everyone nodded. Archie set off again, taking the lead with Duncan a couple of steps behind him.

The path did as Archie said it would, dropping down and

into a u-shaped valley. The wind was funnelling through the valley between two hills, Meall Tuath and Meall Deas to their right and left respectively, negating any perceived benefit from walking at a lower level as they walked directly into a fierce headwind. The recent snowfall was picked up on this wind and gusting straight at them. The group hunkered down as best they could while still pressing forward.

Soon they came to a gate and once beyond it they could all see that the path separated, heading off in multiple directions. Perhaps without the snow cover it would be easy to see which route to take, but here, even Archie paused to think. Duncan came alongside him, shouting to be heard above the wind. The snow was also falling now, and coupled with the drifting was making it difficult to see where they were heading as all nearby markers were lost to them.

"Which way, Archie?" he said, momentarily unnerved by his friend's hesitation. "We can't be caught out here… we have to get to the bothy."

"Aye," Archie said, looking past Duncan and signalling for them to take a route that steadily inclined up the hillside. "That way."

He moved off and Duncan grasped his forearm, stopping him. "You're sure?"

"I'm sure."

He shrugged off Duncan's hand and set off. The others followed. They arrived at the clifftop and another gate, Archie looking far more confident now, holding it open for them and gesturing for them to turn right once they were through it. Duncan waited for him as Archie closed the gate after Russell, the last of their party, passed him. Archie was squinting as Duncan leaned into him.

"The track is on rough ground from here, all the way up to the lookout bothy," Archie said. Duncan nodded and the two of them caught up with the others and let them know what to expect. They took more time now, wary of walking into an ambush. Archie and Duncan took the lead, ensuring Alistair and the others kept a little bit of distance between them just in case.

The bothy, once the permanently manned coastguard lookout with a panoramic view of the Little Minch, was sited on the high point of the cliffs overlooking the headland below and facing the sea. Once the outline of the small building came into view, Duncan took Archie's arm and pulled him down onto his haunches alongside him.

The original building, a white-rendered cube, flat-roofed with a large window facing out to sea, had a newer timber-clad addition almost doubling the size. All Duncan could see was the outline though. The interior was in darkness which unnerved him.

"There are two internal rooms," Archie said, almost reading his mind. "The main lookout faces the water and at the rear, closest to us is the bunk room. Neither room is much more than six or seven square metres worth of space."

Alistair crept up to join them, keeping low. "Seems quiet," he said.

"Something's not right," Duncan said. "Where is everyone?"

Duncan knew there was no other shelter in the area. If anyone was still on Rubha Hunish, then they had to be here.

"They could have taken another path down, couldn't they?" Alistair said, asking Archie the question.

"Aye, there's a route down back to Duntulm..." Archie thought hard. "Or they've gone down onto the headland itself."

Duncan looked at him. "That's a cliff face."

"There's a path down, but it's not for the faint-hearted."

"And in this weather, it'd be for the soft-headed," Alistair said.

"I can't see it," Duncan said. "If they're still here, they must be in the bothy." He pointed to the building. "Is that blue door still the only way in?"

"Aye," Archie said. "Nothing much about the original building has changed since we were weans."

"The forward-facing windows, do they open?"

Archie shook his head. "Nah. They're still steel frames as well."

"One way in, one way out," Alistair said. He looked at Duncan. "Well, we cannae stay here the night."

Duncan nodded. "Archie, you stay here. Keep your head down and stay out of sight."

"You'll get nae argument from me, Dunc."

Duncan scurried back to where Russell, Ronnie and Caitlyn were waiting a little further down the path where they couldn't yet see the bothy.

"We can't see anything going on," he said. "It's all in darkness. We're going to get a bit closer and when we move off, the three of you should come up to where Archie is. Keep low and watch our backs. Under no circumstances do the three of you take any steps that put you in danger, am I clear? Wait here unless we call you in."

"Tell the keck not to get his head blown off, will you, sir?" Ronnie asked. "I'd hate to have to tell his wife that he got killed doing something heroic."

"I'll pass it on," Duncan said before moving back up the path to join Alistair, sinking down in the snow beside him. "Ronnie says don't die, okay?"

"Oh, did he now? That's unusually thoughtful of him."

"It's not altruistic; he just doesn't want to have to tell your wife."

"More like it," Alistair said, smiling. "She'd collect the insurance, mind, so I reckon she'd be all right with it."

Duncan laughed. "Let's not test that hypothesis though."

Alistair nodded and the two of them rose and headed forward. Duncan patted Archie's arm gently as he passed him. Duncan knew the other three would be making their way up behind them. Alistair gestured with his right hand for Duncan to move away from him to his side, his military training kicking in. If someone was to open fire on them, then with some distance between them they'd become two targets rather than one large one.

There was still no sign of movement or habitation from inside the bothy. Once they were within ten metres or so, Duncan silently guessed that Archie was probably correct. They had taken the path back to Duntulm, and probably did so the previous night or, at the latest, first thing this morning. Perhaps they'd slipped by them while the fire at Lorna's had still been raging.

A flicker of movement through the swirling snowstorm caught his eye. Was it his mind playing tricks on him though, seeing something he half expected to see? For a moment he thought the door to the bothy had opened but as he strained to confirm it, he lost sight of all detail in the blizzard. Alistair's voice carried to him on the wind and he looked across, unable to make out what he'd said. In the corner of his eye he saw a flash of light and instinctively flung himself to the ground as the gunshot sounded.

Striking the frozen earth hard, his face hit something with no give and a stabbing pain struck the top of his head. Cursing, he turned to see what was going on and another flash lit up in front of him, another shotgun blast sounding amid the howl of the wind. Was it aimed at him or Alistair, or someone else entirely? Warm liquid trickled from his forehead, catching in his eyebrow and he reached up to touch it but with his gloved hand he was unable to probe the wound.

Alistair was gone now. Likely he too was sprawled on the ground or had broken for some cover. Duncan felt horribly exposed. Looking to his left and right, there was nowhere for him to hide. The thought of returning to his colleagues behind him, crossing that open ground with no cover at all, didn't appeal. He couldn't see any shelter to either side and to go back would leave him vulnerable. He eyed the bothy itself. Aside from the door and the windows overlooking the headland below, there was no other vantage point from which the gunman could operate. The safest place for him to be, paradoxically, was right beside the bothy itself.

Lifting his head, he chanced another look at the building. The door was closed. It was definitely closed. If he was going to go, then he should move now but he was conscious that the door could open again at any moment, and he could face another volley. He'd made his decision. Taking a deep breath, he hoisted himself up and took off at a run through the snow-covered heather towards the bothy, angling his route to his left and trying to steer away from the viewpoint of the entrance door. His eye was trained on that door; if it moved, he would veer to left or right and hit the ground as fast as he could to minimise himself as a target.

His foot caught on a boulder hidden beneath the snow and he stumbled, losing his footing and pitching forward before falling to the ground. He landed in a snow drift, banked up against a bank of earth barely three metres from the southern corner of the bothy. He glimpsed a figure lying on the ground beside him, staring at him on his left. Imagining it was Alistair approaching the bothy, much as he'd done, he looked across and smiled only as he met the man's eye, he knew it wasn't Alistair… and the stare was blank, the eyes cold.

"Holy Jesus…" Duncan said, shoving himself away from the body. The eyes seemed to follow him, but Duncan knew he was dead and had been for some time. Half of the body was covered in snow with only the upper torso, head and right arm visible.

Movement to his right snapped his head around and Alistair startled him, dropping onto the ground alongside him.

"Bloody hell, Alistair!"

His DS chuckled. "Who were you expecting?"

"I wasn't expecting him," Duncan said, pointing a finger at the body barely a metre away from them. "That's for damn sure."

"Aye, there's another one about ten metres that way," Alistair said, waving a hand in the general direction. "Took a shotgun blast to the face… it'll no' be an open casket for that poor sod."

Duncan rolled onto his front, inching forward to peer over the horseshoe of boulders they were nestled into, side by side, looking towards the bothy.

"You're bleeding," Alistair said, looking concerned.

"I'm all right. I hit my head when I went down, that's all. I'll be fine."

Alistair looked doubtful.

"Did you see the shooter?" Duncan asked.

"No. I was too busy getting out of the way."

Duncan nodded. "I hear that. Any ideas?"

"On what to do next?"

"Aye." Duncan looked at him in earnest. "I'm open to suggestions."

A flicker of movement from the side of the bothy saw them both duck down. A shotgun blast went off, followed by another a moment later, but it wasn't in their direction. Then all they could hear was the wind once more.

"They aren't shooting at us," Alistair said.

"The others?"

"I cannae see 'em. They're no' daft. They'll keep their heads down."

"Warning shots?"

"I wouldn't be surprised," Alistair said. "Whoever is doing the shooting, they know we're out here… and they don't want us getting closer to the bothy."

"Why not?"

"For the same reason you and I want to get close to it; their sight lines are buggered once we do. Only one way in and one out, remember? They're giving it beans with two shots and then retreating inside."

"Double-barrelled?" Duncan asked.

"Aye, that's my guess. They duck back inside to reload."

"So… only one weapon?"

"That we know of, aye." Alistair chanced another look across to the bothy. Duncan did the same. Three decent strides and they'd be up against the wall. From where they lay, they could no longer see the door. It would take seconds to cover the distance to the building but if they were unlucky, they could be running into a shotgun cartridge.

"Who goes first?" Duncan asked. "Or shall we go together?"

"Rock, paper, scissors?" Alistair asked, smiling.

"Och… away with you, man!"

Alistair smiled. "I'll see you there."

Before Duncan could protest, Alistair was up and running towards the bothy, almost slamming into the wall as he reached it, pressing his back against the cladding. He gave Duncan a thumbs-up gesture and then inched to his right, heading towards the older part of the building with the steel-framed windows. Duncan stayed where he was, watching

Alistair duck beneath the small square windows of the bunkhouse, edging closer and closer, Duncan feeling his anxiety rising with every step taken. His eyes darted to the eastern edge of the building, and he wondered what he'd do if an armed figure rounded the corner and made for Alistair's position.

"Don't do anything daft, Al... please," Duncan said quietly. He saw Alistair, leaning against the wall beside the old panoramic windows, risk a brief look into the bothy and retreat just as quickly. He made the same move again before edging away, ducking and making his way back to the starting position on the east-facing wall. It was relatively safe there. With no windows on that facing, he still hugged the exterior wall glancing to both left and right, aware of his surroundings. He beckoned to Duncan who took a deep breath and then copied Alistair's route across the open ground to join him against the wall. He was breathing hard when he got there, standing side by side with Alistair. "What did you see?"

"I couldna see anything in there at all. It was way too dark."

"All right... Archie said there were two men he met—"

"And another in the car," Alistair said. "If there were only three then..."

"There's one more; the shooter," Duncan concluded. He looked at Alistair. "If Archie saw all of them?"

"One man... one gun." Alistair shrugged. "Lure him out... and take him down."

"And how do we do that?"

"Well, there are two of us."

"One as bait and the other makes the arrest?" Duncan asked. Alistair nodded. "That's not much of a plan. What would you have done in the Paras?"

Alistair sniffed. "Besides having a gun of my own to shoot back with?"

"Aye."

"I'd have called in an air strike, level the bothy just to be sure."

Duncan smiled. "Not an option. We could always negotiate."

Alistair angled his head. "They dinnae seem inclined to conversation."

"No. So... I suppose it's your plan then."

"Who's going to be the bait?" Alistair asked. He looked at Duncan. "I dinnae want you to take this the wrong way and all, but..."

"I outrank you," Duncan said. "So... I get to choose, right?"

"True. Does that mean I get to be the fox?"

"No. You're right," Duncan said, sighing. "I'll draw him to me and you bring him down."

He couldn't believe he was suggesting it, but the alternative was to get back across what had become a kill zone and then hike back to Shulista, knowing that they were likely leaving Lorna to her fate. If she was still alive. Alistair slapped him on the arm and made his way around to the front of the bothy. Duncan stood on the east corner where it met the southern wall, peering round and watching Alistair lower his body to the ground, enabling him to crawl beneath the windows without being seen. Duncan hurried the other way, pausing at the corner where it met the northern-facing wall, housing the entrance.

He knew that once he rounded that turn, he'd be facing the door. The shooter would have a clear drop on him as soon as that door opened. He looked around and there were no options for places nearby where he could take cover. This was a very bad plan. He had to entice the shooter out and hope

Alistair was in position to jump him from behind. Timing was crucial. Alistair was never late into the office. Today had better not be the first time that he was late for work.

Enough time had passed for Alistair to have made it into position. Between the two sections of the building was a small recess. Once the door opened and the shooter stepped out, Alistair should be shielded from the shooter's view within that recess and then be able to come at him from behind. If he managed to do so before Duncan was shot dead, it would be advantageous.

Duncan steadied himself, drawing a deep breath and considered having a quiet word with the big man upstairs. However, he disregarded the idea. Many years ago he decided if God existed, then he wasn't a fan of Duncan and the feeling was mutual. He was many things, but not a hypocrite. Duncan first glanced around the corner. The door was closed, and he couldn't see anyone, not a shooter and not Alistair. Moving out from his position of safety, he inched his way towards the entrance door located barely two metres from his position.

Coming almost to the base of the three concrete steps leading up to the entrance, he hesitated. There was a small window between him, and the door and he was conscious of not putting his head in front of it, at the risk of losing it entirely. Instead, he put his back against the wall, keeping his eye on the door. The steps led up to a metre-square section in front of the door. Beyond that, the ground sloped up from the level where Duncan was standing. Alistair would have an advantage coming at the shooter from the high ground, but it was marginal.

Duncan braced himself, took a last look around to spot a location he would run for if the plan went south, although he knew if it did, he was unlikely to get away unscathed.

Clenching his left fist, he hammered on the wood panelling, hearing it resound inside.

"Police!" he shouted, mentally toying with the idea of suggesting they were surrounded but that sounded daft. He hammered the exterior again. "Police!" he repeated. "Hold your fire!" He saw the door crack open but only fractionally. Instinctively, he backed away towards the east wall. It would take a couple of seconds, perhaps three, to get back around that corner and out of sight. Unfortunately, it would only take a single second to randomly discharge a shotgun in his direction.

The door eased open and Duncan froze. Should he make a break for safety or stay where he was. The barrel of the gun came into view and Duncan still didn't move. For a moment he thought everything was happening in slow motion, but the shooter came into view, lowering the gun as her eyes met Duncan's.

"Lorna?" Duncan said.

She angled the barrel away from him, casting a glance around the area. She looked pale, gaunt, dressed in a hiking waterproof coat and trousers. Her boots were sturdy, fit for the terrain and she gazed upon Duncan with steely eyes.

"I'm sorry... I didn't know it was you."

Alistair appeared from behind her, and Lorna looked over her shoulder at him but made no effort to bring her weapon to bear.

"Lorna..." Duncan said softly, worried she wouldn't hear him over the sound of the wind, "please can you do me a favour and put the gun down?"

She met his eye, holding his gaze with a blank expression. Then she slowly lowered the weapon to the floor and laid it flat. Alistair was upon it in a flash, removing it from her reach as she righted herself.

"I'm so sorry," she repeated. "I really didn't know it was you out here." She looked around again, as if expecting to see someone else. "I thought you were more of them."

"And who are they, Lorna?" Duncan asked.

She shrugged. "I don't know, but they killed poor Sandy… and then they came for me."

Duncan pointed to the lookout. "Are you alone in there?"

She nodded.

"Then let's get out of this snow and maybe we can sort all of this out."

She smiled weakly and Duncan looked at Alistair who had broken the shotgun, removed the two cartridges inside and had the weapon resting on his shoulder.

"I'll go and get the others," he said, and Duncan nodded. He stepped up to stand beside Lorna who seemed very frail at this point, eyes wide as she stared at him.

"Let's go inside," Duncan said and the two of them entered the bothy.

CHAPTER THIRTY-ONE

THE INSIDE of the bothy was basic to say the least. There was no heating, but to be inside and sheltered from the storm felt like a luxury. They went past the bunk room and into the other room with the picture window overlooking the Minch. The wind buffeted the building, the frames shrieking as the glass flexed and strained against them. There were three old wooden chairs to sit on along with a small table placed against one wall. The window was a bay, with panes facing to either side but the better views lay straight ahead to the north.

"Sit down," Duncan said, and Lorna did so, placing her hands in her lap. Beside the entrance there were some shelves and Duncan found a box of candles along with some holders and a box of matches. There was a leaflet pinned to the wall stating the former coastguard lookout was now maintained by the Mountain Bothies Association. Duncan was grateful for their efforts. The weather had closed in around them and he didn't fancy the walk back down.

He set the candles up on the windowsill, striking a match and lighting three of the candles. He didn't want to use them all seeing as they were there for people to use in an emergency.

There was no fireplace and Duncan briefly wondered what the coastguard occupants would do up here in conditions like these.

The door opened and a draught of freezing air carried to them, making the newly lit flames of the candles flicker. The rest of the team entered, stamping the snow from their boots before coming in. The watch room could accommodate everyone, but it was snug. The bunk room had three racks in it but no more.

"It's blowing a hooley out there now," Alistair said. "I think we're better placed to wait it out here."

No one disagreed and Duncan nodded. Alistair offered Caitlyn the remaining chair and she shot him a dark look.

"You're way older than me, sarge. Take the weight off your feet and I'll sit on the floor."

"Suit yourself," Alistair said, reversing the chair and sitting down close to Duncan and Lorna.

"I think I'll have forty winks in the bunk room," Archie said, looking around at the tightly packed group. "I'm a little peopled-out for one day. No offence."

"None taken," Ronnie said, and Archie lumbered out and into the next room. He pushed the door to, but not closed, indicating that he didn't expect it to be for his sole occupation. The wind swirled around the building, shrieking and howling. Duncan guessed they might be here for the foreseeable future. Hiking down in the early hours was a possibility but the rate at which the snow was falling, it might be prudent to wait for daybreak. He took out his phone. There was no signal. He held it up but the status didn't change.

"Anyone have a bar or two?" he asked.

Everyone checked but soon shook their heads. Ronnie tried his radio, but it too only crackled with static. It was possible the transmitters and cell towers were down or that there had been another power cut. Out where they were, in complete isolation, they had no idea. He looked around the team, a bedraggled group, now trying to get warm. Hypothermia was a real concern. They'd been out at the mercy of Mother Nature for some time and even now, despite finding shelter, they were still at risk.

"Is everyone okay?" Duncan asked. A general murmur passed around the room, confirming they were. "There are some blankets in the bunk room. Gather them up and hunker down. We could be here for a while yet, so it's best to make ourselves as comfortable as possible."

He turned to Lorna. She was staring straight ahead, out into the driving snow. Her forehead and her right cheek were tinged red, visible from the flickering candlelight, and he wondered whether it was a trick of the light. Paying closer attention, it looked sore.

"Is your face okay?" he asked her. She glanced sideways at him and forced a smile.

"I'll be all right."

"Did you come straight out here after the fire?"

"The fire?" she asked quizzically.

"Your house," Duncan said. "It was ablaze overnight."

"Oh…" she said and then shook her head.

"Can you tell me what happened there last night?"

Her gaze lowered from the view outside and down to the floor in front of her. He wondered if she was in shock. The human mind could take remarkable steps to protect itself from trauma. He knew this from personal experience.

"They came to your home last night?" he asked.

She nodded.

"What did they want?"

She remained tight-lipped, pensive.

"There are questions you will need to answer, Lorna,"

Duncan said. "Three men have lost their lives, four if you include Sandy."

"Five."

"I beg your pardon?"

She raised her head and looked at him. "There are five dead. You will find another at the foot of the cliff." She tilted her head towards the outside. "He fell." Duncan exchanged a look with Alistair whose eyes drifted to the window. He might well be thinking about exploring the descent for that man. Duncan shook his head, almost imperceptible.

"What were they after?" Duncan asked.

Lorna shrugged. "Something Sandy had... and he wouldn't give it to them."

"What was that?"

She shook her head. "I don't know. I told them that... but they wouldn't listen." Her expression took on a faraway gaze. "They threatened me." She looked at Duncan, straight faced. "He said he would do to me what he'd done to Sandy."

"Kill him?"

She nodded. "That's what I took it to mean... and it wasn't an idle threat."

"And who was this man?"

She frowned. "He said his name was Michael... something. I don't mind what."

"Tomlinson?"

"Aye... Tomlinson. That was him."

"And he threatened you?" Duncan asked. She nodded. "Can you tell us what happened at the house?"

"I keep a shotgun," she said, looking to where Alistair had set it down against the wall. "I thought he was going to do to me what he did to Sandy... I couldn't give him what he wanted. I managed to reach the gun... my father taught me how to shoot. He took us hunting a few times, in the mountains of my grandfather's hometown." She cocked her head. "Not that I was ever particularly proficient with a gun, but I know the basics."

Duncan met Alistair's eye and he raised a sceptical eyebrow. Lorna didn't see but Duncan understood. There were two bodies in the snow and a further one that had been cremated at her home who might argue she was indeed handy with the weapon.

"Why would he, Tomlinson, believe you had what he wanted?"

She shrugged. "Perhaps Sandy told him I had it... whatever it was. I don't know."

"And you can think of no other reason why he, and his men, might attack you?"

"No, I'm sorry." Her brow furrowed. "You said my house... was ablaze? Is there much damage?"

"I'm afraid so. The main building is completely gutted." She raised her right hand to her mouth, eyes wide, wincing as she touched her face and then briefly examining her hand before lowering it again and cupping it gently in her lap with her left. "But your studio was untouched."

She nodded slowly. "That's something, I suppose."

Ronnie's radio crackled into life. It was the control room. He moved to the far side of the room and there was a brief exchange. He returned moments later. "Mountain Rescue are at the car park making ready to come for us. The conditions are bad, but they'll be with us within an hour. Or we can stay here for the night."

Duncan looked from face to face, and no one seemed inclined to stay put. He nodded. "Tell them we'll be waiting." To everyone else, he said, "Get some rest. In an hour or so, we'll be starting back down."

Everyone made themselves comfortable. Russell and

Ronnie both decided to rest on the spare bunks. Caitlyn was restless, apparently keen to get back down the mountain. Lorna was silent, sitting very still and only after some persuasion, reluctantly accepted a blanket across her shoulders.

"I really didn't know it was you outside," Lorna said after a few minutes of silence. "I would never have shot at you if I'd known you were the police."

"Why didn't you call us last night?"

She frowned. "After I... after the man was shot, I ran from the house. I didn't have a phone and I knew they would follow. I wasn't really thinking."

"Why here?"

She looked around, the trace of a smile crossing her lips. "I've spent many hours here... days and nights. I feel safe."

"Away from people?"

She nodded. "People pass through here, particularly when the weather is fine but when it is inclement, I will have it all to myself. And if you don't know of it, then you would not come up here. I was surprised they followed me."

"Resourceful fellows," Alistair said, and she turned to face him. "A cut above your usual criminals."

"Are they?" she said. "I wouldn't know."

Alistair nodded. "Trust me. They seem like dangerous sorts."

"In which case," Lorna said, placing her hand on Duncan's forearm and meeting his eye. "I'm so glad you came to rescue me."

Duncan looked at the back of her hand, red and sore much like parts of her face. "Well, you seemed to have been managing just fine by yourself, but you're welcome."

"Am I... will I be in a great deal of trouble?" she asked.

Duncan was thoughtful. "In my experience, lethal force in the act of self-defence is considered reasonable. Under the circumstances, I should imagine you will be okay... once everything has been considered."

She exhaled, her expression lightening. "That's good to know, thank you."

Duncan smiled. "Get some rest. It will be a challenging hike out of here and you'll need your wits about you."

She returned his smile with one of her own. "I've managed in worse, but admittedly I was much younger."

Duncan rose from his seat and Lorna rested her head against the wood-panelling, drawing the blanket around her. Duncan saw her eyes were still open, staring out into the swirling snow. Alistair got up and the two of them moved to the entrance door, as far away from Lorna as possible. Alistair lowered his voice.

"There are still a lot of questions I—"

Duncan held up a hand to silence him, glancing towards Lorna who remained staring out of the window. "I know. Now is not the time."

DUNCAN HAD LOST track of time, sitting with his back to the wall and occasionally dozing off. He woke with a start, looking around. Caitlyn was standing at the window looking out over the Minch. The snow appeared to have eased off, light flurries falling steadily rather than the blizzard he'd fallen asleep in. Alistair was still in his chair, the shotgun beside him, stoically watching over the group. He looked sharp and attentive.

Someone hammered on the door before pushing it open. The door juddered, scraping the interior floor as it moved. It must have swollen or warped over time. Alistair grinned as

Willie Maciver walked in, casting a quick glance around the room and making an initial assessment.

"Anyone call for a cab?" he asked.

"You took your time, Willie," Alistair said, rising to greet him with a firm handshake.

"Well, I like to make an entrance, Al." He looked at Duncan and nodded a greeting. "Are we all good to go?"

The door to the bunk room opened and a bleary-eyed Archie stood in the doorway. Everyone made ready, gathering up what few possessions they'd brought with them. Alistair picked up the shotgun along with the box of shells Lorna had inside the bothy, making them both safe before announcing he was ready to leave.

Duncan came over to Willie. "There are two bodies in the snow to the south and south-west. Neither match the age or description of our prime suspect, and so there could well be another body at the foot of the cliff to the north."

Willie nodded soberly. "We'll bag up the two outside and bring them down. As for the other," he shook his head, "that will have to wait until daybreak. I can't risk lives descending in the dark."

"Fair enough," Duncan said. It was unlikely that Tomlinson — if it was Tomlinson — would have survived exposure to the elements even if he'd managed to survive the fall.

They gathered outside, completed a head count and then under the guidance of the mountain rescue team, they carefully retraced their route back down. It felt like it didn't take anywhere near as long to descend as it had to get up to the bothy. Whether that was because of the experienced heads guiding them or the lack of threat to their lives and the uncertainty of what they were walking into. In any event, the relief was palpable once they were on the level moorland with the cars in sight.

Lorna had been walking in front of Duncan but behind one of Willie's team for the descent and she hadn't uttered a word. Duncan noticed her casually staring at the body bags, strapped to gurneys for the descent, on occasion. There wasn't a flicker of emotion from her though. Initially, he'd thought she was suffering from shock whereas now he couldn't make his mind up between his original assessment or whether it was something else entirely.

An ambulance was waiting for them along with a blacked-out van, a mortuary transport vehicle, and several liveried police cars. Angus Ross was also there, a concerned expression on his face, waiting to see the team arrive. His face split into a broad grin as they marched across the cattle grid to meet them.

"Thank God! I tried to phone you guys earlier... but the network has been down. The power's been out for a couple of hours too. It'll be back up soon enough though. At least that's what the Hydro boys have told me, eh?"

Duncan patted him on the back, appreciating his concern for their wellbeing. Lorna, still alongside Duncan looked back in the direction of Duntulm.

"Will we be going to Portree?" she asked.

"Yes, we'll have you checked by the paramedic first—"

"There's no need, Detective Inspector."

"But your face and hand—"

"Believe me, I'm fine," she said, forcing a smile. "But... I was wondering if we could stop by my house before we go down? I have a change of clothes in the studio... I keep things in there for the days where I go out hiking and might get saturated, you know what the weather is like?"

"I do," he said.

"I'd just like to pick them up, so I have something to change into. Is that okay?"

Duncan exhaled, looking around. He shrugged. "I guess another ten minutes won't kill us."

"Thank you. I appreciate it," Lorna said, smiling.

Once the group had dispersed into their vehicles and begun the drive back to the island's capital, Duncan, Lorna and Alistair made the short drive back to her house in Duntulm. What had been smouldering ruins when they were last here had now been fully extinguished by the day's snow-fall. The house was blanketed in white now, charred timbers protruding from their snowy embrace.

Lorna said nothing as they parked next to the property. She cast a forlorn eye across the ruin, pursed her lips and then shook her head. She looked over towards her studio in the sheiling and then at Duncan.

"I'll not be a minute," she said.

"No problem," he replied, leaning against the pick-up. Lorna set off on the short walk to the studio as Alistair got out, coming to stand beside Duncan. There was a silent exchange between them, and Duncan nodded.

Lorna entered the building, glancing back at the two of them before gently closing the door. She looked around the gloomy interior, trying the light switch, which did nothing, before crossing the studio to the rear. From a cupboard she produced a small backpack, opening it and checking there were clothes inside. She emptied out the contents and then moved to the glory hole, prising off the filler piece and peering inside. Reaching back, she fumbled in the dark, cursing quietly.

"Looking for this."

Startled, she spun around to see Duncan standing by the door. He held up the briefcase in his hand.

"I have a matching one in the back of the pick-up."

She didn't speak as he walked over to join her, setting the

briefcase down on the counter and opening it. Lifting the lid, her eyes drifted to the contents, bundles of money and the passports.

"The other one also has cash... along with the details of multiple bank accounts in several countries, Switzerland, the British Virgin Islands... the Philippines. For someone who enjoys living in the outer reaches of the Scottish islands, you do like to travel, don't you, Amelie?"

She exhaled heavily, her eyelids fluttering quickly in an involuntary movement. She smiled. "I didn't have you pegged as an intelligent man the first time we met," she said flatly. "No offence intended."

Duncan inclined his head. "None taken."

"It would appear I may have underestimated you."

"I wouldn't say that necessarily. Perhaps you simply over-played your hand. I have to admit it, you deserve an Academy Award for your depiction of Lorna Somerwell. You played the role magnificently, but you didn't fancy going the whole way and faking the Glaswegian accent as well though? Who was Lorna to you anyway?"

"Nobody..." she said, shrugging. "But if you're looking for a new identity, then it pays to choose one who no one cares about. Fewer questions... or links with reality on which to trip over," she said, leaning against the counter and folding her arms across her chest. "So... you know who I am. What now?"

"I must say, you're looking very well for someone presumed dead."

She laughed. "And I would be, dead I mean, if I'd stuck around to testify."

"Why did you take off like that?"

"Because I had no choice. Not everyone associated with Michael was going to be in the dock... and he had powerful friends, as well as low life ones who wouldn't think anything about killing me, even for a few hundred pounds. Life is cheap to those people." She shook her head. "I had a visit the night before the trial. It was made perfectly clear what was in store for me... and I don't mind telling you, I was terrified. I was a painter... not a... a... an organised criminal."

"So, you did a runner?"

"With whatever I could take from the house in my hands."

"How did he find you?"

She snorted. "Because I got careless... and I broke the rule."

"The rule?"

"The first rule of disappearing to start again," she said quietly. "You not only have to cut all ties with everyone you know, even those you care for the most, but you also have to break your routines; favourite styles of food, holiday locations, sporting activities and... everything you're passionate about."

"Painting?"

She nodded. "It wasn't only my hobby, but also how I earned money."

"Forging artworks and selling them," Duncan said. "Which is where Sandy came in."

"Yes... Sandy was a mildly interesting man. He could be bold... occasionally innovative but he was greedy... and when he dipped his toe into a larger pool found himself completely out of his depth."

"Did you think you could maintain this subterfuge after everything that's happened recently?"

"This changes nothing," she said casually. "I mean, what I told you was true. It happened just as I told you it did."

"Except you do know what Michael Tomlinson was after, don't you?"

She nodded. "Two things." She pointed at the briefcase. "The money held in those bank accounts you mentioned."

"A lot is there?"

"More than enough for a detective inspector to retire on," she said. Duncan tilted his head to one side, glancing at the briefcase.

"And the second thing?"

"Me," she said flatly. "Dead, preferably. The only thing keeping me alive was what is held in those accounts."

"How much is there?"

"All in… just shy of two million pounds."

Duncan exhaled. "That's a lot of money."

"Untraceable," she said. "No one knows about it… no one alive at any rate. No one is looking for it because no one knows it exists."

"That's one hell of a retirement fund. Why stay out here for the last decade if you have access to that?"

She shrugged. "It pays to vanish. If you start spending that kind of money, people will ask questions. Like I said, you have to alter your patterns, be patient and play the long game. Michael will have been looking. I knew that. That's how he found me… my painting." Duncan gave her an inquisitive look. She smiled ruefully. "We were selling paintings through Sandy's gallery but we could only shift so many. It is a small gallery after all, and it is on Skye. Sandy, unbeknown to me, started selling online… then to dealers… like I said," she met Duncan's gaze, "he was greedy. What Sandy didn't realise is that all artists, writers, sportspeople, musicians… we all have ticks. Habits we cannot shake, no matter how hard we try. It's almost like a fingerprint of sorts."

Duncan understood. "Michael Tomlinson recognised your tick?"

She nodded. "Unfortunately, it would appear so."

"The competition Sandy won—"

"A fake," she said, waving her hand dismissively. "A ruse to get closer to Sandy… to get to me." She sighed. "He must have forced Sandy to tell him where I was. Not that the poor sod knew who I was or what was going on. It's not as if I was likely to share my background with him. I wouldn't trust the man as far as I could throw him. He was… a useful idiot. A nice enough guy but…"

"And Tomlinson," Duncan said. "He told you he murdered Sandy?"

"Yes," she said, holding Duncan's gaze, unflinching.

"Then he came for you at your home?"

"Yes. What I told you was true. I managed to get to my gun… I keep it loaded, and I shot the first man who tried to prevent me from leaving. It was him or me. I swear to it."

"And then?"

"I ran," she said, shrugging. "I ran into the hills. I knew I could reach the bothy… and I didn't think they would follow. I've climbed in the Alps… Nepal… As much as these mountains are dangerous, I know my limits and I figured I could lay low for a couple of days before slipping away again after the storm passed… disappear. After all, I managed it once."

"It does sound as if you have everything covered."

She smiled. "Not that I want to tell you how to do your job."

Duncan laughed, shaking his head. "Perish the thought. There is one thing that I still don't get in all of this."

"What's that?"

Duncan rubbed his face with both hands, trying to get colour and warmth into his cheeks. He'd felt cold since they'd hiked up to the bothy and hadn't managed to warm himself through since they'd got back down.

"What is it?" Amelie asked again. "I'll help if I can."

"It's just Michael…"

"Tomlinson? What about him?"

"You see, he's been at the centre of a money-laundering

investigation these past few months. My colleagues in Edinburgh are all over him... not far off bringing forth charges."

"That doesn't surprise me."

"Only, the weekend that Sandy was killed... Michael was in custody, assisting my colleagues with their enquiries. So, here's my dilemma; how could he be in an interview room in Edinburgh and on Skye, killing Sandy Beaton, on the same day?"

Amelie fixed him with a cold stare. She shrugged. "Maybe his people carried it out. How should I know?"

Duncan nodded. "Fair enough. Only... I also have a witness who places Sandy at your house on the evening of the night he died. A visit that you failed to mention despite already being pulled up on your memory lapse. Can you explain that to me?"

"I don't have to," she said. "Your witness... is wrong."

"And I suppose I'm wrong when I tell you that starting a fire with petrol or diesel is very easy, but also carries inherent dangers too."

She frowned. "What are you talking about?"

"You see, when you pour out vast quantities of accelerant and ignite it... the fire tends to flash," Duncan said. "The sudden burst of flame shoots up, feeding off the oxygen in the air, it's worse in a confined space, such as a room in a house. That initial flash-over catches out anyone untrained in fire control or those who aren't practising arsonists. The injuries are often insignificant; singed hair or eyebrows or perhaps reddened skin... on hands and face."

"I... I... don't see what you are getting at."

"Oh... well let me explain. Michael Tomlinson didn't kill Sandy. It is my belief that you did. Whether that was because he was selling you out or you felt the need to stop him from revealing who you are and where you lived, I can't say. The only person alive who would know about that for sure, is standing before me now."

She laughed nervously. "You think I killed Sandy?"

"I do. What are the odds that the impact point of the wound to Sandy's skull will correspond to the angles of the stock of your shotgun? And what's more, I think Michael's people did come to your house. Maybe they knew who you were or maybe not. I don't know. However, Michael was photographed on a speed camera yesterday, heading north from Edinburgh. Was he making his way here? We will check the mobile phone records… see who was calling him the last couple of days. What I do know is that you shot a man to death in your house and then I believe you set fire to the house to cover your tracks. Maybe you were hoping we'd all believe you'd died… again… and you could slip back, collect your money and identities before disappearing once more—"

"They came to kill me! I defended myself."

Duncan shook his head. "Michael found you the same way I did. He knew your patterns and he saw the same paintings from Rubha Hunish as I did. He — or his associates on his behalf — tapped into local knowledge, and then he came looking for you. And you were ready."

"Yes, you're damn right I was."

"You should have taken the money and run, rather than hiding out."

She tipped her head. "Hindsight is a wonderful thing." She met Duncan's gaze and then her eyes flitted to the open brief-case. "Like I said before though. It doesn't change a thing."

"It doesn't?"

"No. I still have nearly two million pounds in accounts abroad. Untraceable. Unreachable."

"And?"

"Do you want to see out your days on this island… the

wind, rain… and the cold? For what? A crappy pension… followed by a heart attack, brought on by dealing with the stress of the job for thirty years?"

"You paint quite a picture."

"It's a talent I'm known for," she said, smiling. "It doesn't have to be that way, you know?"

"It doesn't?"

"Two million goes a long way, even when it's shared. Think about it."

Duncan nodded. "A compelling idea. And what do I need to do for it? Presumably that's what you're suggesting."

"Just look the other way, nothing more," she said, looking out of the glazed wall.

"Nothing more?"

She shook her head. "Nothing more."

Duncan arched his eyebrows, nodding slowly. "Hell of an offer."

"But it's a one-time only deal, and the clock is ticking," Amelie said.

"Sadly, I forgot to wind my watch," Duncan said, glancing over his shoulder. Alistair stepped into view, folding his arms across his chest. Amelie's smile faded. Duncan stepped forward and took her by the arm. "You're under arrest for the murder of Sandy Beaton. You can say whatever you like, and I don't really care to listen." He turned her around and hand-cuffed her. Alistair came to join them. Ronnie MacDonald entered the studio and Duncan passed Amelie to him. He escorted her out to a waiting police car.

"That was quite an offer she made you," Alistair said.

Duncan frowned. "Aye."

"For a moment, I thought you might actually take it."

Duncan turned to Alistair.

"You were joking, right?"

"About what?"

"You don't really think I'd have considered taking her offer, do you?"

Alistair was thoughtful for a moment then smiled at him. "I sure as hell would have."

CHAPTER THIRTY-TWO

ALISTAIR RAPPED his knuckles on the door frame, snapping Duncan out of his daydream. Duncan beckoned him inside and Alistair set a folder down on the desk. The ops room beyond Duncan's office was still quiet. Most of the team weren't in yet. After the drama of the previous night, it had been well into the early hours before things calmed down. Duncan gave them all the option to come in a few hours late today, a day which promised to be a long one. Alistair, much like Duncan, had been in the office since before seven o'clock, disregarding the opportunity for a long lie-in.

"Willie's team found a body at the foot of the cliff beyond the old lookout," Alistair said. Duncan nodded solemnly. "From the description it sounds like it's Michael Tomlinson. He was shot before he fell. He'd have been dead before he landed."

"It would appear that Amelie is quite proficient with that shotgun."

"Aye. Fortunately for us, her aim was a little off later in the day."

Duncan offered him a seat, but his DS declined.

"I have to brief the Edinburgh team in a bit," Duncan said.

"Ah, I can do that," Alistair said.

"You sure? I'd appreciate it."

"No bother. It'll be a short briefing. They're all dead. Case closed."

Duncan smiled. "Afraid so."

"What do you reckon will happen to Lorna, sorry, Amelie now?"

Duncan exhaled, glancing out of the window. The snow had ceased falling overnight and finally the weather front had moved on, the remnants of the Atlantic front were now sweeping across the highlands and things on Skye could return to normal. Power was still waiting to be restored to a few hundred homes, but the worst of it was over.

"Amelie's leverage against receiving a stiff sentence for her part in Tomlinson's fraud was her willingness to testify against him. He's dead," Duncan said, shrugging. "I guess it will depend on who else they were looking to prosecute."

"And Sandy's death? What will the procurator fiscal make of that?"

"Tough to say."

Duncan believed in his heart that his theory was correct. Amelie had walked Sandy Beaton up The Storr and killed him, trying in a ham-fisted way to make it look like an accident. The wound to Sandy's head was ruled as possibly caused by a strike from the butt of Amelie's weapon, but it remained inconclusive. It was a long shot though. There was no physical or forensic trace evidence to tie her to his death. Only the testimony of Dougie Henderson placed Sandy at her home. Everything else was circumstantial. And if there was one thing the fiscal didn't appreciate, it was circumstantial evidence. A decent barrister could tear that to pieces in a courtroom, if the case even made it into one.

The inconsistencies in Amelie's narrative means that they will pursue her for the murder, but aside from the small chance of directly linking her to Sandy's death, they'd need a confession. She was unlikely to offer one. Since her arrest, Amelie had said absolutely nothing, even after consulting with legal counsel. She would no doubt claim self-defence in the deaths of Tomlinson and his entourage. Reading through their criminal histories, she was probably on safe ground. All of this led to her original part in art forgery and fraud. A practice she continued on Skye along with Sandy Beaton, trading from his gallery.

Had Sandy asked for more money in his share? Had he promised Michael Tomlinson that he'd reveal Amelie's where-abouts to him, if he did indeed know her past? There were still so many questions Duncan had, but only one person who could answer them. Amelie Bilodeau.

It was conceivable to him that Sandy may not have known why he was taken to the place of his death. Amelie could well have seen what was coming and taken steps to remove the threat. Had the weather not closed in as it had done, she may have picked up her escape pack, passports, bank accounts and cash, and made a break for it earlier. In which case, Sandy's death would have remained one of the many unsolved mysteries, no doubt featuring in documentaries for years to come. As it was, they might not have all the answers, but they did have a resolution to the investigation.

"Right!" Alistair said. "Leave it with me and I'll feed back to you later."

"What's that?" Duncan asked, breaking his gaze out of the window.

"I'll fill you in later with how I get on."

He nodded. "Great. Thanks."

Alistair's eyes narrowed. "Is everything okay?"

"Yeah, yeah, of course. I was... things on my mind."

Fraser MacDonald appeared at the door, clearing his throat. Duncan looked up at him.

"You wanted to see me, sir?"

"Aye, Fraser. Come in, come in," Duncan said. Alistair nodded to Fraser as he left, raising a curious eyebrow at Duncan but he didn't ask why he wanted to see the constable. "Take a seat."

Fraser sat down, looking slightly awkward. He was a big man and the arms of the chair pressed into his sides. "What can I do for you, sir?"

"Callum... er..."

"Mcinnes."

"Aye, the Mcinnes lad," Duncan said. "What's happening with all of that?"

Fraser blew out his cheeks. "Er... driving without a licence or insurance... likely be a hefty fine, points and a disqualification to take effect once he actually passes a test."

"Will he be going to court?"

Fraser was uncertain. "If he hadn't stoved the thing into a tree, then maybe it'd just be the fine and points... but the injury to the sister..." Fraser wrinkled his nose. "I cannae say just now. The weather for driving was awful... so that counts in his favour that he wasn't doing anything daft behind the wheel." He met Duncan's eye. "It's no' my decision though."

"No, of course not. I just..."

"Asking for a friend like?"

Duncan nodded. "Aye, that's it."

"It'd probably help his cause if he explained why he was driving that night."

"Has he not said?"

Fraser shook his head. "He's not offered any explanation at all... which I find odd." Duncan looked at him quizzically.

"Well, I kinda think there's a reason behind it. I know the Mcinnes family... a little, not closely, but Callum has always been a decent enough lad. Quiet... but never been in trouble. It seems very much out of character."

"That should help if he does go to court."

"Aye, it just might," Fraser said, delivered in his no nonsense, emotionless tone. "If he could offer a plausible reason as to why he got behind the wheel, it might help. Can I ask your interest, sir?"

"Family friend," Duncan said immediately. Fraser nodded, accepting the statement at face value but his expression suggested he knew there was likely to be more to it. He didn't labour the question though. "Thanks for stopping by, Fraser."

"Nae bother at all, sir. Anytime."

Fraser left and Duncan sat alone in his office, considering his options. Alistair caught his eye, talking on the phone, but he was also watching Duncan surreptitiously. Rising from behind his desk, Duncan gathered his coat and left his office. Alistair covered the mouthpiece of his phone as he passed him.

"Ducking out for a bit, Alistair. I'll get you a coffee on the way back."

"And a sausage roll," Alistair said. "Square, not link."

Duncan nodded. "See you in a bit."

DRIVING through the small crofting township of Maligar, Duncan slowed the car as he came upon Becky's cottage. Several times he'd almost turned the car around and returned to Portree but he knew, this time, that he couldn't run away.

Turning off the road and through the gate onto the drive-way, he was surprised to see Becky standing beside her car, the door open. She had a coat pulled about her and she looked back nervously towards the property as she saw him at the wheel. It was too late to turn back now, even if he wanted to. He switched the engine off but before he could get out, she'd already closed her door and was striding across to meet him.

He cracked the door, and she forcefully pulled it open, glaring at him.

"What the hell are you doing here?"

Taken aback, Duncan still got out. Becky took another look back at the house and Duncan followed her gaze.

"Are you expecting someone?" he asked.

She turned on him. "I'm just leaving for the hospital."

"Right. How is Eilidh?"

"She's improving… but it'll be a long road."

"Aye, well if she's as tough as her mum then she'll be doing okay—"

"What do you want, Duncan?"

He scoffed. "What do I… seriously? After what you said to me the other day, you can't expect me—"

"I don't expect anything from you, Duncan," she said. "Not for me… for your son."

She'd lowered her voice, looking at the house again. Davey's pick-up wasn't in the drive, so it could only be Callum she was concerned about.

"Is Callum in the house?"

"Aye," she said, keeping her voice down. "And he knows nothing of any of this."

Duncan laughed. "You think I'm going to walk up and introduce myself or something?"

She stepped into him. "Don't joke, Duncan. I mean it!"

He held his hands up. "I'm not here to cause trouble for you, Becky."

"Then why are you here?"

It was a good question.

"I've spoken with the officer dealing with... the accident. He says Callum is a good lad, and that he'll likely face a fine, points and a disqualification."

Becky's stance softened. "That's... good. Thank you."

"He may still need to attend court," Duncan said. "He's not out of the woods yet. The injuries suffered by his sister complicate things somewhat." Duncan was pensive, looking around. The air was chilly, but the wind had eased to all but a gentle breeze now. "Apparently, Callum offered no explanation for why he took the car that day."

"Oh..." she said, shaking her head. "I didn't know."

"Neither has Eilidh. I checked. Why might they both be silent, do you think?"

Becky lifted her eyes to meet his. They both knew, he was certain, but he wasn't going to make her say it.

"If there was a reason," he said thoughtfully, "a special set of circumstances that made him feel he had to take the car... that drove him to act out of character, then it might help."

"I see."

He held her eye, but she averted hers from his gaze, brushing the hair away from her face, catching on the breeze as it was.

"Of course, I can imagine what might have driven Callum to taking your car that night... and trying to get his sister to safety."

Becky shook her head slowly, still looking down.

"Bex?"

She lifted her head, and he could see her eyes were glistening. She looked pale, the skin beneath her eyes was dark and puffy. He wondered how long it had been since she'd had a decent night's sleep.

"I... I don't know what to say."

"The truth would help—"

"Screw you, Duncan."

"Come on, Bex—"

"No!" she said, a veil of frustration and anger crossing her face. "Do you know what you're asking of me… of us?"

"I've been in the polis a long time, Becky. I know what I'm asking, and I know what it would likely mean for you and for the weans."

She smiled ruefully, shaking her head. "The conse-quences… if it all comes out into the open…"

"I know," he said softly. "I'm sorry… but you came to me for help and…" he shrugged "I'm sorry, but this is all I have."

Her head snapped up. "Then you're still a disappointment, Duncan."

He felt that comment cut him. She was lashing out, he understood that. There really was nothing else he could do. The bruises he'd seen on her, still fresh and developing in the days after Callum's accident told him what had been going on in their home that night. He was certain Callum was fleeing the house, possibly at Becky's request, and took his sister with him. It was the only conclusion to draw from the children's reluctance to explain how the situation came about.

Duncan was well aware however, that for any of them to speak out, it would destroy their family. Everything would change. Arguably for the better, in his opinion, but it wasn't his life. It wasn't his choice. He couldn't force them to do anything.

"You need to leave," Becky said.

"Now?"

She nodded.

Duncan heard the sound of an approaching car. He looked towards the road, spotting a pick-up approaching. It slowed and then pulled into the drive with Davey behind the wheel.

He stared at Duncan, parking in front of the small ancillary barn next to the house and got out. Duncan sensed Becky tense as her husband approached. She looked down at the floor and Duncan could see the power Davey exerted over her in that brief moment.

"Hey, Duncan," Davey said, flashing him an artificial smile. "I didn't expect to see you back here so soon." He offered Duncan his hand. Duncan looked at it, thinking he'd rather take it and pulverise every finger with a hammer rather than shake it. Becky's eyes flicked up at him and he knew what was best for her. He accepted the offer of the handshake. Davey's smile broadened. "Listen, Dunc. I was a wee bit off with you the other day. I had a rough couple of days... you know how it is, with everything going on, right?"

Duncan nodded, releasing his grip on Davey's hand. "Aye... I know the feeling."

The door to the house opened and a young man emerged. It was Callum and he tentatively approached the three of them. He was wearing jeans and a thick hooded sweatshirt, but was still feeling the cold, his arms clamped to his sides.

"Mum... can I come with you to see Eilidh?"

Becky smiled warmly, reaching out and putting her arm around his shoulder. He was quite small, much smaller than Duncan had been at the same age. He found himself studying the young man for the first time since Becky had told him, subconsciously looking for similarities, mannerisms... he wasn't sure what exactly.

Becky's eyes darted between Davey and Duncan, hugging Callum in an almost involuntary gesture to break what was an awkward moment for the three adults.

"Callum... this is—"

"Detective Inspector McAdam," Davey said evenly. Callum

immediately flinched upon hearing he was a policeman, likely fearing why he was here.

"I'm an old friend of your mum's," Duncan said, extending his hand warmly. Callum looked at it sceptically, and then took it. His grip was quite feeble, but he was clearly on edge. "Good to see you're up and about, young man."

"Thanks," Callum said, smiling nervously. Becky shook him gently.

"Of course you can come with me," she said. "But I want you to get a proper coat to bring with you."

"Are you sure?" Davey said, frowning. "The boy needs his rest. It's been a lot for him to take in and seeing Eilidh in the hospital might do more harm than good."

"Oh, it'll be all right," Becky said. "I'll be there too."

"Even so," Davey said, shaking his head. Callum looked crestfallen. "I reckon it'd be best—"

"For him to spend some time with his little sister, surely?" Duncan said. Davey's eyes narrowed as they drifted to Duncan, clearly unhappy with his intervention.

"I think I know what's best for my family, Duncan."

"Perhaps not in this case," Duncan said, holding the eye contact. They remained in silence for a moment, Callum waiting expectantly for a response. Davey acquiesced.

"All right. It probably won't hurt, but don't tire yourself out, wee man. Okay?"

Callum smiled. "Thanks, Dad." He took off back to the house. Becky looked nervously between the two men.

"Right, well I'd better get the car warmed up." She looked at Duncan. "Thanks for calling by with the update."

"The update?" Davey asked.

"Oh... Duncan was saying Callum might be okay with a fine, some points and..."

"A period of disqualification in the future," Duncan said. Davey nodded. "Best case scenario… as things stand."

"Right… that is good news. Thanks, Duncan."

Becky smiled at Duncan and made to leave.

"Hey!"

She turned back to her husband.

"You forgetting something?"

She smiled nervously, quickly returning and leaning in to give her husband a kiss on the cheek. She hesitated before making contact. It was a brief hesitation, but Duncan noted it, nonetheless. Unbeknown to Davey, her eyes flitted to Duncan before she moved away. Duncan looked away so Davey wouldn't clock the eye contact between them.

"I'll see you later," she said, unclear who she was speaking to, and walked to her car, getting in without looking back. Callum appeared from the house, clutching a coat in his hand. He waved to Davey, who waved back as Callum hurried around to the passenger door and got in. He had such a youthful gait about how he ran, making him look far younger than he actually was.

"He's a good lad, that boy," Davey said. "Real character about him. Gets it from his mum, I reckon."

Duncan remained tight-lipped. He looked at the car, clouds of exhaust vapour drifting from the rear in the cold air. From his vantage point, Duncan could see Becky's eyes in the door mirror. She was watching them. Neither man spoke and Becky must have realised she had to go. She reversed the car and made for the road, the wheels crunching on the gravel. Both Duncan and her husband watched them go.

"So, Duncan," Davey said with a dark grin. "I'll guess we'll no' be seeing you again for a while."

"You don't reckon?"

Davey cocked his head. "No. I think you can see Becky's made her decision."

"Did she have a decision to make then?"

Davey turned to face him, the smile gone. "You had your time with her, Duncan. It's in the past and that's where it will stay."

Davey turned away, making to set off for the house. Duncan was torn, either respect the promise he'd made Becky the previous day and keep out of it or give in to his desire to stove Davey's face into the ground.

"I'll see you around, eh?"

"Davey…"

He turned back to Duncan, inclining his head as Duncan stood in the middle of the driveway, saying nothing.

"What?" Davey asked.

Duncan quelled his anger, willing himself to get into his car and leave. He knew that's exactly what he should do, but he didn't. He stood there, feeling the rage growing. Davey took a couple of steps back towards him.

"If you've got something to say, Duncan. Say it."

The arrogance – the smugness – seemed to ooze from him; revelling in the joy of some perceived victory.

"Do you read your Shakespeare, Davey?"

Davey's eyes narrowed, his expression puzzled. He shrugged. "No' for a while. No' since school. Why?"

"Macbeth," Duncan said, coming to stand within an arm's reach of him, pulling himself upright. Davey was a good four inches taller than him. "If I get to hear of you laying a finger on her again… or either of those bairns… I swear to you, there is not enough ocean that will wash your blood from my hands."

Davey stood open-mouthed as Duncan backed away, their eyes remaining locked together until Duncan reached his car, turned and got in. He slammed the door and started the engine, looking in the rear-view mirror and adjusting it so he could see Davey.

Davey Mcinnes stayed where he was, sporting an impassive expression as he watched Duncan pull away. This was far from over, and Duncan knew it.

FREE BOOK GIVEAWAY

Enjoy this book? You could make a real difference.

Because reviews are critical to the success of an author's career, if you have enjoyed this novel, please do me a massive favour by entering one onto Amazon.

Type the following link into your internet search bar to go to the Amazon page and leave a review;

http://mybook.to/JMD-skye2

If you prefer not to follow the link please visit the sales page where you purchased the title in order to leave a review.

Reviews increase visibility. Your help in leaving one would make a massive difference to this author and I would be very grateful.

THE TALISKER DEAD
PREVIEW

The voices are muffled. Both of them are trying to keep from being overheard. Is that for my benefit? Probably. Mum seemed off when she picked me up after school this afternoon. She asked me how my day was, much as she always does, but something was different with her today. She was quieter. In general, recently, she is quieter.

The thin shaft of light stretching out from between the door and the jamb hurts my eyes as I peer through into the front room. The fire is lit. I can't see it, but I can smell the peat and feel the warmth leaving the room and mixing with the cold air in the draughty hallway where I'm sitting. My toes are already numb. I should have brought my duvet, or a blanket, but then they'd know I was here. I definitely should have worn my slippers. Dad will be upset if he finds me out here, listening. I should be in bed at this time on a school night.

"We can't go on like this!" Mum says. I can hear the tension in her voice. That isn't just a comment; she really means it. "We had another letter through this morning."

"From the bank?"

My mum is looking tired. I mean, she always looks tired

but now it's not just the usual fatigue of a normal day... it's more world-weary, worn out. As for my dad, he's himself. He doesn't say much at the best of times. Gran said he was always like that. How did she once describe him to me? Removed. That was it.

"We're falling further behind..."

"I know."

Tension in his voice now too. This never ends well.

"On the mortgage and the—"

"I bloody well know, woman! What do you expect me tae do?"

"Pay it!"

My dad is exasperated. He's up... pacing the room.

"How can I pay it when we don't have any money?"

Mum is on the brink of tears now. I know. She cries when dad is out on the boat sometimes, always at night, and only when she thinks I'm asleep. Often times, I'm just pretending though.

"Can we... try something different?"

"Different how?"

Mum is shaking her head. She's clutching at straws now.

"I don't know... maybe we could modernise—"

"Modernise?" Dad says with a dismissive laugh. "What with?"

He's becoming angry, or as angry as he gets at any rate. He's giving her that look; the one he does when he's feeling uncomfortable and wants to exert control over the conversation. He's frightened. It's not something I see routinely in him but it's there, even if he won't allow himself to show it openly.

"We're not bringing in enough to cover our costs as it is. You know I've had to let wee Connor go already."

"I know... but you have to do something!"

"The big ships are coming in and trawling everything in

sight. We're having to go out to deeper waters… it's dangerous and we have to spend longer out—"

"I know all that but—"

"But nothing! After all this time, you still don't get it, do you? The stocks have been decimated. There are too many of us going out after the same catch. Something's got to give. We all need to row back on the take."

"And how are you going t' feed your family if you do that? We're your priority – or should be – and not the bloody north Atlantic."

"I'm well aware of my responsibilities."

Dad looks straight at me. I swear he can see me through the crack in the door. I'm holding my breath. If I move, he'll see, if he hasn't already.

"Things have to change… for everyone, not just for us," he says quietly.

"Do you think the rest of them will accept less? Don't be so naive!"

"Change is coming to this industry, whether we like it or not. I cannae hold it back, no matter how much I might want to."

"But you don't, do you?"

"What?"

"Want to. You think it's time for people to come away from the sea, don't you?"

Dad is looking at her. He doesn't want to say so – fearful of her reaction, I suppose — but she knows what he is thinking. He's talked of little else for ages.

"Aye. Things have to change. Like it or not."

"Then… what are we going to do?"

I've heard frustration in her voice a lot recently, tension, even a little anger but now she is scared. That's both of them.

"A lot of the boys… are talking about heading down to the

docks. There's still good work to be had in the yards on the Clyde."

"The shipyards?"

"Aye."

"What do you know about building ships?"

"I've spent ma whole adult life at sea—"

"In a boat, not building one."

She's angry now. He's not though. What is that expression? I've not seen it on my dad's face before. He looks like the boys at school did when the fourth goal went in at the weekend; accepting their fate that it wasn't going to be their day. Resignation, that's it. Dad is looking away from me now, away from mum too, and out into the darkness. During the day you can see all the way across Loch a' Ghlinne to Rùm and the Isle of Canna beyond that, but now, all that can be seen is darkness, with the rain striking the window in earnest. It seems like Mother Nature is keen to reflect my parents' mood.

"I dinnae know what else to do. I really don't."

"And what about us? Do you expect to drag us down to Glasgow as well?"

"It'll be grand."

"For you maybe. But what about—"

"I said… it'll be grand. The bairn will adjust."

"She's never known anything but the island. It's a big ask at this age…"

"Aye… well, sometimes I wonder if we'd all be better off if I wasnae here at all!"

"Don't say that…"

I've heard enough now. I don't want to leave my friends, my home. I don't even want to leave my school, and I hate school. There's the sound of movement from the room. They must have heard me, so I hurry back upstairs, avoiding the squeaky floorboards with the skill and poise of a professionally trained Scottish dancer and I'm back into my bed, under the covers, before I hear a single footstep on the first squeaky tread at the base of the stairs.

My door creaks open a few moments later and I lie facing the wall, away from the door, keeping my breathing slow and measured. It's my mum. I know it's her. She has a reassuring presence that I can feel by sense alone. She is always the one to check in on me. The door closes and I am alone again. For the first time in as far back as I can remember, I feel something I haven't in a long time.

Now I'm scared too.

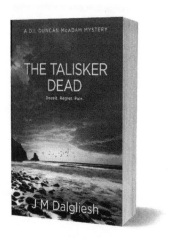

Publishing January 2024

'Digging up the past… is enough to kill you…'

ALSO BY THE AUTHOR

In the Misty Isle Series
A Long Time Dead
The Dead Man of Storr
The Talisker Dead *PRE-ORDER*

In the Hidden Norfolk Series
One Lost Soul
Bury Your Past
Kill Our Sins
Tell No Tales
Hear No Evil
The Dead Call
Kill Them Cold
A Dark Sin
To Die For
Fool Me Twice
The Raven Song
Angel of Death
Dead To Me
Blood Runs Cold
Life and Death**
**FREE* EBOOK - VISIT* jmdalgliesh.com*

In the Dark Yorkshire Series
Divided House
Blacklight
The Dogs in the Street
Blood Money
Fear the Past
The Sixth Precept

AUDIOBOOKS

In the Misty Isle Series
Read by Angus King

A Long Time Dead
The Dead Man of Storr
The Talisker Dead (January 2024)

In the Hidden Norfolk Series
Read by Greg Patmore

One Lost Soul
Bury Your Past
Kill Our Sins
Tell No Tales
Hear No Evil
The Dead Call
Kill Them Cold
A Dark Sin
To Die For
Fool Me Twice
The Raven Song
Angel of Death
Dead To Me
Blood Runs Cold

Hidden Norfolk Books 1-3

AUDIOBOOKS

In the Dark Yorkshire Series
Read by Greg Patmore

Divided House
Blacklight
The Dogs in the Street
Blood Money
Fear the Past
The Sixth Precept

Dark Yorkshire Books 1-3
Dark Yorkshire Books 4-6

Made in the USA
Monee, IL
13 February 2024